UNEXPECTED

Suzanne Biggs

Eva —
nice to meet you!

Suzanne Biggs

Frank. John. Lindsey. Wyatt. James.

Thank you all for the main thing, and thank each of you for your particular things .

Chapter 1

As Walter walked by Jack's cubicle, he rapped on the glass.
"Come to my office for a minute."

Jack saved what he'd written and heard the faint beep as his
computer stored the first part of tomorrow's article. He stared at the print on
the screen for a long moment before getting up. Another story retelling
an overworked subject.

Normally he would be caught up in the exhilaration and adventure of an
election. But this year offered nothing more that a rehash of old,
unsatisfactory ideas, tired slogans, and feeble candidates – even though it
would seem to be a time that called for something – someone -- more.
The various candidates, some once again, some for the first time, were
feeling their way through the treacherous political swamps leading up to the
coveted party nominations.

Even my articles, thought Jack, have a strange sense of sameness. He
was tempted to get out the pieces from years past and simply change

names as appropriate. He wondered if anyone would notice. Jack got up and walked to Walter's corner office.

"What's up?" he asked, as he settled into the soft chair opposite Walter.

"How do you feel about a trip out to Oregon?"

"Depends on the purpose."

"We'll be generating plenty of copy on the major contenders..."

"Amen to that," Jack said under his breath.

Walter smiled and continued, "...so I want the paper to run a series on presidential hopefuls who are, shall we say, outside the mainstream — why are they trying for something that seems so hopeless, what do they hope to gain. You can see the angles."

"So you want me to interview an unknown presidential candidate from Oregon. Who might that be?"

"Her name is Helen Conner. Have you heard of her?"

"Guess I've seen her name."

"She's written a book entitled "If You Don't, Who will?" She shows some low-level, grass-roots support and already has her name on several state ballots. Although she is relatively unknown, her supporters are active and willing to get petitions signed."

"I seem to remember seeing her book in a bookstore. Seen some things on the internet. What's her party affiliation?"

"You can ask her yourself on Friday."

"Friday? Geez, Walter, I have plans."

"The interview is already set up. See Annie about the details."

"Walter, can't someone else do it? What about Jessie or Sam? Yeah,

Sam. He'd be great."

"No. I'm sure you will bring that certain *je ne sais quoi* to the story. Maybe you can even do follow-ups throughout the campaign year."

"Really, what gives?"

"Go on Thursday. Spend the weekend. Have a little vacation. You sit at your computer, staring at the screen with a grimness that is not like you. Have fun with the story. Besides, it wouldn't hurt to get in on the ground level — she may be the next president of the United States of America. Think how grateful she will be to the reporter who first blazes her name across the pages of the 'Washington News.' "

"I don't need a vacation...."

"Go. Interview her. Write a good story. Maybe you should read her book, too. Annie's trying to find one. "

"Yes, boss."

"Once this story is done, I have more of the same."

Jack couldn't hide his distaste, but Walter only laughed. "It will be a good series. I'm going to have Sam doing some also."

Jack got out of his chair saying, "O.K." The assignment had been made and Jack would do it. He started to walk back to his desk, but then checking his watch, decided on an early lunch. He picked up his coat and headed for the elevators. Sam caught his eye and beckoned him over.

"Got a hot story?"

"Right. Actually I'm going to lunch. Want to come?"

"Some of us have to work. Maybe I'll join you later."

Even though it was cold out, Jack didn't go straight to the restaurant. The bite of the wind on his cheek felt good, reassuring him that he was alive in body, if not in soul. Even Walter saw the malaise that gnawed at him.

Jack saw his trouble as a pale reflection of the malaise that gripped politics in general, and Washington politics in particular. Politics — the whole reason he was a journalist. How he had loved the drama, the gritty reality, the digging and digging to get a story, the surprises. Now it was all so heavy — as though the sheer weight of government bureaucracy was smothering the final sparks of life.

Walter was right. It would do him good to get away. He could do the interview and then spend the weekend on the coast. He'd been out there a few years ago and always been meaning to go back. Maybe he'd even catch a winter storm rolling in off the Pacific. Should he take Nora? No. He needed the time alone. She'd understand.

He walked into the restaurant with thoughts of a room looking over the stormy ocean, a cup of steaming coffee in his hand, and...and...nobody at his side. The unconscious smile that had played across his lips disappeared. Finding an empty booth, he sat down and ordered lunch — his thoughts turned to his present article and how he was going to finish it.

When Jack was nearly done eating, Sam came in and sat down.

"Has Walter assigned you an interview with one of his 'presidential unhopefuls,'" he asked after ordering a burger with the works and a diet Coke.

"Yeah. What about you?"

"The first one I have is Harry Something who lives here in Washington and has run for president every four years, I don't know, since the Civil War."

"At least I get to spend a few days in Oregon. I'm doing some lady who wrote a book and thinks she should be President. How many of these people do you think Walter has?"

"Maybe enough so we can skip all the real candidates until after the conventions. Then we wouldn't have to write article after article endlessly comparing them all."

"Sounds great. Bring on the droves of nameless, faceless public-spirited souls who have a plan for us all. I don't know. Maybe Walter's right. It'll be refreshing to talk with people who believe in something so passionately that they launch an unrealistic bid for President."

"Here's to unrealistic dreams."

Sam raised his glass as Jack got up and said with a smile, "See you back at the office."

Later that afternoon, Jack returned to his apartment, his notebook loaded with all the information Annie had provided. It included travel arrangements for his trip out west, background on Helen Conner, even a download of the woman's book. He put his things on the table, and opened the refrigerator. Leaning on the door, he tried to decide what to eat.

Nora had left a phone message at the office saying she would stop by later. He could go out and eat, but didn't relish the prospect. In the end he made a ham sandwich and carried it to the table. As he ate he glanced at the information on Ms. Conner. There was her book and seemingly endless chatter on the internet and other social media and yet he wondered if she had truly been heard of anywhere other than her home territory — or even there. The book had rave reviews and implied a large following.

But then all book publishers did that regardless of the quality of the book.

He knew he should read, or at least skim through it, but decided to wait until he was on the airplane on Thursday. He'd do this interview for Walter and then enjoy himself for several days.

The last bite of sandwich was in his hand when he heard the door open and Nora walked into the apartment.

"Hi. I was finished early and decided to come by before going on to the Kendall's."

"Want a sandwich?"

"No, thanks. I'll be eating there."

Jack wanted to say something, anything, that wasn't so impersonal, so like the conversation of two acquaintances passing on the street. Nora poured herself a drink and stood by the bar sipping it. She was still as good-looking as the day four years ago when he'd met her at the media awards. He had a series up for consideration. She was a shoo-in as the best local T.V. news reporter.

It wasn't as though he'd been looking for anyone. Carrie's death several years earlier had left an empty place that he wasn't sure he wanted filled. He hadn't dated at all, even though his friends dropped subtle, and not so subtle, hints. Regularly he'd arrive at a dinner party and find himself seated next to this or that eligible woman, "my dear friend Mary," "Paul's cousin Tiffany." Everyone thought that they knew what was best for him and ignored his pleas that they stop.

He and Nora dated for a while and then drifted into an easy, ill-defined relationship. He didn't love her — not that way — the way it had been with Carrie, but he liked her. They were friends, sometimes lovers — not committed to each other, but not really seeing anyone else either.

As he watched her now, he again considered inviting her to join him on his trip to Oregon. However, when he spoke there was no invitation in his words or in his tone.

"I'm leaving on Thursday and won't be back until Monday."

"Where are you going?" she asked, more out of politeness, it seemed, than real interest.

"An interview in Oregon."

"I'm going to be gone tomorrow and the next day, so, I guess I'll see you when you get back." She glanced at her watch. "I've got to go." The perfunctory kiss just grazed his cheek as she breezed by, grabbed her coat, and went out the door.

Jack looked for several moments into the empty space she'd left behind, then picked up his dishes and set them in the sink.

Chapter 2

Thursday arrived, cold and dreary, a threat of snow in the moist, gray air that hung low over the city. Jack just hoped it would hold off until he was on the plane to Oregon.

He'd packed with speed and precision. By now it was something that came as naturally as brushing his teeth or shaving. The trips had taken on a decided sense of sameness. He could remember when this trip would have excited him — but it was only a memory. Sometimes he wondered whether it would have made a difference if he'd been home, instead of on a hot story, seven years ago? Seven years ago. Seven long years ago. Carrie. Her face remembered now from photographs.

In his more honest moments he saw that he had never really been fair to Nora. He was the one who always held back. And in the end, the cool, albeit friendly, distance between them became a habit.

The taxi was out in front so Jack took a quick look around the apartment. Of course, everything was in order. If it wasn't, Mrs. Stempel, the housekeeper, would see to it. He went out, got in the taxi, and was driven to the airport.

The flight was uneventful and Jack actually slept through most of it. Annie had booked him into the Sheraton at the airport in Portland, but he wanted to be downtown, so he rented a car and drove there. He remembered Portland as a lovely city and wasn't disappointed, even though a soft drizzle was falling. Sitting in his room reading Ms. Conner's book was the right thing to do. Instead he went to the Japanese garden up the hill, and turned out to be almost the only one there. He found a bench with a panoramic view and sat, his umbrella keeping out most of the gentle rain, and let the stillness, the simplicity, weave a quiet pattern in his thoughts.

The damp, blue-gray winter afternoon turned quickly toward night. When Jack stood up he felt stiff and slightly chilled, but good, really good. On the way back he saw a theater playing a movie he'd been meaning to see. Back at the hotel he warmed up and then got a bite to eat. He thought guiltily about Ms. Conner's book, but opted for the movie. The interview wasn't until tomorrow afternoon. That gave him plenty of time to page through and get the highlights.

That night he left no instructions for a wake-up call, and was startled the next morning to see how long he'd slept. If nothing else this trip was letting him catch up on his sleep.

After doing everything he needed to do, including the finishing touches on another article he wanted to email to Walter, there was no time to give more than a cursory glance at the book. Part of him rebelled against the lack of professionalism that he was displaying, but another part knew that Walter had given him this assignment to allow him a short vacation. Walter wasn't looking for a hard-hitting, deeply researched piece. The whole concept was a joke after all. "Ms. Helen Conner, President of the United States." Right.

Jack followed Annie's impeccable instructions and arrived at Ms. Conner's in good time. One question was answered as he drove up the driveway — she probably had enough money to try for the Presidency. It wasn't that the house was unusually large. In fact, it was modest in comparison to some of the others he'd seen on the way there. It was the grounds, so beautifully landscaped, and the obvious quality and workmanship that went into every detail of the house. They radiated refined taste and un-ostentatious, comfortable wealth. Was this from the husband, or from her?

What little background reading he'd done told Jack that Ms. Conner was a 44 year old widow with two teenage sons. Pictures he'd seen on the internet showed an attractive woman, but pictures so easily lied. A mental picture began to form as Jack walked up the steps to the front door: salon-styled and dyed hair, a little too much make-up for his taste, thin and angular, but expensively dressed in a filmly, floaty dress — no, wool slacks and a blazer, season tickets to the symphony, two cocker spaniels, passionate about her cause, whatever it was; her sons, no doubt, misunderstood and spoiled, with long hair and sullen faces. The vision made him stop at the top step and reconsider before he rang the bell. What had Walter gotten him into?

He'd reported from war zones. He could handle a woman who thought she should be President. He rang the bell.

After a short pause, the door was opened by a young man. If this was one of the sons, Jack's imaginings were way off. This boy was about sixteen, tall, all arms and legs, but a sweet face. Jack was surprised that the word 'sweet' came to mind, but there was no getting around it – he looked like a nice kid. And he had a spark of intelligence that one didn't always see.

"I'm Jack Kelly here to interview Helen Conner."

The young man held out his hand. "I'm Chris Conner. Mom's in the back. If you will come this way please."

Well-mannered, short hair, clean shirt and jeans. Well....

Jack followed Chris through the beautifully decorated house. The interior matched the exterior in understated good taste. He was surprised again when Chris showed him into the huge, bright kitchen.

"Mom, Mr. Kelly's here."

The woman who came toward him was about five feet six or seven inches. Her brownish-blond hair was pulled back in a knot at the back of her neck. She had on a rust-colored sweater over a white blouse and longish skirt. Around her waist was an apron. She wore no make-up that he could see, except a touch of lipstick. A smile lit up her face as she stretched out her hand.

"Hello, I'm Helen Conner."

"Jack Kelly."

"Forgive me for meeting you in here. I'm nearly finished and then we can go to the study."

With that a buzzer went off and Helen Conner turned away to the oven. As she removed a sheet of what appeared to be chocolate chip cookies, Jack realized that ever since entering the house he'd been wrapped in the warm, pleasant aroma of baking.

Jack walked over and looked out the window onto the winter landscape. Meanwhile, Ms. Conner was removing the cookies from the sheet. She was telling Chris not to eat any now. She'd make more later if necessary. So far none of this was as Jack expected. At the moment he mostly hoped she'd offer him a cookie. He hadn't even spoken with her yet and already a story was forming. He smiled.

His mind was still on his opening paragraph when she spoke to him. He turned to her.

"Mr. Kelly, would you care for a cookie? I'm making them for an event tonight at Chris's school. I thought I'd be done before you arrived."

"Yes, thank you."

"Would you like some milk to go along with them, or a soft drink?"

"Milk sounds great."

"Chris, will you bring everything to the study for us? And you can have a couple, a couple, yourself." Mother and son looked at each other with humor in their eyes, as she took off her apron, folded it and set it on the counter.

Cookies and milk. Sam was going to love this. What a story.

The study walls were lined with bookshelves on three sides and had large windows on the fourth. A fire was smoldering in the fireplace. Ms. Conner added a log and poked it a bit as Jack set up his recorder. They sat in comfortable chairs facing each other. Chris came in with the cookies and milk and then excused himself.

"Ms. Conner, you are running for President of the United States."

"Yes, Mr. Kelly, I am."

"Why?"

Her laughter was low and melodious. But her voice as she answered was serious. "Nobody is articulating what is truly important. I am at a time in my life when it is possible to do this, so I am."

"What is 'important' to you?"

"I love the idea that is America. Since the country came into being it has been a place where the possibilities are endless for people with the will to embrace the idea of freedom and individuality. The United States of America was founded on the underlying principle that freedom is an inherent right of Man rather than a dispensation from government. I believe that it is important that there be at least one place in the world where this sense of freedom can flourish.

"Individual politicians seem more interested in gaining and keeping power than serving the citizens. The minor parties have single or limited ideas and goals. Everyone recognizes that there are problems in our country, but no one seems willing to deal with the causes. They either hide from the issues, or try to tinker only with the symptoms. Then they wonder why nothing changes."

So here it comes, thought Jack, her recipe for the Saving of America. Let them eat cookies and milk, perhaps. "And how do you define these 'root causes'?" he asked aloud.

She looked at him for a long moment before answering.

"I wrote a book that discusses this subject. Perhaps you are familiar with it — 'If You Don't, Who Will?'"

Jack started to make an excuse, but she cut it off with a knowing smile. "Let me explain it to you. I feel that one of the main ingredients missing from our present American society is the willingness to take responsibility for our own actions."

"Lack of responsibility?" He knew he sounded a little incredulous. He got his voice back to his normal, noncommittal interview tone. "And how can the government affect that?"

"In countless ways. But to put it simply, every time the government says that they can help us, or our neighbors, better than we can help ourselves, and we believe them and allow it to happen, we take a step closer to the destruction, and yes, I mean destruction, of all that America stands for."

"I suspect that you come down on the side of smaller government?"

"Government bureaucracy is not a suitable resting place for our hopes and dreams. Government consistently, in every nation in the world, shows itself unable to regulate satisfactorily the day to day lives of citizens. The more they try the worse it gets. Every step toward centralization of decision-making is a step away from freedom. Government-sponsored national health care, or agricultural policy, or welfare -- even personal security. It is impossible for the government to make decisions about your life as well as you can. The government cannot begin to know enough to make sound choices. They will always end up with the least common denominator and then pass laws in the attempt to force us to go down and live in that little, super-regulated, 'fair' place.

"And yet you are running for President. You aspire to be the head of that sprawling government bureaucracy. It seems slightly inconsistent."

"Do you care for another cookie?" she asked, passing him the plate.

"Thanks. These are incredibly good."

"Thank you. I'm running for the Presidency because I see the office as a place from which I can spread my ideas. We can either change the system legally from the inside, or live with the results of unlawful forces that try to coerce change. The President has extraordinary power. I want to use that power to change the direction of this country." Seeming to read Jack's mind, she continued, "And, no, I cannot make someone be responsible for their own actions. It is not the sort of thing one can legislate — just as one cannot legislate any sort of right thinking. But one can set an example, help to change the mood of the country, and, perhaps most importantly, make sure no legislation is passed that takes away a person's natural inclination to be the best he can be."

"For example...?"

"There are two things that I will institute immediately. The first: I will veto all bills that deal with more that one issue – every time, across the board. Legislators need to start taking responsibility for their actions and not hiding behind the statement, 'I had to vote for those earmarks because they were in the military expenditures bill.' Second: when I am President my first responsibility will be to maintain freedom. We are all aware of 'Environmental Impact Statements'. I will institute 'Freedom Impact Statements'. BEFORE being enacted, every bill, regulation, or policy needs to have a well thought-out Freedom Impact Statement – what will this law do to take away the citizens' inherent right to freedom? Is whatever this regulation is about so important that individual freedoms must be sacrificed? Does this policy take away the individuals' need to take responsibility for his or her actions and inactions? Does this bill make groups more important than individuals?"

"And I will insist that government employees take full responsibility for presenting these Freedom Impact Statements. Every – and I mean EVERY – single enactment of government takes away some measure of freedom. If it did not, then there would be no reason for it to exist. Laws, policies, regulations exist only to control behavior. Some are necessary, but most are not."

"You wish to see a drastic cutback of government?"

"I believe that will be the inevitable result as people begin to realize that they can make better decisions for themselves than the government can."

"I guess you can't count on the vote of government employees."

She laughed.

"I absolutely reject the idea of gathering votes by blocks. I will make no effort to appeal to special interest groups. I will seek no endorsement from the various leaders of organizations. My campaign aims at the heart of each individual citizen and asks them to decide for themselves what they stand for. If it is the ideas I am presenting, great. If some other theory, at least make a reasoned decision and be prepared to be responsible for the consequences."

"Tell me about your campaign."

"I have people working to get my name on the ballots of all fifty states.

I see the look of disbelief on your face, but I assure you, it will happen. I will be included in the debates with the major party candidates. I will be there to offer an alternative. I'm about to launch the first of a series of cross-country trips to get my name out to the general public. I already have a large presence on all the social media and now I am going out in person. Television and radio talk shows, town meetings, living room get-togethers. My message will be spread as far and as wide as necessary. I am a serious candidate. And I have every intention of being in the White House."

Jack couldn't fault her confidence. "How is this being financed?"

"I have some money, well, a lot of money, but the bulk of it is coming — you must note, I say, is coming — from people who agree with my message. There are actually a large number of people who have read, and liked, my book."

She looked at Jack with a bland, open expression, but her eyes were laughing.

"I know that you live in the famous 'blindness zone' inside the Beltway. The fact is, a lot of people from all walks of life are reaching out, really want to be more than spineless lackeys of a government gone out of control. People want to be their best. They want to strive, work hard, achieve. They don't want to work hard and then pay exorbitant taxes to a bloated, inefficient government which grandly gives them in exchange a lower lifestyle, lower self-esteem, and crumbs, mere crumbs, from the trillion dollar trough where the hogs feed. Hard as it is for Washington to understand, really important ideas, sound decisions, wise actions, true caring, go on daily in nearly every individual's life. The government needs to get out and stay out of that."

"You say you don't want the backing of special interest groups. What about the woman's vote?"

"First of all there is no more a 'woman's vote' than there is a 'man's vote.' There are women's groups who optimistically claim to speak for 'women.' They don't speak for me, and I am a woman. I hardly think I am the only one. Again, I am appealing to each individual, man or woman."

"Ms. Conner," said Jack, already writing the article in his head, "Can you tell me a little about yourself, your family?"

"First of all, you may call me Mrs. Conner. I have always been proud to think of myself as Edward's wife, as he, I believe, was proud to be my husband."

" 'Ms.' is the wisest and provokes the fewest reactions. Also, it is editorial policy at the paper. Even if I wrote the story using 'Mrs.,' the editors would change it."

She laughed that pleasant laugh again. "Ah, the tyranny of the right-minded. To answer your question: I have two sons, Christopher, whom you met, and Alexander, who is in his first year at Berkeley. My husband, Edward, died several years ago. I've always had a deep interest in politics and theories of government. I'm sure you've read the background sheet — the degrees, business interests, etc." She paused and looked at him with a skeptical half-smile.

"Yes, I do have that information." Well, he'd look at it carefully later. "What do your sons think of all this?"

"Alex is thrilled. He is going to take time off from school in the spring and begin to campaign actively. His interests already lie in this direction. He looks forward to being the 'First Son.'" Chris is putting up with us graciously and with good humor."

There was a knock on the door and then Chris stepped in.

"Excuse me, Mom, there is an important message for you."

"Thank you, Sweetheart. Will you entertain Mr. Kelly for a moment."
To Jack she said, "I'll be right back. Chris will take good care of you." She
touched Chris's arm as she passed by, a gesture of maternal affection.

Chris seemed almost to blush. He looked at the empty milk glasses
and asked, "Can I get you something to drink?"

"No, thanks, I'm fine." Jack wasn't sure it was fair, but he asked
anyway, "What do you think about your Mom's bid for the presidency?"

"She'll be an excellent President," he replied with no hesitation and
more poise than Jack had expected.

"So you believe she'll win? Isn't that being overly optimistic —
even unrealistic?"

Chris didn't reply. He just raised his eyebrows slightly and gave
a quiet laugh. A quiet, knowing laugh.

Helen Conner returned and Jack began to gather his
paraphernalia.

"Ms. — Mrs.— Conner, thank you for your time."

"My pleasure. Will you be staying in Portland for a while?" she
asked, making polite conversation to cover his really too obvious desire to
be done.

"I'll spend the night and then head out for a day or two on the coast
before I fly back."

"Which part of the coast do you plan to visit?"

"I'll just go west until I hit the coast and then find a good spot."

"There are lots of wonderful places over there for you to discover. Let me give you the names of several restaurants we enjoy."

She went to her desk, opened a drawer and pulled out a piece of paper and pen. Jack had a nearly irresistible urge to sneak a couple of the cookies and put them in his briefcase. She wrote something on the paper, turned, and handed it to him.

"There you go. I hope you have a lovely weekend. I look forward to seeing your article. I know your work, and appreciate your talent."

"Well...thank you." Was she sincere, or just buttering him up so he'd write a complimentary story?

She walked to the coffee table, picked up several cookies, and wrapped them in a napkin. She handed them to Jack and said, "Take these. They will make a nice snack for later."

Was she psychic, or was he so transparent?

"Thank you. And thanks again for the interview."

She showed him out and stood at the door as he got in his car and drove away. He felt a huge sense of relief. It hadn't been a hard interview — why had he been feeling so tense? And he hadn't even realized it until he left.

Back at the hotel he sat down to write the article and eat dinner from room service. He barely re-read the story before emailing it off to Walter. Well, that was done. He lay back on the bed, turned on the T.V., and within moments was sound asleep.

Chapter 3

Next morning the sky was brightened by a watery sun. Jack drove west and upon hitting the coast, headed south until he found a motel that had rooms with an ocean view and a restaurant nearby. The next two days were spent reading or walking on the empty winter beach or just sitting in his room watching the waves and sea birds. At odd moments thoughts of Helen Conner intruded. He had pangs of guilt when he thought of the half-hearted article he'd written. But Walter didn't expect anything serious. And her ideas might be passionately held, even well thought out, but how realistic was it for her to think she could mount a successful, serious national campaign?

Early Monday he returned home and was back at work by noon. He went straight to Walter's office.

"Jack, how was Oregon?" asked Walter as Jack walked in. "Great story on the Conner woman. We ran it yesterday."

"Already?"

"Yes. Is that a problem?"

"No...no. Let me see it."

Walter shoved a copy of the paper across his desk. "Page one of the Lifestyles section."

Jack found it immediately. There was a photo of Mrs. Conner that didn't do her justice and a headline that said, "Super Mom: Presidential Campaign and Still Time For Cookies." It wasn't his headline but Jack had to admit to himself that his article probably did emphasize that aspect, although she herself had not projected that image. It was too late to do anything about it now, and it certainly wasn't going to make any difference to her campaign, such as it was. And the article wasn't too badly written....

Sam came by and poked his head into the office.

"Cookies? My guy just spouted rhetoric for two hours and didn't even offer me so much as a glass of water. So, Walter, do you have any more of these for us? Next time I get to go on the trip."

Walter leaned back in his chair, relishing the moment. "Actually, I have five or six more, but I'll space them out over the next few months. Now both of you get back to work. Jack, which story are you on now?"

"An overview of the Democratic and Republican contenders — stand on issues, experience, chances..." Same old boring, useless stuff, he thought to himself.

"How much more work?"

"A couple days."

"Have it for the Sunday edition."

"Right, Chief." Jack gave a mock salute and joined Sam at the door. They walked to the coffee machine.

"Some piece of work, that Ms. Conner," said Sam. "Does she really think she can be President?"

Jack thought a moment and then replied, "Yeah, I think she does."

"And you?"

"How can she? She has no party – and doesn't even want one. I'm certainly not going to think about it anymore."

"Think of the possibilities — third party headed by a woman. I like it. Think of the special interests that could flock around her."

"Actually, she disavows special interests. Says she is interested in the hearts and minds of each individual American."

"Even better. Imagine the uproar and confusion caused by someone who couldn't be bought. Washington would fall apart."

"If she gets that far — a gigantic if — she'll be right in there with the rest of them."

"No faith in her good political intentions?"

"About as much as you have."

They both laughed and went back to work.

Shortly after Jack got home, Nora arrived. They worked comfortably side by side in the kitchen making a light dinner.

"I saw your piece on the Oregon woman."

"So how'd you like it?" asked Jack thinking he knew the answer.

"Regardless of what you think, she probably really believes in this bid for the presidency."

"Was it too terrible?"

"I wasn't there, so I don't know what she's like, but I went out and got her book. You should read it."

"Tell me."

"I don't agree with a lot of what she says...."

"I can believe that."

"...but there is something underlying her whole message that gets to me. This may sound silly, but I ended up wanting to be 'better'. "

"Ah, Nora, how could you possibly be better?"

"Laugh if you must, but I wish you'd read it."

"What makes you think I haven't?"

"Have you?"

"I read the blurb."

Nora, who had her hands under the faucet, flicked her wet fingers in his face. "Jack Kelly, famous in-depth reporter, once again shows us mere mortals how he got where he is today."

He got his hands wet and flicked at her. "Well, Ms. Campbell, we can't all be brilliant, beautiful T.V. stars."

"You're just jealous."

"Absolutely. Let's eat."

"Maybe we can make cookies after dinner."

Jack laughed and shook his head.

The evening progressed pleasantly, but Nora didn't spend the night. Although expecting her to, Jack wasn't all that disappointed. A part of him wanted her to stay, move in even, get married maybe. He wished he could tell her that he loved her, but didn't want to lie to her. At least he cared for her that much. So they said goodnight at the door. He read awhile and then slept.

In the following weeks Jack interviewed several other 'Potential Presidents,' as he and Sam had taken to calling them. Most were sincere, several quite strange. One Jack felt glad to get away from with his life. Fred Summers bore a striking resemblance to Elvis Presley, but talked a hard-core Nazi line.

Meanwhile the Republicans and Democrats were starting to warm up. Battle lines were drawn between and within the parties. The field was wide open because the serving President was folding up his eight years in a cloud of inefficiency and bad choices. His vice-president was not running, being too old and in questionable health.

In Congress both parties were claiming to be the ones who either brought the present prosperity or fought against the terrible policies, depending on which issue was at hand. Polls showed voter apathy at record levels.

Jack plowed through the thick, lackluster atmosphere and tried to find stories, any stories, that held his, let alone the reader's interest. It was rough going.

Chapter 4

Stories about Helen Conner appeared daily in all the various outlets including social media. Curiosity prompted Jack to read much of it, while pretending to himself that he had no real interest. One day an advertisement in the paper caught his attention — on Saturday Ms. Conner was going to be in Washington to give a talk. He noted the time and place on his phone calendar only half-expecting to go. But then Saturday came around and it wasn't raining and Nora was out of town and there was nothing he had to do so he decided to go — just to see how she handled herself in public.

He arrived at the hall with only minutes to spare, figuring that seating would not be a problem. He ended up having to stand against the back wall with other late-comers. The hall was packed with a crowd that was hard to categorize. People from many different backgrounds seemed to be present. Jack whispered to the man next to him.

"What do you know about Helen Conner?"

"Don't you know?"

"Not really."

"She's going to be the next President."

Oh great, he'd ended up next to one of her campaign workers. Jack couldn't deny that these workers had certainly done a good job of getting out the public. Now a middle-aged, well-dressed woman walked out on to the platform followed by the guest speaker. Ms. Conner looked elegant, but not over-stated. Somehow Jack had forgotten how attractive she was.

The woman gave a short, flowery introduction and then enthusiastic applause welcomed Ms. Conner. She moved to the microphone and stood there with a quiet smile acknowledging the applause. She looked completely at ease. Her eyes roamed across the audience as she waited for the clapping to die down. He knew the trick of seeming to have eye-contact with each member of the audience, making them feel they were special to her. She hadn't even spoken, but already he knew — she was good. And he was glad he was there. Just before the applause died down, he had the sensation that she looked right at him. Did he see something in her face? A flicker of recognition? But then her eyes were off him and she was beginning to talk.

Jack had to admit it was an excellent speech. She knew how to work the audience — one moment a joke, the next dealing with issues, then calling on their deepest sense of themselves. Time went by quickly and he was surprised after glancing at his watch to see that nearly an hour had passed. At the end of her talk she called for questions from the floor. There were some from obvious admirers, but several attacked her and her ideas. She handled them with grace and ease. All-in-all, Jack was impressed and had to admit he had seriously underestimated her.

On the way home, he began to formulate a plan for another interview. Only this time he'd be ready. Back at the apartment he opened the hard copy of her book he had purchased, sat in his most comfortable chair, and began to read, red pen in hand. He slashed and marked, scoffing at many of her ideas, but in all, the book was very readable and its message did have a certain appeal. He figured that someone with an unsophisticated political mind might think her ideas were workable. The fact is, she was idealistic and unrealistic. Nevertheless, he looked forward to interviewing her again.

But what if she didn't want to give him an interview? The first had been so half-hearted and the resulting article had such a condescending tone. Was she the type to hold a grudge? Jack was busy for the next week or so, but then he had some free time. He'd see what Walter thought of the idea.

Before going in to see Walter, he organized a file on Ms. Conner. He also checked to see if she was on any more state ballots. To his amazement she was on twenty-five. Why wasn't this a big story yet? Walter was impressed.

"Get another interview. It'll make a great follow-up on the cookies story.

Annie will make arrangements for you. "

As Jack walked out of the office, Walter said, "Good work, Jack. Follow your instincts on this one. There may be more going on here than we know." Mostly to himself he muttered, "Twenty-five states...."

Jack thought of what Ms. Conner said about the 'Beltway Blindness Zone' and wondered as he walked back to his desk.

After a variety of calls and call-backs, Annie said Ms. Conner's schedule was full, but she could see Jack either in three days in Springfield, Illinois or in a week back in Oregon before she headed off to California. He considered the lure of Oregon, but wanted to catch her in mid-campaign, so he had Annie firm up the Illinois date.

Three days later he was in Springfield. Ms. Conner was at a fund-raising luncheon in the banquet room of a downtown restaurant. Jack had no qualms about quietly crashing the party. He arrived in time to hear part of the speech which was short, to the point, and, once again, very well presented. One long round of applause came when she said, "You cannot expect the government to make your life better. It is something you have to do for yourself."

Here was a crowd that already seemed to know and love her. What Jack didn't understand was where all this support came from. He'd find out though.

The speech was over and Ms. Conner came down to sit at the head table. As she sipped from her water glass and glanced around the room, her eyes fell on Jack. He'd been trying to blend in with the wall next to the double doors. She smiled and gave a slight nod of her head. To his own annoyance he felt himself blush, but he trusted that no one noticed. He nodded back to her, tipped a non-existent hat, and went out.

The interview was set for three o'clock in her hotel suite. He went back to his room in the same hotel and waited. He couldn't prepare because he'd already done that. He tried to watch T.V. but couldn't get interested in what was happening to Brooke and Cliff and Storm and Amanda on the soaps. The talk shows were worse — they actually pretended to be about real life. And how many reruns of NCIS could one watch? He looked through his notes — they were in order. He was nervous. This was really stupid. He was never nervous. Why be nervous? Finally it was time.

He was met at the suite door by an older woman whose appearance shouted out efficiency and calm good-sense.

"You must be Mr. Kelly. Mrs. Conner will see you in a moment. This way, please."

"Thank you, Ms....?"

"Mrs. Edith Kramer."

"Thank you, Mrs. Kramer. May I ask how you fit in the campaign picture?"

"I am Mrs. Conner's assistant."

"How many people does Mrs. Conner have working on the campaign now?"

Jack wasn't sure if Mrs. Kramer was being cool toward him, or was simply brusque by nature when she answered, "Enough to get the job done."

He was stopped from thinking about it when Ms. Conner came in the room.

"Hello, Mr. Kelly. I see that you have met Mrs. Kramer, the backbone of our operation. She'll be working in the next room. Shall we...?" Ms. Conner indicated two chairs near the window. There was a low table between them, a small box wrapped like a present sitting on one end. She didn't refer to it, so he didn't either, as he put his recorder down and took out his note pad. She waited for him to speak.

"Ms...Mrs. Conner, before we start, I have to apologize...." She looked at him questioningly, as he went on quickly, "I don't know if you ever saw the article I wrote after our last interview...."

"Yes, I did." Her smile was enigmatic.

"I wasn't fair to you. I didn't care. The whole thing was more of a lark than anything else. I barely even re-read it before sending it off. I'm sorry."

"Don't be. The fact is, it was a very useful interview for me."

"In what way?"

"You were the first big name reporter to interview me. I needed to learn some lessons and you were a good teacher."

Jack thought back and could only remember her poise and ease and the fearlessness with which she conducted herself. He was the one who'd done a sloppy job. His confusion must have shown.

She just smiled and didn't help him other than to say, "Don't give it another thought. You truly did help me."

"You won't explain?"

Her smile remained in place. Jack decided to think it out later if it seemed important enough. Now he had to get on with the interview. He didn't like this feeling of being slightly off-balance — usually he was the one putting the interviewee on the defensive, because that was when interesting things came out.

"I saw part of your talk today..."

"Yes. Also in Washington, I believe."

She had seen him. "Yes, Washington, too, and the fact is, I'm intrigued. You seem to be largely unknown and yet you are already on twenty-five state ballots."

"And within the next few months will be on the other twenty-five," she interrupted quietly.

"It doesn't make sense. This should be a big story."

"The thing you don't see is that it already is a 'big story' — I have a huge following. This campaign has been organizing for years, all over the country. And people have waited, not even knowing they were waiting, for the message I bring them, the hope I give them — that, yes, it is possible to slow, maybe halt, hopefully even start to reverse, the current trend in American politics. The media tends to work hand-in-glove with the status quo, and can barely see what is under their noses if it doesn't conform to their preconceived notions."

"So you think that is why I wrote the first article the way I did?" Stupid question. Talk about defensive. Jack wished he could take it back. Mrs. Conner answer surprised him.

"No. Last time you had an assignment you didn't care about and just wanted to be done. I've read the other articles you've written about presidential long-shots. I suspect I was just one of a group of people that you consider to be kooks. And I didn't help you to get beyond that. Of course, I didn't know about your series. I thought it was a real interview."

Jack didn't know what to think. Her words were like a reprimand and yet he had the feeling she was teasing him. Her face was serious, but an imp lurked behind her eyes. And did the corners of her mouth twitch ever so slightly toward a grin? He was torn between annoyance and laughing out loud. The laugh was what came out.

"Mrs. Conner, I'd like to do a real interview this time, and I hope I never underestimate you again."

"Do you think I have a chance at the presidency?"

He decided to be honest. "No, I don't think you do."

She laughed and said, "Mr. Kelly, it's always nice to deal with an honest, if confused, man." She glanced at her watch. "At five o'clock I must go out, but until then I'm at your disposal."

"When we talked before you mentioned that you didn't wish to seek the support of various special interest groups. Once you burst into the national spotlight — as I admit you soon will" – at her raised eyebrows, he added, "perhaps already have – you'll be inundated from all sides by the various factions wanting you to endorse their ideas in return for money or a guaranteed block of votes. If your stated policies are in agreement with any of these, will you 'join up'?"

"I feel very strongly about this. I want individuals to vote for, or against, the ideas I present. I have no specific quarrel with the concept of special interest groups of any sort — in fact I like the idea of people going all out for what they believe in. I try to listen and respect all sincere points of view. If someone has an idea I haven't thought about, I'll consider it. But I will be influenced by the validity of the idea, not by the money they can offer. I do not accept money or endorsements from any group."

"Changing the trend of human thought is not usually an overnight process. It has taken a number of years to get where we are today. And yet, is the fact that it might be difficult any reason not to try?"

"You want to turn back the clock to a 'simpler' time?"

"No, not really. Life was very different a hundred years ago. I'm not nostalgic for an imagined past where everyone was kinder and better. I doubt it even existed. I prefer to go forward, starting now. We have what we need right here, right now, to achieve anything."

"You plan to legislate values?"

"No. Just the opposite - with some obvious exceptions. There needs, for example, to be a codification of the idea that if you murder someone you will suffer this or that penalty. But legislators need to ask themselves — what will the true effect of this law be, will it do anything to detract from the human spirit of those it touches? I wonder if they ever think about this?"

"Your stand, your goals, will not be very popular with some people."

She nodded in agreement, then added, "I don't mind. I'm running on the assumption that these ideas will be popular where it counts. I say again, I am not out to show how many different opinions, how many different agendas, I can represent."

"You are running for president. How much effect do you really think you will have over Congress if you win? Am I correct in thinking that you are not affiliated with either major party?"

"First: no, I'm not declaring with either party because that would stamp labels on me which would be difficult to shed. I don't want people..." here she grinned at Jack... "able to categorize me without thinking. Both candidates from the major parties — whomever they turn out to be — will carry baggage they'd probably prefer to be rid of. But it also allows them to get away with things. They can give the impression that they believe in something without actually having to say it.

"As for the Congress — obviously, they are free to act as they will. However, you may not be aware of one aspect of my campaign. Every citizen must learn about his or her representatives from the local to the national level. Are your elected officials doing what they say? Are they doing what you want? What do you truly want? If you are dissatisfied, find others for the job. Run for election yourself. Take responsibility. Think. Be brave.

"As of today, we the citizens of the United States still own the government. The government does not own us. Citizens need to remember that every single person employed in government service at any level is simply an employee of the citizens – never the bosses. As with any good employee, we, the bosses, give our employees a certain amount of responsibility. Never should the employees take this responsibility and then begin to think and act as though they are the bosses.

"In America we still have the ability to vote out every elected official and start with a new batch of government employees. If the citizens can develop the will to repeatedly vote out incumbents until those who work for us get the message that we are the bosses and not them, then there is hope that freedom will survive. And those who are elected need to understand the importance of reining in all the non-elected segments of 'government'.

"In government, we get what we deserve. I want us to deserve better than we've got. We need people in office who believe they are there to represent us — not to become our bosses. Americans are fed up — will the inevitable change come peaceably, or do we wait until despair and distrust turn to anger and violence? Even if by some slim chance I lose the presidency, perhaps my message will catch on with the public."

"Suppose you win, but Congress remains essentially the same — what then?"

"Oh, the president has ways. The power of the veto, as I've mentioned before, for example. Sure, the legislators can override the vetoes, but I will be out there explaining to the public what is going on and why."

"I can't see that being very popular on the Hill."

"I have one advantage over everyone else who is running — politics is not my life so I don't have to be afraid of failure. I am not a career politician. Everything I do is not partially (or fully!) aimed at maintaining or furthering my personal power. What I most want is for the citizens to remember that THEY are the bosses and all – yes, ALL – government employees elected or appointed or hired, work as servants to the citizens. Never as bosses."

"Frankly, many of your plans seem unrealistic," Jack interjected.

Mrs. Conner laughed quietly. Then she rose from her chair and walked to the window that looked out over the parking lot. She turned and looked him in the eye for one long moment. When she spoke her voice was gentle.

"To you, being 'realistic' means being hopeless,- giving in just because that is what many have done before. In that sense, I want very badly to be unrealistic. You've got to understand, Mr. Kelly, I am not foolish or naively ignorant. I know what I'm up against. I'm just not afraid to try."

There were moments when he thought she was a crazy zealot, completely out of touch. Right now he wanted it to be possible that she could become president.

She helped him pull out from under her spell by asking if he'd care for some tea or coffee.

"No thanks, maybe just some water."

She got ice from the bucket, and water from the wet bar. He noticed that there was no alcohol in the cabinet.

"Are you a non-drinker?" he asked, indicating the empty bar.

"It seems to me that one must choose between alcohol and clear thinking. They are mutually exclusive. Through the years I've opted for clear thinking."

Jack was pleasantly surprised. He'd come to the same conclusion one night at a fraternity party. The party was in full swing when he'd arrived, but because of an important exam early the next morning, he had no intention of ending up with a hangover. He figured to party without the liquor. Everyone thought they were having such fun. Everyone thought they were getting wittier by the moment — he knew that if he'd been drinking he would have felt the same way. Seeing it sober, his friends just looked pitiful and foolish. He never really drank again — oh, some champagne at a wedding or one glass of wine at a friend's dinner party, but that was about it. But here today, he was a reporter, so he asked, "Does it take the form of a crusade with you?"

"Not a crusade — a conviction that I hold dear. I'm grateful to say that so far the boys have agreed with me. And as President, I will not drink to suit any perceived social convention. I'm not running on a temperance platform, I simply and emphatically live the life of a non-drinker."

"You seem to be such an outsider. Where do you expect to find the people to fill out your administration?"

"I have plans for streamlining the administration to have far fewer people between me and the decisions that are made, a reversal of the current trends. However, this is because the idea is right, not because I don't know suitable people. There is a part of you — I suspect a very big part of you — that believes I am a widow with nothing to do and more money than sense, who is running for president to relieve the boredom of endless bridge parties and tea with the ladies club. Am I right?"

"I'll admit that had crossed my mind...."

"Yes, I'm sure. But don't worry. It may take time, but you'll begin to understand."

Once again feeling slightly off balance, Jack said, "My question still stands: Where will you find the people?"

"I have a wide and deep acquaintance with many eminently qualified people. As it gets nearer to the election, I will bring the main ones forward for public inspection."

"Nothing now?"

"Nothing now."

"What about a vice president?"

"I have some thoughts on the matter."

"But nothing now?"

"That's right. You'll just have to be patient."

They sat down again and continued to talk. Jack pushed and challenged and probed. No matter how hard he pressed, Mrs. Conner remained cool and collected. In fact she seemed to enjoy the battle and rose up to meet it head on.

Sooner than he wished it was time to stop. "I can see that it is nearly five. Thank you for your time. I have more questions I'd like to ask — perhaps we can do this again?" Jack stood up and gathered his belongings.

Mrs. Conner stood also and nodded, saying, "It's been my pleasure." Then she reached into her pocket and handed him a card. "I believe your secretary had quite a time getting through to arrange this interview. I'm afraid our organization has blossomed even faster than we anticipated. We have added a number of lines to our 800 number so it shouldn't be quite so difficult next time."

Taking out a pen, she wrote on the back of the card and handed it to him. "This number will get you through to my assistant, Mrs. Kramer."

"Thank you. I look forward to doing this again."

As Jack started to leave, Mrs. Conner picked up the package that had been sitting unobtrusively on the end of the table and handed it to him.

"This is for you, Mr. Kelly."

Jack was surprised, even somewhat taken aback.

"What is it?"

"Open it later and you'll see." She smiled. "And now if you'll excuse me, I have another appointment — an interview with the local T.V. station, as a matter of fact. I suspect you are flying out shortly, but if not you can catch my two minutes on the ten o'clock news."

Jack still stared at the small, beautifully wrapped package in his hand, wondering if it was something he should accept. Mrs. Conner touched his arm lightly and steered him to the door. "Good day, Mr. Kelly. I look forward to seeing your article."

"Yes...thank you. We'll speak another day."

Then the door was shut behind him and he was in the hall. He wanted to rip open the package right then and there, but decided to wait until he was up in his own room.

As he walked up the stairs, he thought about Mrs. Conner and the interview. She was so smooth, so sure, so articulate, occasionally even eloquent. But he had come away from both interviews feeling unsettled, as though he had not been the one in control. It was a new feeling. He was beginning to think that this year's presidential campaign was going to be interesting after all. He had a challenge now. Who was this woman — this upstart — thinking she could come out of nowhere and become president of the United States of America? He'd find out. He was smiling as he opened the door to his room.

He set his notes and recorder down and then studied the package in his hand. It was about three inches wide, six inches long, and two inches high wrapped in shiny white paper with red and blue curled ribbons cascading over the edges. There was no writing and no card. He unwrapped it carefully and lifted the lid. Inside were four perfect, very fresh, home-baked chocolate chip cookies.

He tried one. It was as good as he remembered. He smiled. Yes, it was going to be an interesting campaign.

Chapter 5

Walter read Jack's article and then called him into his office.

"You seem to be taking this Conner woman seriously."

"She's hard to figure out. Conventional wisdom says she hasn't got the slightest chance, but her support is broad-based and growing. I've heard her speak several times — she has charisma. It's been a long time since I've seen that."

"How will she hold up in the rough and tumble of hardball politics?"

"I don't know, but I plan to be in the front row watching."

"I take it you plan to continue following her campaign."

"Yeah, I'd like to."

"Good. How's your research on special interest groups coming along?"

"As you know, right now I'm mostly sorting through all the groups, making a list of every group that has the potential for influencing politicians — everything from the AARP and the NRA to small fringe groups that hardly anyone hears about. I'll describe the groups themselves and who they contribute to, finally comparing voting records with contributions. I can also see a story dealing with the tactics they use to get their way."

"Sounds like a quagmire that could easily bog you down."

"It'll take time, but once I've gotten into it, it's fascinating. I can sympathize with the special interests who believe in something so strongly that they will fight for it with any method at their disposal. I can sympathize with the politicians who respond to those who importune them the most."

"And the public?"

"If they don't like it, they need to do something about it." Jack realized with a start that he sounded like Helen Conner.

Walter said, "Well, turn in those stories as you have them. And keep track of Conner."

Jack returned to his desk and continued to work — he certainly had plenty to do. First thing was another piece on the Republican and Democratic contenders. No clear winners were emerging from the primary contests so the field was wide open. The Democrats had seven running with one senator wavering, perhaps hoping to be called upon by his 'people' to step in. The woman who had been considered a frontrunner – almost a shoo in – had dropped out for 'personal reasons'. Apparently the sensational tabloid stories were turning out to be true. The Republicans had six major contenders and three on the fringes. There were two nationally known independents who were making noises about running, but seemed to Jack to lack the necessary support. Of course, he'd thought Mrs. Conner had no support, so there was no telling what was going to happen.

And then there was the special interest research. For every group he found and documented, five more seemed to be lurking in the background. It wasn't always easy to discover who was doing what to whom.

Sam stopped by Jack's desk and asked, "Are you and Nora still on for dinner tomorrow?"

"Sure. You and Carol — I should say, Carol, always puts on a great spread. How many are coming?"

"Just ten counting us."

"Sounds great."

"By the way, you might want to check out Internet. There is a hot debate comparing the domestic policies of the Democrats and the Republicans. And they are comparing Ms. Conner as well. She's being taken seriously by some of the contributors."

"Where do I look?"

"It's called NLE. There's a link from Econonet."

"I haven't looked at this before. Do you know anything about it?"

"Not really. Seems to be some economists who formed an electronic newsletter. There is some talk that the 'NL' stands for Nobel Laureate. The writing certainly indicates such a possibility, but it is all anonymous. All questions about identity are either ignored or scoffed at."

"Thanks for the tip. I'll look into it."

Sam returned to his desk and Jack logged on to Econonet and found the NLE writings. It was fascinating reading. Mrs. Conner, while considered meaningless by some, was praised by one or two of the contributors. Jack bookmarked it and made a note to himself to look into this more. He even inserted a request for an interview, in person or on the net, with any of the principals behind NLE. Finally he got back to work on his present article and returned to calling up data on the records of the candidates.

The next morning Jack called Nora to arrange to pick her up for the dinner party. She declined the ride and said she'd just meet him there. Jack agreed, but was disappointed. That meant she'd go home alone, too.

Sam and Carol had a beautiful townhouse on a historic street. The dining room looked out over the garden that in summer was an orchestrated riot of color, but now had the subtle colors of early spring.

Peter Holderman was across from Jack at the table. Between mouthfuls of black bean soup he said to Jack, "I read your article on what's-her-name — Ellen Conner."

"Helen Conner."

"Right. You sound as though you take her seriously. Who is she?"

Kara Swindell broke in, "I was wondering about that, too."

Nora asked, "Who are you talking about?"

"Helen Conner," Jack replied.

Nora asked the table at large, "How many of you have heard of Helen Conner?"

The response was mostly negative.

Nora said to Jack, "This is really amazing. According to you, she has no doubt that she'll be a major contender. And she's on how many state ballots?"

"Twenty five at last count."

"And yet nobody knows about her."

"Jack's story should open a few eyes," said Peter. "But you don't really think she has the slightest chance, do you? I mean, her ideas are something out of a 'let's all feel good' seminar. Just close your eyes, say 'everything is going to be all right' and if you really believe it, then — poof — everything IS all right."

Kara spoke up, "I didn't get that out of Jack's article. I don't think she has a chance against political pros, but I like her ideas. It's time someone said those things."

"Do you think she's serious?" asked Sam from the end of the table.

"She's running a very serious campaign," replied Jack.

"No, I mean, do you think she is sincere, or has she just found a good marketable line? I've read a bit about her and she seems to be extremely bright. Maybe she's doing this as a way to get power and influence. She can't really believe she'll be elected president come November."

"I don't know. I've interviewed her twice, heard her speak in public twice, yet remain unsure what the answer to your question is. She has a quality about her, a charisma really, that makes her seem sincere. I don't know yet if it is just 'seeming', or if it really is sincerity."

"And you intend to find out?" asked Peter with a slight leer.

"Yes, I do," replied Jack, ignoring Peter's tone. "Her candidacy will make this a memorable election year."

"Will you vote for her?" asked Kara.

"Interesting political races and who I vote for are two very different things. I'll wait and see who the candidates are before I decide who to vote for."

Later over coffee in cozy corner of Sam's living room, Nora said to Jack, "You are really excited about the prospect of Helen Conner being in the election, aren't you?"

"I think she'll bring a spark that's been missing lately. Whatever else happens, she's not someone who will be ignored."

"Maybe I should try to get an interview with her next time she's in Washington."

"You should," said Jack. "I have the number of her campaign headquarters if you want to set it up." In a quieter voice he asked, "Do you want to come over after the party?"

She didn't look him in the eye as she answered, "Not tonight. I need to get right home. Big day tomorrow."

"I understand," said Jack, trying to sound more sympathetic than he felt. It must not have worked.

"I really do need to get straight to bed. I have to be up at five thirty tomorrow morning. The reason I drove here tonight was so I could leave early." She didn't bother to hide her annoyance.

"Got to get that beauty sleep." Jack knew this was an unfair dig. Nora was getting touchy about that subject. There were so few women reporters who were able to stay on top as years began adding wrinkles to the corners of their eyes and laugh lines around the mouth. Nora never quite believed that she had what it takes to be one of the winners. Jack knew it was talent that was driving her career — he wished she believed it. And now he was digging at that tender spot just because he was annoyed that she was going her own way. He had no right. There were no promises, no commitments.

"Let's not argue. I'm sorry. I just hoped to see you," Jack apologized.

Nora smiled, apology accepted. "I know. Things are hectic right now. This is very hush-hush, but Henderson told me that I am up for an anchor job."

"Nora!" Jack quietly exclaimed, "That's great. When will you know?"

"It's still just rumor..."

"You'd be perfect. The guys at the station are finally using their heads."

"I'll believe it when I see it." She hesitated, then added, "If I get the job, well, I'll be a lot busier..." Her voice trailed off, but Jack grasped her implication — even less time together.

Peter came up and said, "You two are always off in a corner nattering away, all lovey-dovey."

Why Sam included Peter in his guest list was outside Jack's comprehension, but Nora and Jack just smiled and return to the party.

Chapter 6

Over the next weeks the stories about Helen Conner gained in frequency and seriousness. Her name appeared regularly over the wire services. She got on the TV news occasionally. Bumper stickers began to show up on cars. And, of course, the electronic networks were a-buzz with ever escalating updates, tweets, and conversations. Jack continued to follow NLE and it's running debate about the effect on the economy of Mrs. Conner's policies.

However the mystery of NLE itself remained. No one knew the source or the identities of the major contributors who logged on under obviously false names. And all attempts to follow the electronic trail back to the senders had failed. Apparently, it was harder to break into NLE's computers, than to access the C.I.A.

Several of the NLE's regulars were blasting Mrs. Conner, but one defended her with great vigor. Subscribers who logged on also tried to influence the debate. When he had a free moment, Jack enjoyed 'listening' in. He had tried before and he continued to try to get those behind NLE to allow a real face-to-face interview. Over the electronic highways, they always declined, enjoying the power their anonymity gave them.

Jack now had a bulky file on Mrs. Conner. He was beginning to think it was time for another interview, when Walter came out of his office and pointed to the T.V. monitors next to the wall.

"Come see this."

Jack, and others nearby, walked over. The screen was filled with a twisting, pushing, angry tide of bodies. Some carried placards, all were shouting or chanting. They were shown pushing their way past ineffectual security guards into an auditorium. On the platform behind the podium stood Helen Conner. The voice-over announcer explained that this was the scene at a speech being given by the presidential hopeful in Eugene, Oregon. The picture switched to the reporter who stood with the building in the background.

Then the announcer explained that the pictures had been taken earlier at a rally in which Conner supporters had clashed with several groups of protestors. Three individuals had been treated for minor injuries and released from the local hospital. The authorities whisked Ms. Conner away against her wishes because they could not guarantee her safety. The reporter was trying to get a statement from the Conner people and from those who had been protesting. He would report when he had further information. The reporter's tone suggested he thought it was all a bit of a tempest in a teapot — why would protestors worry about Ms. Conner's candidacy anyway?

"Well, Jack," said Walter, "Your friend seems to be stirring things up. Do you want to look into it?"

"Sure. I'll see if I can get through on the phone."

He knew it was a terrible time — no doubt countless reporters were all trying to get through to satisfy their editors. Jack tried anyway. The 800 number was busy, so he decided to try the other number Mrs. Conner had written on the back of the card. It went through and was picked up on the fourth ring.

"Hello."

"Hello. This is Jack Kelly of the 'Washington News'...."

"Yes, Mr. Kelly, this is Edith Kramer. How may I help you?"

Jack was surprised, but glad, to have gotten right through to the top.

"Mrs. Kramer, I was hoping to have a chance to speak with Mrs. Conner. Is she available?"

"Did you wish to set up another interview?"

"Actually, yes. But right now I was hoping for a clarification of the business in Eugene."

"One moment...."

There was a silence at the other end for nearly a minute and then Mrs. Kramer was back, "Mr. Kelly?"

"Yes, I'm still here."

"If you will hold for several more minutes, Mrs. Conner will speak with you briefly."

"Sure, I'll hold." Jack didn't know what to think. His timing must have been perfect. He waited.

"Mr. Kelly?" Her voice came across bright and clear with no hint of stress.

"Mrs. Conner, hello. I was wondering if you have a statement regarding the incident in Eugene earlier this morning?"

"My, my, how news travels. Where did you hear about it?"

"Over the T.V. down here at the paper. What can you tell me?"

"At this point, I know little more than you do. The security who were hired as a standard procedure, were unprepared for the crowd, and please don't quote this, but I think they panicked. They dragged me away as I protested that I'd rather stay and deal with the situation. A most ignominious retreat."

"Who were the protestors?"

"We are trying to sort it out now. It seems to me there were some with environmental causes, a women's group or two, and several others who were convinced that they were the victims of one thing or another. The fact is, no one is sure yet if they were supporting or rejecting me."

"So you are already drawing protestors."

Even over the phone he could sense to smile on her face. "Yes. It seems there are those who are taking me seriously — although whether it is as a real candidate or a freak sideshow is still unanswered."

"What do you think it is about your, shall we call it 'platform' that upsets these people?"

"Although they haven't stated it precisely, the underlying reason seems to be that I encourage people to make up their own minds on issues after finding out as much information as possible. The leadership of many of these groups who claim to work for the public good, even those who probably started out with high motives, end up grasping personal power. And to get it they are often willing to lie or shade facts. For example, many of the claims of the ardent environmentalists cannot stand up to rigorous independent research."

"That's a strong statement."

"Yes. And they obviously don't like it said. Instead of trying to shout me down, I wonder why they don't just prove me wrong?"

There were voices in the background and Mrs. Conner said, "Excuse me a minute." When she came back on the line she said, "I'm sorry, Mr. Kelly, there are some things I need to take care of. Feel free to call again if you wish."

"I would like to set up another face-to-face interview."

"I'll get you Mrs. Kramer."

"Thank you for your time."

"My pleasure." Then she was gone and Mrs. Kramer's no nonsense voice came back. In ten days time Mrs. Conner was planning to take a break in her hectic schedule and relax on the Oregon coast. She was willing to offer Jack a couple hours of that time. He agreed immediately.

Jack hung up the phone. Sam walked over.

"What did you find out?"

"I spoke with Mrs. Conner."

"You're kidding!"

"No. I must have gotten through at the right time to the right place."

Sam looked at him for a moment. "Maybe it's more than that. Maybe you've got a special in with someone down there."

"I don't know," grinned Jack. "I have made a effort to get on good terms with the personal secretary. She's a tough old bird, but maybe she finds me irresistible."

"Well, you'd better take good care of that 'old bird'. You'll be glad to have her on your side in the next months."

"I'm going to interview Mrs. Conner again in ten days — out on the Oregon coast."

"Think of me slaving away.... "

"Wasn't it Las Vegas where you were going to do that story?"

"Oh, yeah, well, anyway...."

"I'm going to write up my report. There must be something you need to do?"

Sam cuffed him on the arm as he headed back to his desk. He called over his shoulder, "Still on for the game tonight?"

"I think so. Unless something happens with this story."

Forty-five minutes later Jack's phone rang. It was Edith Kramer calling for Mrs. Conner. "She asked me to tell you the names of the groups who got out of hand at the speech."

Jack was impressed, although he thought it was simply a standing order to provide follow-up to the media.

"Thank you. Go ahead."

Mrs. Kramer gave him the names of several groups, all of which he had in his files on special interests. None of it seemed new or surprising except that they seemed to be starting so early in the campaign. There were still so many Republicans and Democrats in the race it must be hard for the protestors to zero in on any particular one. Mrs. Conner just made an early, easy target.

But the ranks were beginning to thin. An ex-senator dropped out citing 'health reasons' after three women, each claiming to be his mistress, began to fight it out in the tabloids. Jack wondered if these politicians would ever learn. Did they think these things stay hidden? That made him wonder what was going to pop out of Helen Conner's closet as the campaign heated up. He'd always been willing, even eager, in the past to dig out whatever he could on candidates — while trying to reserve some place for that which was truly private to stay private. He realized that with Mrs. Conner he'd made no attempt to look deeply into her background.

Who was she? Where did she come from? Her family? Her friends? Her husband? Their business? Their finances? Did she have a boyfriend waiting somewhere in the wings? She was attractive and had been a widow for years — naw — leave that angle to the sleazy reporters. But the rest — it was time for some deeper digging. He wanted to be very prepared for the Oregon coast interview.

Nora walked into the newsroom looking radiant. With a guilty start Jack realized he hadn't seen her for a number of days. But she waved at him gaily as he rose to greet her. She gave him a big hug.

"It happened!" She was simply bubbling.

"What happened?"

"You are looking at the new anchor for Channel 4 T.V., Washington, D.C. Not co-anchor, mind you. Anchor. Me."

"Congratulations. This calls for a celebration. Let's go to dinner."

"Oh, no, I can't. Not tonight. I'm sorry, but I did want to tell you about this job. I beat out John. It's a miracle."

Jack wondered what else she had to do that was so important she couldn't celebrate with him, but knew asking her would spoil the mood. Instead he congratulated her again.

"And something else," said Nora when the excitement level died down. "I'm doing a short interview with Helen Conner for the Sunday news program. I wondered if there are any tricks to dealing with her?"

"No, so far she has seemed to be fairly straightforward. No strange moods or unreasonable requests. I'd say don't assume anything about her. She'll surprise you. She's bright, articulate, confident. You're a good reporter. You'll get a good interview."

"Next week. She'll be in Washington for the day, and the station managed to arrange the interview."'

"You make it sound as if it were difficult."

"The talk is that she is becoming sought after — and then that business this morning in Oregon. My producer has been trying to get through to her all day. Her people have put out a press release and that's what we'll air on the news tonight."

Jack had kept Mrs. Kramer's number a secret from everyone, even Nora. He felt a vague sense of disloyalty, but on the other hand if they wanted others — Nora — to have it they would give it out. Was he being mean-spirited, or simply protecting a potentially valuable source? Nora didn't need special help. She was making it just fine on her own.

Jack had dinner in front of the T.V., with the DVR going as well. He was gathering everything he could on Mrs. Conner. Channel 4 ran the story of the disrupted speech about five minutes into the news. It was basically the same footage as earlier, but this time there were comments from Mrs. Conner and a spokesperson from the Green Eagles, one of the protest groups.

Mrs. Conner wondered what the environmentalists had to fear — all she called for was rigorous independent scientific testing before environmental claims were used as the basis for public policy decisions.

In a separate statement the spokesperson said Mrs. Conner was trying to destroy all the progress that millions had sacrificed and worked for, that she didn't care what became of the earth or the life of all creatures and plants on Earth. Having her as president was the most dangerous thing that could happen to America.

Mrs. Conner came across as dignified and reasonable — the environmentalist as articulate and intense. Jack added to his notes for the Oregon interview. Then he called Sam and told him he'd meet him at the game.

Chapter 7

On the way to Mrs. Conner's beach property in a car he had rented at the airport, Jack compared his present attitude with that of the last time he'd been in Oregon to interview her. He didn't kid himself. Had he done the proper research the first time, he would have known that she was a legitimate candidate, even if a long shot. His first article had been so condescending. The second was better, but this time he felt really prepared. And far in the back of his mind an idea had begun to grow. Whatever the outcome, by the time this election was over, Mrs. Conner was going to be a household name. The story of her campaign would make a great book and who better to write it than Jack Kelly. As he drove through the forested Coast Range, he began to imagine the form such a book could take. It filled his thought until he reached Highway 101. Then he had to concentrate on the directions he'd been given.

The whole area was beautiful, but the Conner house was situated on spectacular property. The house was nestled into the side of a hill with an open view of the dunes below and ocean beyond. There were no houses anywhere nearby and Jack suspected that the Conners owned the whole area.

The house was solid but simple — weathered gray boards, cedar shake roof, landscaping that was subtle, done mostly with natural coast vegetation such as salal, rhododendrons, and evergreens. But the entrance walk was lined with bright, spring flowers. Jack walked up and knocked.

Somehow he'd expected Mrs. Kramer to answer, but it was Mrs. Conner herself who welcomed him in. She led him to the front room that had long windows giving an unobstructed view of the ocean down beyond the dunes.

"You have a beautiful place here, Mrs. Conner."

"Thank you. I take credit for the house, but God surely did an excellent job on the rest. It's always been a good place to get away."

"A sort of 'White House West'?"

"I know you are kidding because you don't think I have a chance of winning, but I, knowing otherwise, have actually considered it, and I'm not sure it would be fair to the old place. Can you imagine fifty Secret Service agents, the White House press corps, not to mention various secretaries, advisors, and hangers-on here? I'm afraid some part of the essential nature of the place would be lost. What do you think?"

Jack laughed. "You're probably right."

"Is this a good spot for you?" asked Mrs. Conner, indicating a soft chair near the window.

"It's fine, and thank you for allowing me to come here to interview you during your time off."

She smiled and sat down opposite him. When he first came into the house he had hoped for the scent of fresh-baked cookies. He was tempted to say something. Oh, why not.

"I was wondering where the cookies are," he said with a straight face.

"That's not until later," was her enigmatic response. Wordlessly, they looked at each other, both waiting for the other to smile first. Neither did. Jack started the interview.

"Mrs. Conner, some of your recent speeches have drawn controversy. What can you tell me about these occurrences?"

"People don't like their cherished notions to be challenged."

"Will you elaborate?"

"We live in a wonderful society. We are allowed to believe whatever we want to, and most of the time may act on those beliefs. Occasionally, however, and with increasing frequency, people get the conviction that those who disagree with them are not just 'wrong', but are evil. I am standing up in front of the nation and saying things that are disturbing, not only to the status quo of big government, but to the status quo of various groups, some relatively mainstream, some on the fringes, who have begun to take for granted that if they speak, the nation trembles. I'm not trembling and they are seriously annoyed."

"I know that environmentalists were among those protesting. Where do you stand on environmental issues?"

"Basing the policy of the United States on pronouncements of doom and destruction that get their value not from research and deep thought, but from fear-filled, emotional rhetoric is a bad idea. And if real problems can be shown to exist, then the first line of defense is in the private lives of each of us. The government has a role, but not the only role in this issue. The government must take part only if it is clearly necessary and there is no other option. We have developed the terrible habit of thinking that the government is the answer to most of our problems. There are many other, better solutions based in free enterprise."

With barely concealed amazement, Jack said, "That is easy for you to say. Look at this place. You don't have to live in the middle of a city where the air is bad and garbage spills out into the streets, or in an African village where over-grazing has denuded the hillsides."

"You're right. I own this property and am able to make decisions about it. Those decisions that my husband and I made are responsible for the man-made additions you see about you — additions that only moments ago you were complimenting. Why is it beautiful? — because we love it, and care for it, and are able to make decisions based on our intimate knowledge of this particular piece of property.

"If you look at our cities or in some of the areas in the world such as you mentioned, what will you discover? Quite regularly you'll find that government regulation on the local, state, federal, tribal levels is the root of the problems. There are always some people who will behave badly — but the vast majority of people care for that which they own. Just look at China — with the government in charge of everything you'd think that they would make wise decisions about the environment. There were no 'greedy' individuals to get in the way of 'sound' policy. But the reality? Terrible pollution."

"You sound like a hard core conservative to me."

Mrs. Conner laughed. "You want very badly to paste a label on me

— one that will clear up your confusion. If you can just label me, you won't have to think about what I say. You'll be able to pretend you already know what I think. If conservatives have some good, wise ideas, I delight to share them. The same goes for liberals, Republicans, Democrats, Libertarians, Independents, whoever. A good idea is a good idea. However, just because some Nazis loved their children as I love mine, does not make me a Nazi.

"There are areas of environmental concern where the federal government is the best place to look for solutions. All I ask is that the decisions be based on research, wisdom, logic, common sense — not on hysteria or on the pronouncements of those who hate humanity."

"You feel that environmentalists hate humanity?"

"Most do not, of course, but some do. There is a clear, outspoken element in the environmental movement that feels that mankind is the enemy. And if only we could get rid of most of the people, then 'nature' could return to...nature. I sometimes wonder where exactly they think people came from."

"What do you think Man's place is?" Jack could hardly believe he was asking an ontological question in a presidential interview.

"I think we are incredibly special. Whatever you believe — that the primordial soup danced an extraordinary dance and suddenly life was there, or life is the result of divine intervention, God being God, life being the result —whatever you believe, I don't see how you can get around the fact that humans definitely stand out from the rest of 'nature'. We have a creativity, a sense of the possibilities. It's a big responsibility, but one we can shoulder with grace and wisdom and fearlessness."

It was hard to think of a smooth shift into his next line of questions. He wanted to ask about foreign policy, crime.... Just then two young men came running up the path from the beach. One Jack recognized as Chris. The other he assumed to be Alex, the older son. They were clearly having a race, with Alex only barely in front. Jack glanced at Mrs. Conner and saw the love with which she watched them. A pang shot through his chest. He and Carrie had tried to have children. The doctors all said there was no hope unless they wanted to go the surrogate route. Neither of them could face that. An adoption was being considered when the accident happened.

The boys burst into the room, tumbling and laughing and smelling of salt air. They stopped when they saw Jack. Chris smiled, Alex's appraisal was cooler.

Mrs. Conner, ever gracious, spoke, "Mr. Kelly, you remember Chris." They shook hands in greeting as Jack replied, "Yes, of course."

Chris said, "Hello, Mr. Kelly, How are you?"

"And this is Alex."

"How do you do?" Alex's greeting was polite, but he clearly did not have Chris's open willingness to be friends.

Mrs. Conner, speaking to both boys, said, "Wash up and then bring out some refreshments, will you please?"

When they left, the room seemed suddenly very still. As if reading his thoughts, Mrs. Conner said, "Young men have a way of exuding life."

They both laughed.

The next few moments were filled with chat about the commonplaces — the weather, the view, and then the boys were back. Chris carried a tray full of treats — little cakes, pieces of fruit, and in the middle, a huge pile of chocolate chip cookies. Chris set the tray down and Alex said, "The hot water will be ready in a minute. Mom, tea or coffee?"

"Tea."

"Mr. Kelly?"

"Tea sounds good to me, too."

Alex turned and was gone. Jack looked at the cookies and then at Mrs. Conner. "Chocolate chip cookies. Did you make them?"

"Why yes, I did."

"And tell me, will you be making such cookies when you are in the White House?"

"I feel that if there is one thing that will enhance this country, it is having someone in the White House who knows how to make good cookies. As far as I know this question has not been asked of the major candidates as yet, but mark my words — the country needs to know, the country deserves to know every candidates' stand on this issue."

Jack finally couldn't help laughing. "You'll never let me live it down, will you?"

She just grinned and raised her eyebrows. Alex came back with the tea service. He poured out for all of them as they sat, chatted, drank tea, and ate treats.

Chris asked what it was like being a reporter, about stories Jack had covered. Alex remained more distant, while still joining occasionally in the conversation. Jack noticed that Mrs. Conner made no effort to steer the conversation in any particular direction. She certainly didn't seem concerned that the boys might say something untoward to this reporter from a major Washington newspaper.

Jack decided to see what the limits were. "Alex, what do you think of your mother's bid for the presidency?"

Alex spoke with no hesitation. "I can't think of a better person to lead this country for the next eight years."

"That's very loyal."

"Yes, but also reasonable, thought out, and a conclusion based on facts."

"Do you agree with her on all subjects?"

Here he paused and glanced at his mother, a question in his eyes. She gave silent consent. Alex continued, "No, not always. But I've learned, sometimes the hard way, since I was quite small, that most of the time she is right."

Something about the statement caused the three Conners to all laugh. Jack was left out of the family joke. Mrs. Conner said, "Forgive us, Mr. Kelly. As I'm sure you know, families tend to share certain memories...." They all laughed again.

"May I know?"

Mrs. Conner looked at the boys. "It's up to Alex."

Alex stopped laughing and looked at Jack. The distance, the distrust, came back to his eyes. "Maybe another time. I've got to go now. Coming Chris?"

Both boys stood up and after the proper farewells were gone into the back reaches of the house. Shortly the sound of music wafted faintly to the front room.

"More tea, Mr. Kelly?"

"Yes, please."

Jack felt comfortable here and fairly sure he was not over-extending his welcome, so he began the interview again. They spoke on a variety of issues. Always the overriding theme was that individuals made their own choices and even if they made stupid mistakes the government had no right to step into the process. It was exemplified in Mrs. Conner's ideas about crime and gun control.

"Everyone who commits a crime is making a conscious decision to do so. Part of that decision-making includes whether or not to use a gun to assist in the crime. We already have fairly strict gun-control laws — what we need now are laws that are clear and unequivocal about their use. If you use, or even have a gun with you when you commit a crime, you have to know absolutely that you will be punished severely — no plea bargains, no shortened sentences. You do it, and you're in serious trouble every time. Criminals are pretty stupid, but not completely so. It won't take long to see a dramatic reduction in the use of guns in crimes."

"What about the various shootings at schools, airports, malls, etc.?"

"I don't believe it is a good idea to make laws in the hope of stopping crazy or out of control people. Those people still exist and everyone else suffers under the laws. There are already plenty of laws dealing with these and other related issues. Murder is already against the law. The most stringent military state and draconian laws will not stop an individual bent on destruction."

"Do you expect the support of the NRA?"

"Mr. Kelly, what do you think my response will be to that?"

"That you don't care what the organization says, you just hope that the individuals who make it up will hear your message and decide for themselves."

"A plus, Mr. Kelly. Perhaps you have been listening after all."

"The groups will come. They will want to endorse you. How will you deal with that?"

"I refuse money except in small amounts from individuals. I can't be bought. It's that simple. If ideas are good I'm happy to include them, but only for the sake of the idea itself." Mrs. Conner was silent for a moment, looking out toward the sea. Finally she spoke, her voice somber, "Actually the biggest problem are those who want to get rid of me and these ideas."

Nothing up until now had led Jack to suspect her of paranoia. His skepticism barely hidden, he asked, "What are you talking about?"

"I did lots of research before I made the final decision to run for president. Much of it was to help strengthen my views, get my facts straight, that sort of thing. But I also wanted to find out the impact on my life and, more particularly, on the boys. What it would 'like' to run for president — to be president. I've known from the start what I was facing. And yet, I wonder if anyone gets used to it — to the threats. I don't know if you noticed when you came in that we have guards now."

He hadn't.

"They are good at being unobtrusive. Soon the Secret Service will be watching. It's strange. Of all the candidates, I'm probably the one most willing to listen to all voices. I'll even change my mind if it is proved to me that my stand is flawed. I'm not some crazed demagogue who needs to be stopped at all costs."

"Who do you think is threatening you?"

"I wish I knew. I have people trying to sort it out. Lots of it, of course, is just garbage, but some...some of the threats — they call them promises — have a ring of cold-blooded, murderous determination."

"What would it take to get you to quit?"

"That won't happen. They misjudge me completely when they think their threats will scare me off."

Jack had not seen this side of her before and was not sure what to make of it. This also added a dimension to his work on special interest groups. How did other candidates deal with serious threats? Did they even receive them? Were they a normal part of being a candidate?

Mrs. Conner smiled, breaking the somber mood. "That is not the essence of my campaign, only a small distraction."

Changing the direction, Jack said, "I have been following a discussion on the internet — NLE — have you seen it?"

"Chris, who is the computer wizard of the family, has pointed it out for me and, I must say, we have been enjoying it. We follow the dialogue and even occasionally try to get a word in."

"You've contributed? Under what name?"

"I get to keep some secrets. When you log on, try to guess."

line lay between a good interview and an imposition. He knew that he was getting special treatment and he didn't want to jeopardize that. He wanted to stay longer, but finally forced himself to stop.

As he drove out, he looked for the guards and saw two. Each was armed and had state-of-the-art communications equipment. An air of complete professionalism surrounded them. On the way in he must have been recognized as well as expected, hence allowed to pass. He wondered how tight the security would get before this was all over. It was hard to decide if the benefits of being famous could outweigh the dangers. He'd had his share of death threats through the years. Certain kinds of stories always seemed to bring the weirdos out of the woodwork, but he assumed that the vast majority were just people with nothing better to do than write nasty letters, rather than people with truly murderous plans. He used care as it was appropriate, but he never held back because of fear. In that regard he understood Mrs. Conner. On the other hand, he didn't have two sons to factor into the picture. What would he have done if the threats had ever been aimed at Carrie?

Chapter 8

That night Jack spent in Portland. His flight was scheduled for early afternoon of the next day, so he used his morning to check out Mrs. Conner's campaign headquarters. They occupied the ground floor of part of an office building just off the main downtown. There were the standard posters and bunting as he walked in. The large front reception area had many desks full of people busy on computers or talking on phones. There was an air of barely submerged excitement, almost electric, in the air. He'd

Jack walked up to the nearest desk. The young woman was on the phone, but glanced at him and smiled. She held up her hand to indicate that she would be with him in a moment and then finished her call. After gently replacing the receiver on the phone, she asked if she could help him. He explained that he was a reporter and wondered if there was someone here with whom he could speak. She looked about eighteen, but may have been twenty-four. Was he getting so old that he couldn't tell anymore? Smiling brightly, she directed him to an office in the rear. She waved good-naturedly with her fingers as the phone rang and she picked it up, spreading her cheer to the next person to enter her life.

As he was nearly to the back offices, Mrs. Kramer stepped out of one of them. Jack went up to her and was about to re-introduce himself, but she spoke first, "Mr. Kelly, how are you?"

"Mrs. Kramer, how nice to see you. You are looking lovely today."

She gave him a stern look, but smiled when she asked, "What can I do for you?"

"I wanted to see this place, talk to some of the workers, get a feel for the mood of the campaign. How about you? May I interview you?"

She scoffed at the idea, dismissing it out of hand, "I hardly think so."

A partially opened door behind Mrs. Kramer swung open wide and a young man stepped out. "Edith, I think I should be the one to talk with...."

"Jack Kelly," she supplied. "Mr. Kelly, this is Will Camden."

Before she could say anything else, Camden took Jack by the hand, half leading, half dragging him into the office. He dismissed Mrs. Kramer with a curt thank you and closed the door.

"Kelly, this is an honor. Please have a seat." He indicated a chair and waited for Jack to sit down. Camden was a good-looking boy...well, young man — he was probably all of thirty years old. His face burned with intensity and enthusiasm as he spoke. His simplest statements sounded as though they 'mattered'.

"What can I do for you, Kelly?"

"Answer some questions, give some background."

"Sure. Anything."

"What is your position here, Mr. Camden?"

"Please, call me Will."

"Will."

"I'm the coordinator. You could call me the chief-of-staff."

"I thought that was Mrs. Kramer's place."

"No, she's more of a personal secretary."

"How did you get involved with the campaign?"

"When I found out that Helen was running for president, I said to myself, 'Yes, that is just right'. I came to her immediately and volunteered."

"Are you and the others I saw outside all volunteers?"

"No, Helen has far more important things to do. Of course, she has hired some of the staff."

"Do you agree with her 'platform'?"

"Yes, of course, she is amazing. There are one or two things I hope to persuade her to reconsider," Camden chuckled, well, snickered, it seemed to Jack who had the irrational desire to put his fist through Will Camden's elegant, chiseled, smug nose, but instead asked, "What are your responsibilities?"

"I make many of the day-to-day decisions, things Helen doesn't need to be involved in, talk to supporters, accept contributions, plan publicity."

"And before you were here?"

"I was at Hansen, Hansen, and Bailey."

"Who are...?"

Camden looked at Jack as if wondering how it was possible for him to be unaware of Hansen, Hansen, and Bailey, and then answered. "The most prestigious law firm on the west coast."

"And you left them because...?"

Camden's eyes narrowed ever so slightly, but then he smiled what he probably assumed was a disarming smile, "When the opportunity came to help Helen, I had no other choice. We all come to times in our lives when we have to decide what is important — money, fame, prestige, or doing the right thing. I'm sure I chose wisely. Helen's going to be president."

Jack wished Camden would stop calling Mrs. Conner 'Helen'. It sounded so familiar. And this young man's barely hidden ambition seemed so out of sync with the Conner campaign as he had come to know

it. And yet Mrs. Conner was really such an unknown quantity at this point.
Sure, he'd interviewed her a few times, and found her open and appealing
in personality. But he had also seen her speak and knew she was excellent
at working her audience. She had the power, the magic, of charisma. And
she knew she had it. The question was: was she using the power of
seeming sincerity to hide something not so pure — to want to be
president implied extraordinary ambitions. He'd certainly seen plenty of
cases when goodness was a mask. Fortunately, masks eventually fall. Was
Camden the first crack?

Camden, meanwhile was explaining his latest promotional idea that he
was about to present to 'Helen'. There was a knock at the door and
Mrs. Kramer walked in.

"Excuse me, Edith, we are busy here," said Camden.

Ignoring his testiness, she said to Jack, "You have a message, Mr.
Kelly."

Jack got up and Camden handed him a card — perhaps to make sure
Jack wouldn't misspell his name in the article. Jack was grateful when
Camden's door closed behind him.

"This way." Mrs. Kramer motioned him toward her office. Once
inside she said, "There is no message. I just wanted to give you the option
of being able to get away from Will...

"May I ask you a few questions?"

Mrs. Kramer was immediately back to her old efficient, unflappable self. "I'll help you in any way I can."

"You have already helped a lot," said Jack thinking of the quick phone access he'd had to Mrs. Conner. "First of all, what are your duties in the Conner campaign?"

"I do what's necessary," was the simple, yet forceful reply.

"Mr. Camden says that he is chief-of-staff and you are Mrs. Conner's personal secretary. Is that fairly accurate?"

"Perhaps in Mr. Camden's mind."

"And you would say…?"

"That things are not always as they seem."

"You don't wish to speak ill of Mr. Camden?"

"All it takes is for him to open his mouth — no other 'ill speaking' is required."

"I must say, all of this surprises me."

"Mr. Camden has not been with us long, and may not be."

"Are you going to fire him?"

"Mr. Kelly, there are any number of truly important things going on in this office and in Mrs. Conner's campaign in general. What becomes of one Will Camden is not important enough to demand all this attention."

It is if it shows the underlying nature of the campaign, thought Jack. At this point, however, he wanted to continue on Mrs. Kramer's good side so he didn't push it. There were other ways to find these things out. He glanced at his watch. "I've got a plane to catch. Thank you for your time. Perhaps we can talk more when I come again."

Chapter 9

As he drove to the airport, Jack pondered his encounters at the campaign headquarters. A question that he didn't want to think about forced its way out. Were Mrs. Conner and Camden lovers? She was older than he was, but a very attractive woman, widowed for a few years, and in a position of great power. Camden had those flashy good looks that some women found appealing. It was possible, but Jack couldn't make himself believe it. He pictured Mrs. Conner at her beach house, her two boys running up the path, her face full of love. She seemed too fine for the likes of Will Camden. And yet....

shady dealing or corruption. No lawsuits past or pending. The finances seemed strong. Mrs. Conner had been involved as a partner — whether in fact or only in name Jack was hoping to find out.

Jack could usually tell if people were giving him the run-around or stonewalling him — but his visit to the corporate headquarters left him wondering. Try as he might he couldn't find anyone who had anything but praise for Mrs. Conner or her late husband. They all seemed very enthusiastic about the prospect of her as president. "Conner for President" buttons were everywhere. The only concern seemed to be that Mrs. Conner wouldn't be available to run the company. In anticipation of the campaign, she'd removed herself from the day-to-day workings and was in the process of organizing her affairs so she could be away for eight years. Jack couldn't fault her confidence.

One of his questions in the interview dealt with her view of business:

"Mrs. Conner, as a partner in your husband's company, you have had a close-hand look at business and labor. As president, if dispute arise, which side do you think you'll favor?"

"Business and labor are one. Business needs labor. Labor needs business. If anyone takes 'sides' they are missing that essential point. You visited our company, did you not?"

"Yes."

"Did you see great forces in conflict with each other?"

"No. In fact there seemed to be an unnatural harmony."

Mrs. Conner laughed. "You think you were set-up."

"It crossed my mind."

"I assume you know that I am no longer a part of the day-to-day operations. You may not know I'm considering a buy-out offer."

"No, I didn't know that."

"The point is, I am really no longer a part of the company. They are free to do and say what they want. In the early days of the campaign I spoke to the people of the company. I explained that the time would come when reporters began descending on them, bringing a plague of repetitive, never-ending questions. My one request to them was that they try to be patient and ultimately forgive me for putting them in that position. My information is that so far they are taking it well. I trust they will not mislead anyone.

"Business in all its forms, is the backbone of the American economy. We need to welcome and embrace new enterprise — not regulate it to death."

"Anything goes?"

"No, sir. Remember my basic tenet — responsibility. The aim is for everyone to be responsible. And, ideally, irresponsibility should bring with it its own consequences — no government bail-outs, for example."

"I have to say, Mrs. Conner, that I can't get over feeling that just whistling in the wind. How do you seriously make everyone responsible for their own even by your own stated principles, n

"Exactly. And yet for a long tim its way into that very position — arbiter of every aspect of our lives. happen simply because they were their lives. And now that I, and n

there will be a re-thinking, a renewing of individual pride, and a willingness to think for themselves. If I can just facilitate a start in that direction, I'll be satisfied."

"Where is the concrete evidence that this is possible?"

"You don't have to look much farther than the burgeoning success of my campaign. There is a mood in the country that is ready for this."

Sitting in coach on the plane back to Washington, Jack thought about the idealism of this woman. The taped interview played softly through his earphones as he lay back listening and thinking. He wanted to believe in her sincerity, even if he couldn't believe in her plan, but that would seem to require him to believe her naive. And she was too much in control to be that naive. He wished he understood her master plan — knew the true target of her ambitions. Ambition, idealism, charisma. He thought of history, of other times of discontent and confusion, and leaders who rose up — ambitious, charismatic, with sweet words on their lips. Would it be wise to fear her? But he listened to the tape and smiled, because he realized with a start that he liked her.

The Republican and Democratic conventions were coming up and then more months of intensive campaigning. What needed to come out would. He'd see to it. He and countless other reporters were digging, always digging to find the true story. He laughed at his own arrogance and continued listening to Mrs. Conner's voice spin its beautiful web.

Chapter 10

The next few weeks were a jumble of activity for Jack. None of the primaries had spewed out a clear-cut winner. The Republican convention was coming up first. The field had narrowed down to three likely candidates and endless copy was being generated. He didn't have time for any more articles on Mrs. Conner, although he kept up with her activities through various sources. At this point his computer was stuffed with files relating to her. He hadn't even gone through much of it.

Mrs. Conner continued to be adept at the campaign process itself. The Republican convention was in full swing — only one final day and then the candidate would be chosen. That evening Mrs. Conner had a short news conference that was covered by three out of the four major networks as well as CNN and other cable and satellite stations. The convention coverage was preempted for thirty minutes because Mrs. Conner announced that the fiftieth state had just put her on the November ballot. She was now a viable, unquestionably real candidate and could no longer be ignored by the Republicans and Democrats. Helen Conner had arrived.

Every journalist in America and half of those from other countries 'discovered' Mrs. Conner. Jack wondered if it was worth a try to contact her. For that matter, his special number may no longer be of value. Perhaps Will Camden had supplanted Mrs. Kramer completely. And if there was an idea Jack dreaded, it was the thought of trying to get on Camden's good side.

Jack was in Philadelphia for the Republican convention and he'd had the news about Mrs. Conner while grabbing a quick meal at a nondescript restaurant with Sam who was also covering the convention action.

"She really did it," said Sam, shaking a bottle of ketchup over his fries.

"Yeah," was Jack's noncommittal reply.

"The contact you've had with her so far gives you an inside track, don't you think?"

"She had attention before, but this is a whole new ball game. The rules might be different."

"You mean you are a big-time reporter and she needed you then, but not so much now?"

"Something like that."

"I say go for it. Maybe she likes you." Sam laughed as if that was very unlikely.

"She knows what she's doing. And has reasons for her actions. I wonder if she has made any missteps so far," Jack mused, half to himself.

"Have you made up your mind about her yet?"

Jack was startled. He hadn't shared his doubts with Sam. "What do you mean?" he said more sharply than he intended.

A question rose in Sam's eyes. He said, "Hey, I don't 'mean' anything. I was just wondering if you think she is really presidential material. What did you think I meant?"

"Sorry, my mind's on other things. I don't know if she can, or should, be president. That's what the next months are for."

First thing next morning, Jack couldn't resist any longer. He called Mrs. Kramer's number. It rang four times, five times. He was about to give up when a voice answered. It was Mrs. Kramer.

"Mrs. Kramer, hello. Jack Kelly here. What are my chances of getting an interview with Mrs. Conner?"

"I'm glad you called. Mrs. Conner is giving a press conference tomorrow. We hope you'll be able to attend."

All right, Mrs. Kramer, you sweet crusty old thing you, thought Jack. Out loud he just thanked her and asked for particulars. On impulse, he asked, "And how is Mr. Camden?"

"Mr. Camden is no longer with us," was her short, precise reply that invited no elaboration. "Tomorrow then, and good day to you now, Mr. Kelly." The line went dead.

He'd finish his work on the Republican convention. He'd be at Mrs. Conner's press conference tomorrow. And he'd look into what became of Will Camden.

That night the new Republican candidate was announced to the wild cheers of the conventioneers and the huge collective yawn of the rest of the nation. The Republicans had taken no chances. The candidate was conservative, but not too conservative. He'd chosen the runner-up as his vice presidential partner. After months of sniping at each other, they were suddenly the best of friends, ready to rule the country with stale ideas and half-hearted cries that now there was going to be "real" change.

Jack smiled during the acceptance speech. In places there were veiled references to rogue, outside forces that dreamed of upsetting this country's move onward and upward to greatness under a Republican administration. They weren't ready to name Mrs. Conner yet, but think of all the months ahead.

Mrs. Conner's press conference went well. All the big names from print and visual media were there. The questions were pointed and no holds barred. Mrs. Conner gave different kinds of answers than she gave when Jack interviewed her. Oh, the substance was the same, but here she was succinct — saying no more than she absolutely had to. If they wanted more information they had to ask follow-up questions.

Mrs. Conner stood behind the mike-infested podium, the T.V. lights glaring down on her, and remained calm and poised during the whole ordeal. The reporters saw her as fresh meat, but she wouldn't satisfy their blood-lust. She was in control of every single moment of the nearly two hours of questions and answers. The only question Jack was able to get out was about when she was going to announce her V.P. decision.

She smiled at him and said, "In good time. Mr. Kelly. All in good time."

From then on Helen Conner garnered at least as much publicity as the Republican and Democrats — perhaps even more. She was a fresh new commodity, largely unknown. Everyone wanted to know everything there was to know about her. It was rumored that the Democrats were searching for a woman to put up at least as vice president, since the one likely woman candidate had dropped out earlier, just to show that they recognized the value of women in high places — just as long as they held the 'correct' views. Both parties were searching for ways to ignore Mrs. Conner while trying to incorporate as much of her clearly popular message as they could without denying their own dogma. It was too late for the Republicans, but the Democrats were seen shifting from one front runner toward another whom they perceived as able to 'look good' against not just the Republican, but against Mrs. Conner as well.

In the midst of all this Jack was as busy as anyone else. He was the paper's resident 'expert' on Helen Conner, a position he began to regard as a dubious honor. Colleagues expected him to know the details not only of her political ideas, but of her private life as well. On several occasions he was even one of the guest panelists on national television news programs. He continued his work on special interest groups and saw some patterns emerging as he followed the paths of money, influence, and intimidation. He also did not forget about Will Camden.

Jack had trouble tracking him down at first. After leaving Mrs. Conner's campaign he seemed to drop out of sight for many weeks. Jack kept looking.

Chapter 11

About a week after the Republican convention, Nora phoned Jack at the office. He tried to remember the last time he'd seen her — two, no three weeks earlier. She asked if they could have dinner together. Jack said, sure, and they agreed to meet at 8:00.

As Jack got ready he was feeling nervous. Things had changed and he wasn't sure how he felt. Should he try to win Nora back, ask her to marry him? Should he let their slow drift apart continue? Or perhaps end it here and now? He didn't know her feelings and wondered if he ever had. He redid his tie three times and then changed his mind and took it off. As he left, he grabbed it again and put it on without even looking as he walked to the car. She was already there when he arrived at the restaurant. They got an out-of-the-way table and ordered. Nora looked beautiful, and Jack told her so.

"Thank you," Nora replied with a big grin. "Its good to see you."

"It's been a long time."

"These are busy days. Your lady is causing quite a stir."

Calling Mrs. Conner 'his lady' seemed slightly absurd, but Jack ignored it.

"I always like to be the first on a big story, but this time it seems to be a mixed blessing."

"How so?" asked Nora, her cheeks inexplicably turning pink.

"Everyone thinks I have some sort of magic inside track, some deep hidden knowledge about Mrs. Conner."

"Well, you do, don't you?"

"I've just been at it longer than the others. They'll catch up."

"But those long exclusive interviews you had with her, and you seem able to get information and direct statements almost immediately. You know someone on the inside."

"Nora, you know how it works. I try to keep on good terms with my sources."

"Who is it? Who helps you?"

"What's this really about?"

"I want to get an exclusive interview with Mrs. Conner. There is talk of a network special. If I can come to them with everything already set up, they will surely go with me. This could be my big break. I've talked to her people and they just say they are thinking about it. I know you can help me on this."

"You have too great a confidence in my abilities here."

"I think not. Will you try, please?"

Jack looked into her beautiful, pleading eyes and knew that there would never be anything, except casual acquaintance, between them again. Did Nora already know? For that matter, did she even care? As a farewell gift he could make this one, probably futile, effort for her.

"I'll try, but I can't promise anything."

"Oh, Jack, you are a dear."

They spent the dinner chatting about politics, what they were doing at work, gossiping about friends. Afterwards, Nora gave him a peck on the cheek and he promised to be in touch as soon as he knew anything. Then she was gone. It was a warm, sultry evening — too warm for a tie. Jack loosened his and undid the top shirt button as he climbed into his car and drove home.

As he brushed his teeth before bed, he looked at Nora's toothbrush. It had been there unused for a very long time. He picked it up and dropped it into the wastebasket.

Next morning Jack had some regrets about his promise to Nora. On the other hand, didn't he use Mrs. Kramer's number so that he could get special treatment? And didn't he keep it a secret? Nora just wanted him to share a little. She hadn't pressed for the name of the source, hadn't asked for the number. He picked up the phone and speed-dialed. True to form, there was Mrs. Kramer at the other end.

"I know you must be very busy now, but if you have a moment?"

"What can I do for you Mr. Kelly?"

"For myself, very little, although I would certainly like to have another chance to interview Mrs. Conner soon." He'd almost added, 'now that she is a real candidate', but stopped himself in time.

"She is extremely tied up for the coming week, but how about next week?"

"Yes, please."

"I'll be in touch."

"You're the best Mrs. Kramer."

"I believe there was something else...."

"A friend of mine asked me for some help." Jack went on to explain about Nora.

"Yes, I am aware of her desire for an interview." There was some talk in the background and Mrs. Kramer said, "Excuse me, Mr. Kelly, will you hold?"

Jack waited and a voice came on the line. "Mr. Kelly?" It was Mrs. Conner herself.

"Mrs. Conner, congratulations on the fiftieth state."

"Persistence and dedication can achieve wonders." Her laugh was low and gentle. "Tell me about your friend, Nora Campbell. I am, as you can imagine, suddenly swamped with offers and requests. I will have to be selective from now on and use the utmost wisdom."

"Things are going well and you don't want to blow it?" suggested Jack.

"Something like that. The image I project becomes especially important. At this point it seems best to avoid interviews that wish to focus on me as the widow with two kids — how do I manage to get food on the table and run for president? You know the sort of thing."

"Yes."

"And you see, I learned my lesson about this from a pro."

"Your lesson?"

"One of my earliest interviews with a nationally known journalist was completely skewed because the reporter saw me in the kitchen with cookies in my hand. Although that was only about three minutes worth of our time together, the impression was so vivid that it colored his whole perception. I took his lesson to heart and so far have not made the same mistake."

"Mrs. Conner, I am before you as a humble reformed reporter, who, I hope, has also learned his lesson."

She chuckled softly before turning serious. "Tell me why I should accept Ms. Campbell's offer?"

"I don't know if you should or not; Nora is intelligent and savvy. She won't let you get away with anything, but I don't think she will waste her or your time."

"Anything else?"

Jack decided to be honest. "Nora has ambition. She wants to break into the big-time."

"And delivering me might get her closer."

"Yes."

"Is she good enough to make it?"

"Yes, I think so, with or without your interview."

"Thank you, Mr. Kelly. I have to go now. Mrs. Kramer tells me I will be seeing you next week. I look forward to it. Good bye."

Two hours later Nora called. "Jack, you are wonderful. I knew you could do it."

"Nora, slow down. What happened?"

"Helen Conner's people have been in touch with my producers, and I have it — a half hour exclusive. The station brass are already negotiating with the network."

"What makes you think it was me?"

"Last night I ask you, this morning they call. One plus one equals two."

"And did they tell you it was me?"

"No. I didn't really want to ask 'why did you choose little old me'. But it had to be you."

"They probably looked at your credentials and saw what the rest of us see. On the other hand, maybe they put up a dartboard with all recent requests and let fly with a dart. Whatever, I'm happy for you."

Nora wasn't about to let his teasing dampen her spirits, "I'm sure it was you, so thanks."

The pace continued to pick up. The Democratic convention was a short three weeks after that of the Republicans. Nora did her televised interview with Mrs. Conner and it aired across the country. Jack's next exclusive was ultimately scheduled for the day after the convention. He'd hoped for an earlier date, but realized the value of knowing who the Democratic nominee would be.

After Nora's story aired, Jack gave her a call.

"Congratulations, it was a good interview."

"Thanks."

"What was she like to work with in front of the camera?"

"She's a real pro. Knew exactly what she wanted, and, more particularly, what she didn't want."

"What do you mean?"

"She was adamant that there be no, what she called, 'women's magazine' questions. She said if I asked any she'd not respond at all — so there would be no way to put that slant in the final edit. She said there was a time and a place for everything."

"Had you planned for any such questions?"

"Actually, yes. I referred to the original article you wrote — you remember, cookies warm from the oven for the boy's school program."

Jack was glad they were talking over the phone so Nora couldn't see him cringe.

"What did she do when you asked the question?"

"It was amazing. She simply sat there, not saying a word. Her expression was of expectant waiting for a question. We couldn't use the question in the final piece because she gave no response at all."

"Are you willing to let me see the uncut tape. I know it's asking a lot."

"I'll send over a copy. It's the least I can do for your help."

Jack wanted to see the tape so this time he accepted the credit she gave him.

Later that day the DVD arrived by messenger. Jack was so busy he had to wait until he got home before he found time to stick in his computer. Everything was there, including the careful placement of Nora and Mrs. Conner just so in comfortable chairs, the checking, rearranging and checking again of the lights and sound. Mrs. Conner sat quietly through it all with gracious patience.

The questions and answers didn't bring out anything with which he was unfamiliar. When Nora asked the 'women's magazine' question, the expression on Mrs. Conner's face made Jack laugh out loud, but a fraction of a second later she had the expression described by Nora — a smile of expectant waiting. Jack played it back again and recognized the start of a look he'd seen before. So it seemed Mrs. Conner could suppress some of the ready humor Jack had come to know. Why? He'd seen her in a variety of settings and she seemed to fit perfectly in each. Who was the real Helen Conner?

Chapter 12

Jack was in Denver for the Democratic convention. He particularly enjoyed the Democrats' convention because, try as they might to change their image, the Democratic Left always included large numbers of special interest groups — some more mainstream than others, but all playing the theme 'if you cared, truly cared, you would...." The blank was filled in with whatever cause was being pushed at the moment. It was a carnival. Jack was able not only to cover the convention, but could gather information for his special interest series from first hand sources — often without even having to leave his hotel.

This time he was still checking-in at the front desk when he caught sight of a familiar face. The name escaped him for a moment and then he knew — it was Will Camden. He asked the desk clerk to excuse him for a second and made his way over to the group of gray-suited young men that included Camden. Jack touched his shoulder and Camden turned.

"Will Camden? Jack Kelly. I talked with you in Portland a while back. Do you remember?"

"Sure, Kelly, I remember."

"Do you have a moment?"

Camden nodded and stepped away from his friends. "What can I do for you?"

"I tried to reach you again at the Conner campaign headquarters, and was unable to find you. I wanted to talk some more."

"What did they tell you about my leaving?" asked Camden.

"Not much. Just that you were gone. Why did you leave?"

"When I found out what it was really like, I got out of there."

"Meaning...?"

"What she says sounds good until you start thinking about it, and it's true implications. She's living in a la-la land. At first I wanted her to be president more than anything. Now I feel the need to stop her at all costs. I'm involved with the Democrats again. They know what it means to represent the people. They know how to govern."

"What's your job here?"

Camden smiled, "I'm doing my part."

"Do you have any specific complaints about Mrs. Conner, or her campaign?"

"What needs to come out will. She'll never be president."

The reaction to the sudden hate that radiated out from Camden must have registered on Jack's face, because Camden quickly softened his tone.

"Her ideas are like paint over rust, they seem good, but do not attack the real problem. What is her plan to help — truly help — the millions of Americans who are in need, who are scared, terrorized, hopeless? What about our cities in decay, our farms disappearing, racism, destruction of the environment? Tell me how she plans to deal with these problems."

"I'll be sure to ask. And if I don't, others will. Do you feel that the Democrats have solutions to these issues?"

"Wait until Friday. The new nominee will outline a real course toward greatness."

The lobby was becoming more crowded. Camden's interest drifted from Jack toward someone on the other side of the room, but Jack couldn't tell who. As Camden edged away, Jack said, "Thank you for your time. Where can I find you if I want more information?"

In a vague manner that suggested that Jack no longer held the slightest interest, Camden replied, "I'll be around," and then was gone through the crowd. Curiosity prompted Jack to follow him, wading through the sea of committed, caring conferees. Camden seemed intent on catching up with a man who was heading into one of the hotel's private dining rooms. Jack got only a glance at the man when he turned his head back toward the lobby before entering the dining room. The face was vaguely familiar, but here everyone was somebody. When Camden got to the door it was apparently locked, because he tried it and couldn't get in. He seemed more resigned than upset as he returned to the lobby.

Jack finished checking-in, took his bag to his room, washed up, and went out to mingle. The town was alive and he was completely and happily in his element.

Late that night he found a message from Walter waiting for him in his room. Apparently, Mrs. Conner was at it again. On the day before the Democrats were to finish, she was calling a press conference to announce her vice presidential running mate. The next day the news was full of speculation. No one knew how to guess the direction she would go. As she had no doubt planned, the Democrats were getting second billing.

Jack was torn, but in the end, he hopped on a plane and headed for Portland. He could catch the Conner announcement in person and still be back in Denver for the final day of the convention. And then it was back again to Portland for his interview with Mrs. Conner — assuming it was still on.

The hall Mrs. Conner had chosen was packed with reporters. It seemed that Jack wasn't the only one who opted to come.

At precisely three o'clock, Mrs. Conner came out to the podium followed by a man...was it?...yes. Jack had to laugh. So, Mrs. Conner, what does this mean? Jack had to wait just like everyone else to find the answer. At least he had a good seat up front.

Mrs. Conner looked around the room nodding at this or that reporter whom she recognized, Jack included. When the noise died down, she spoke.

"Thank you all for coming. As you can see I have with me here Thomas D'Arcy, the present governor of the state of Washington. We share many common goals when we look at the future of politics in this country. He has agreed to join me as my vice presidential candidate. He'd like to say a few words to you and then we will be open to questions. I give you Thomas D'Arcy."

Jack tried to remember everything he knew about the man. The Washington governor's race four years ago had been exciting and closely contended. In the end D'Arcy emerged victorious. Mrs. Conner claimed not to be playing for the vote of various blocks, yet here she was, a woman candidate choosing a black man as her running mate. If that didn't have the ear-mark of pure politics, he didn't know what did. He wished he remembered more about the man, what he stood for. Of course, he'd left word for researchers at the paper to dig out information on whomever the V.P. was, so that it would be readily at hand the moment he got out of this news conference. He just wished he already knew.

What he did know was that D'Arcy won the top office in a state with only a minimal black population. Mrs. Conner from Oregon. D'Arcy from Washington. The Pacific Northwest was leaping up and forcing its way into the national spotlight. Jack admitted to himself that he knew so little about D'Arcy because he'd always written off that part of the country as, well, meaningless in the big picture. Sure, because of the right to public access to the ballot and a huge streak of individuality, the Northwest was a hot-bed of interesting, if occasionally kooky, reform ideas, but mostly he thought of the area as a place for a secluded vacation. Mrs. Conner's words about the 'Beltway Blindness Zone' once again intruded uncomfortably upon his mind.

Meanwhile D'Arcy had come to the podium and begun to speak. His words were about the joy he felt at being a part of Mrs. Conner's vision of America. He said he agreed with her on most points and looked forward to helping her see the light on a few others. That got a chuckle from the assembled reporters. He spoke of his hopes for a nation where freedom truly mattered. He said we as a nation must be willing to look clear eyed at all threats -- domestic, foreign, terrorism, tyranny, racism – and we must do that by looking into our own hearts, our own actions first.

Jack began to remember some of the controversy that surrounded him. D'Arcy was not well liked by some of the black leadership. Apparently, he believed that what we each achieve in life is up to us. If we fall back on excuses or try to paint ourselves as victims of unfair forces outside of our control, we are just lying to ourselves and setting ourselves up for failure. So what, D'Arcy said, if we come from what is considered a hard or underprivileged or even systematically down-trodden background – what if we are defined as part of a minority? Each of us is a new person — free at any time to break the bonds of traditional beliefs, to destroy the evil of mental slavery that held us back.

He wasn't going to let anyone say that he had to be an un-wed father, endlessly and hopelessly discriminated against until he was dead by the hand of a rival gang member just because statistics indicated that outcome based on his early family life. He was an individual. And he was free. He was not an African-American. He was an American. And despite any obstacles carelessly or maliciously put in his way, as an American, as an individual, he could achieve anything.

Among the attending press corps were local journalists who were familiar with D'Arcy. They asked the most direct questions. A woman who identified herself as from 'The Oregonian' asked, "There are those who suggest that you ignore or simply don't care about the bigotry and racism that runs through the very core of the nation; that you have gotten where you are today by glossing over the truth and making white people feel good — you allow them to forget their guilt and prejudice. How do you respond to that?"

D'Arcy smiled down at the reporter. "Ms. King, isn't it? I'm glad you have the courage to come right out and ask that. Bigotry, hatred, prejudice, racism. I wish there was no one in the world who harbored such feelings, but unfortunately my wishing doesn't make them disappear. My Mom told me I'd have to work twice as hard to get anything good in my life. Well, I fooled her. I worked three times as hard — four times as hard. Whatever it took. I ignore the bigots. Who cares what a small-minded minority of people think? And, incidentally, I do believe it is a small minority."

Ms. King was not satisfied. "But, Governor D'Arcy, how can you deny the legitimate anger, the rage, the hopelessness felt by a whole race of people — your people — who, with a few notable exceptions, have been systematically held back, put down?"

"Do you suggest that it is not reasonable for 'my people' to be thoughtful, to look beyond prejudice? You think that the best we can do is lash out mindlessly — perhaps as an animal, scared, confused, trapped, lashes out at its captors? Perhaps you yourself don't think very highly of 'my people', Ms. King?"

Ms. King had turned a decidedly red color. "I never suggested...."

"Prejudice is wide-spread and deep-rooted, but it can only touch me if I give my permission. I am presently Governor of the state of Washington and soon will be Vice President of the United States. And it is because there are many people who are open-minded and respond to sound ideas regardless of the color of the lips they pass over. Helen Conner is one such person. It is an honor to be joining her in her bid for the presidency."

That got the questions back toward how realistic this third party candidacy really was since, realistically, there was nowhere to go with the whole "can or should a black man hold high office" issue. Throughout the questioning, Mrs. Conner allowed D'Arcy to be the center of attention. Jack watched her as much as he watched D'Arcy. D'Arcy was a consummate politician. He kept perfect control of the press conference. He was a tall man, matching Jack's six four — Mrs. Conner only came up to his shoulder and yet, even standing quietly to the side letting D'Arcy speak, she was a dominant presence. D'Arcy was unquestionably a leader, but he deferred subtly to Mrs. Conner. It wasn't put on for this crowd. D'Arcy clearly and unmistakably respected her. For the first time, Jack began to question his conviction that she could not win.

Back in Denver again, Jack covered the official nomination of the Senator from New York as the new Democratic candidate and heard him speak of a new day and a new way. Rumor had it that they had found a woman to put up as V.P., but apparently they opted out at the last minute and chose a California Representative of Hispanic ancestry. Their analysts apparently decided they would get the women's vote anyway, but the Hispanic community was iffy — not to mention California's many voters. Also those western states needed to be courted. All-in-all, a reasonable theory.

Down on the floor, delegates and Democratic enthusiasts milled around Jack as he got comments speaking to the point of an inevitable, landslide victory — carrying on the present administration's successes, onward and upward. They simply glossed over the fact that the sitting president had been making one misstep after another for the past several years. The Democrats, of course, blamed this on the Republicans who kept blocking

meaningful reforms the Democrats tried to put through. But this year —
this year — the Democrats would take it all. Jack smiled and kept his
own counsel.

Jack knew many of the people here and some he planned to know
better. There was Paul Sutcliffe, spokesman for the Green Eagles. They
were one of the most vocal of the environmental groups that Jack was
researching — and they had taken part in the demonstration against Mrs.
Conner in Eugene. The throng made a nearly impenetrable barrier as Jack
made his way toward Sutcliffe. Sutcliffe, while the public face of the
organization, liked to be the one setting the time and place for public
pronouncement, so Jack was surprised to see him here — and standing
next to Will Camden.

Being very nearly rude, Jack pushed his way past ecstatic
conventioneers and shouted out to Camden, "What do you think of the
new candidate?"

"You've heard the next President of the United States here tonight."

"You like the choice?"

"Of course, they will make a good team to lead this great
country."

Sutcliffe was edging away, and Jack didn't want to lose his chance.
Indicating Sutcliffe he asked Camden, "Your friend is...?"

"Paul Sutcliffe. Paul, this is Kelly, a reporter..."

Sutcliffe broke in, a pleasant smile on his lips, "I know Mr. Kelly and
am familiar with his work."

"Thank you," Jack replied apropos of nothing. "I've been hoping for a
chance to interview you. When all this is over perhaps we could

arrange something."

"Fine. Fine." Sutcliffe handed a card to Jack. "Get in touch with me." And then he drifted into the press of humanity and was gone.

Camden was still there.

"A friend of yours?" Jack asked.

"An acquaintance, really," said Camden with a detached smile, his eyes elsewhere. "If you'll excuse me...." And then he was gone, too.

Jack saw the chairman of the Democratic party just a few feet away. And from the look on his face, he was not all that happy to be down here with all his people. Jack wormed his way through and managed to get a statement.

Later when Jack got back to his room, he realized he had a message from Walter. Jack called him.

"Are you loving every minute of it?" Walter's voice boomed through the cell phone.

"You know me — nothing like sincere politicians telling their deepest inner-most feelings and thoughts to bring out all my warm, fuzzy sentiments. I couldn't ask for more."

Walter guffawed.

"Listen, Jack, the paper is going to set up an interview with each of the three main candidates. But this time I want different perspectives, so you will do the Republican, Jesse will do the Democrat, and Sam will do Helen Conner."

"I'm interviewing her tomorrow in Portland."

"That's why I wanted to talk to you."

"No way you are sending Sam in my place."

"No, no. You do your interview. Just put in a good word for Sam."

A small knot that had suddenly twisted his stomach relaxed and Jack replied, "Sure, happy to do my part."

In a different tone of voice Walter asked, "What's she like?"

"You've read my stories."

"No, I mean as a woman."

Jack thought for a moment, then answered, "I don't know. I guess I just think of her as a political candidate."

"She seems very attractive."

"Yeah, I'd say she is. What's your point?"

"Nothing. Just curious."

"Right."

"Well, you ought to get some rest. Big interview tomorrow. She's an official candidate with a new V.P. and both the Democrats and the Republicans are decided. I trust you to find out whatever needs finding."

"Good night, Walter."

"'Night, Jacko."

Chapter 13

The Portland airport was beginning to seem like an old friend. And the desk clerk at the hotel looked at Jack with a smile of half-recognition. The interview was set for after dinner so Jack had time to wander around the city before he needed to be there. His steps took him past the Conner for President headquarters that had expanded to take in a space at least twice as large. He was going to walk by, but then he saw a flower vendor on the corner. He bought a bouquet of mixed flowers and went inside. A young man at a desk just inside asked if he could be of help.

"Is Mrs. Kramer in?"

"Yes, but I think she is busy."

"I have a delivery for her." Jack indicated the flowers. But, of course, he didn't look much like a flower delivery man. Suspicion creased the young brow as he said, "Well, just follow me," and lead the way to the back. Mrs. Kramer's door was open and she was in deep conversation with two other people. She looked up in annoyance at the young man's knock, but then she saw Jack.

"Thank you, Gary," she said, dismissing the young man. She got up and left the other two in her office. She guided Jack back out into the hall and then asked, "What can I do for you, Mr. Kelly?"

"Not much really. I was passing by, saw these flowers and thought of you."

He presented them to her. She looked delighted and confused. "What are these for?"

"You are always there for me, and I seldom get a chance to thank you."

Mrs. Kramer thought that over for a moment and then began to laugh as if Jack had told a humorous joke. He didn't know quite what to say. Through her chuckles she took the flowers, buried her nose right in their midst, and finally said, "Oh, Mr. Kelly...." She seemed about to say more, but didn't. Instead she chuckled again and simply said, "Thank you. These will brighten my office as your kindness has brightened my day."

"I don't want to disturb you any further," said Jack, turning to go.

"Mrs. Conner looks forward to seeing you later," she said, the smile still lingering about her eyes.

"Me, too," he replied. "I'll see you later."

He headed back out on to the street and found a Mexican restaurant that pulled him right in off the street with it's wonderful spicy aromas.

When Jack arrived at Mrs. Conner's house it was still light enough for him to appreciate the landscaping. On his earlier visit it had the bareness of winter. Now everywhere he looked the beauty bathed his eyes. Some was subtle — large open areas with one tree or plant placed just so, or plants with gray-green thick foliage next to ones with darker sword-like leaves. Other spots were vibrant with intense color. He wished he could wander around and see more, but it was time and he wanted to be prompt.

As he started toward the house, several armed guards stepped out and challenged him. He was required to show his identification and submit to a quick metal detector test. He was passed and allowed to continue up to the front door where he rang the doorbell and waited — as always, expecting a servant even though he'd never seen one. Once again, it was Chris who opened the door. Surely the boy had grown another two inches since he'd last seen him. He had the same friendly smile, but added to it was a residual of what seemed to be laughter. Before coming to the door he must have been doing or talking about something very humorous.

After a polite greeting and a few quick pleasantries, Chris led Jack to the kitchen. Jack was intrigued. What did Mrs. Conner have planned?

Chris opened the kitchen door and a wave of fresh cookie aroma washed over Jack. He had to laugh. There she was in her apron again pulling cookies out of the oven.

For her part, Mrs. Conner kept a perfectly straight face as she greeted him. But it was there. He saw the humor lurking behind the bland expression.

"Aren't you taking a big chance?" he asked her.

"It seemed like time to come full circle," was her reply.

He thought he understood, but asked anyway, "Meaning…?"

"This truly is part of who I am, just not the essence of who I am. We are each complex beings. We can't choose one aspect of a person and think we have the whole picture. I can make cookies, but I am also going to be president. Would you care for a cookie?"

Her eyes flashed a challenge. And he replied, "Thank you. You make very good cookies."

Finally she laughed. "The day you believe I can win, I'll know I have a chance."

"I'm just a reporter, ma'am, writing up the facts."

"Yes, of course."

She put some cookies on a plate and headed for the study. Jack followed.

"You have a beautiful yard," he said as they reached the study and could see the back garden through the windows.

"Shall we walk out there for a few minutes while it is still light?"

"I'd like that."

She opened large French doors and stepped onto the patio.

"You must have a wonderful gardener," Jack said.

"It's been hard. This is one of the things I have had to give up. Turning this over to a gardener is much like leaving your children with a babysitter. You know that no matter how conscientious they are or how much you pay them, they will never care as much as you do."

"Did you do all this?" Jack asked in wonder.

"Essentially. It evolved over a number of years."

"You are obviously well-to-do, and very busy, but I never see cooks or maids or other servants."

"Oh, I've always been quite willing to have help. One of the advantages of having money is that one can pick and choose which activities to do and which to give to others."

"What will we find when we start looking into the way you have dealt with your help?"

"You mean, do I hire illegal aliens for low wages and not pay social security taxes for the maid?"

"Yes. That sort of thing."

"What do you think of politicians, Mr. Kelly?"

"Excuse me?"

"How would you characterize, stereotype, politicians?"

"Ah..."

"Power-hunger? Saying whatever was necessary to get elected? Considering themselves above the law, and perhaps a little better than other people? Untrustworthy?"

"I've known many who weren't like that," said Jack, actually thinking of only one or two.

"Of course, but generally...?"

"I've been reporting on politics and politicians for a long time and, yes, I tend to disbelieve first. Although I'm willing to be proved wrong."

"Then I won't tell you I'm honest. I won't tell you that as far as I know, I've not once lied to you or anyone else during this campaign. All I'll ask is that you have an open mind. Dig where you will, search for whatever dirt you think you can find, but if you don't find it, be willing to report that, too. And if you think you've found something, be sure to question it closely because I doubt it will be true."

"Mrs. Conner, no one's that perfect."

"I'm hardly perfect," she smiled, but then turned serious again. "However I have always operated on the principle that it's actually easier to do what's right. Why cheat? Why try to hedge? Why say what you don't mean? Lies are too hard to keep track of. Do you know I've never even had a traffic ticket?"

"Come on — never?"

"It drove Edward mad. He was an excellent driver, but he managed to get several speeding tickets through the years. I think all of us go faster than the speed limit occasionally, but my theory is that I did it inadvertently, while he sped on purpose if he was in a hurry."

"O.K. What about drugs? You were a youth in the time when drug use was rampant. You never even tried? Or maybe you tried but didn't inhale?"

"I don't drink. I don't do drugs. I don't smoke."

"You'd better not say that publicly unless it is strictly true."

"Are we not speaking publicly now?"

It was strange. He'd noticed it before. When he was interviewing her sometimes he forgot.

"Yes, I suppose we are."

"This may surprise you, but I don't even use legal drugs very often."

"Legal drugs?"

"Aspirin, cough syrup, that sort of thing."

"Why not?"

"With the boys growing up in the house, with so many outside pressures, I didn't want them to think that the solution to every little problem or ache or pain was to pop a pill and drift, even ever so slightly, into a comfortable haze. There is a time and a place for such things, but its not as often as those pushing their drug products would have you believe."

"The pharmaceutical companies aren't going to be too crazy about you as president."

"I guess they will just have to take their chances with the rest of you unsuspecting public." She paused and then continued. "Excuse me, I shouldn't joke about such things with a reporter. The fact is this is a very personal stand and I can easily understand the other point of view. There are so many ideas that I want to place out there in the front of Americans so everyone can give them a good looking-over — this is a tiny one, a thread — what matters is the whole fabric. The essence that runs throughout this fabric is, as I repeat endlessly, responsibility for our choices, for our actions."

"Aren't you setting yourself up to seem 'better' than the rest of us?"

"I hope not. Self-righteousness includes enormous, opaque blinders as part of its baggage. If I turn out to be an unknowing hypocrite, ignorant of my own faults, I'm sure I can depend on people like you to spell them out clearly and concisely in very large letters."

They had wandered back into the house by now. It was quite dark outside and the summer night had cooled down. The guards were unobtrusive, but always there.

"Will Camden," said Jack, hoping for a reaction. He couldn't read the reaction that came.

"Yes? What about Will?" Was she just curious about Jack's interest, or caught off-guard?

"He worked at your campaign headquarters for a while and then left. I've run into him several times since. I was wondering what your side of the story is."

"I wouldn't have thought there was a story there."

Was she stalling? Did he really even want to know?

"You tell me."

"He is bright and enthusiastic. He came to work for us, moving into a position of influence fairly quickly. Some questions arose, and we asked him to leave."

"Can you be more specific?"

"I would prefer not to be."

"Why not?"

"I ask in return: Why do you feel the need to write about this? I don't understand."

"He implied some things. He said you would never be president when the truth came out."

"What 'truth'?" Mrs. Conner sounded mystified.

"He wasn't specific."

"Can we talk off-record for a moment?"

"Sure."

"Turn off your recorder, please."

"I won't use what you say."

"Please. Turn it off."

Jack did so.

"It's not fair to have my speculations on tape," she said by way of explanation, then continued, "Will came to us with a desire to be part of this 'historic campaign' as he called it. I'm afraid that his skills were not equal to his dreams. Winning was more important to him than principle. He accepted a large donation from a group that he thought should support me. He did nothing illegal, but it was in direct opposition to everything I stand for. Apparently, he had never believed me — thought my stand was just a good political move. He showed me how we could cover the donation and make it look like it came from individuals. I made him return the money, and explain the reason why to the donor. He was furious and humiliated. He became bitter. He said things. I asked him to leave. I assume this is what caused him to speak to you as he did."

"That's the whole story?"

"Enough of it."

Were you lovers? The question rested on the tip of his tongue, but he swallowed it. Better not to know in case the answer was yes. And he was beginning to believe that if he asked she would tell him the truth.

"On the record again...?"

"O.K."

He started the recording again.

"As far as you are concerned, Will Camden is a non-story?"

"Yes."

Jack nodded, looked down at his notes and went on with the interview.

"The field is set — Democrats, Republicans, and you. How do you think you stack up against your opponents?"

"A political campaign is inevitably described as a race. We are all three contending for the hearts and minds of the people. But I don't feel I am running against the other two. What I do or say will be colored only slightly by what they do or say. I am appealing to the American people with ideas that I hope they will accept. I hate to say it, but the Democrats and Republicans are only peripheral to my campaign."

"And yet you announce your fiftieth state during the Republican convention and your V.P. during the Democratic convention."

"Oh, I'll play that game with them, and do my best to beat them at it. One would have to be very naive politically and hardly a suitable choice for president if one could not play that game. But I intend to 'play' within the context of my convictions."

"Willing to grab the spotlight, but no dirty tricks?"

"Something like that."

"It's safe to say that right now within the Democratic and Republican organizations there are people working tirelessly to find dirt about you to have ready in case you actually start to look like a winner. Do you have such people doing the same job for you?"

"If there are any, they will be fired the second I find out. I can see you don't believe me. However, by my way of thinking, there would be no point in winning if I did it that way."

"That seems rather magnanimous of you."

"Only if my aim is to beat the other two. Beating them is an inevitable part of my becoming president, a sort of side product. It is not my goal. The presidency is my goal."

"Does D'Arcy share your views?"

"On this issue, he'd better, or I'll fire him." Mrs. Conner smiled, but Jack saw that she actually meant it.

"How did you come to choose D'Arcy?"

"I've known him a long time and I respect his viewpoint and his courage."

"His courage?"

"I don't know how deeply you've been able to research Governor D'Arcy's background, but when you do you'll find him to be an extraordinary man. I think I should let you find out for yourself rather than try to form a character for him."

"Fair enough. I look forward to interviewing him."

"Give Mrs. Kramer a call when you're ready. She'll know how to arrange it."

Lovely Mrs. Kramer, thought Jack.

"But again, Mrs. Conner, you who set yourself up as slightly above 'politics as usual' chose a Black man as your running mate. That seems a blatant attempt to curry favor within a certain block of American voters."

"You don't mean to imply that the only reason I've chosen Governor D'Arcy is because of the color of his skin? I'd hoped you could see a little deeper than that."

Feeling a bit defensive, Jack replied, "I know something about D'Arcy's views and see how they mesh neatly with yours, but it's a big country out there, with many uninformed people...."

"Yes. How easy to assume that others are not capable of grasping what we can."

Jack could see he was being teased, but it didn't make him any more comfortable. Mrs. Conner became more serious again.

"I hope that by the time November rolls around, the public and the media will be considering the ideas that the candidates put forth. I know there is a certain optimism in this hope — the media is so consumed with surface appearances. Perhaps one of the gifts my campaign will give to America is the realization that we are better, collectively, than we have given ourselves credit for."

"Do you still believe you have a chance of winning? You are getting lots of attention, but the polls show you way behind both the Democrat and the Republican."

"Polls are interesting and occasionally have some value. Apparently, if the election was today, I'd not win. But the election is not for several months. And no matter what the polls say, in the end it is the people who vote."

"Can I take that to mean, yes, you feel you have a chance?"

She laughed. "You must always bear in mind that you may very well be interviewing the next President of the United States."

"I'll do that."

The study door burst open and Alex Conner came part way in. He sounded angry as he spoke, "Mom, I...." He stopped when he saw Jack.

Mrs. Conner got up and excused herself. She and Alex went back out and closed the door. Jack heard low voices, but was unable to make out the words. He was tempted to listen at the door, but hated the thought of being found eavesdropping. So he waited, staring out the window into the summer night.

Shortly Mrs. Conner returned. Her face was grim as she entered the room, but softened as she spoke.

"I'm sorry for the interruption, Mr. Kelly."

He waited expectantly, willing her to say more so he didn't have to ask. She walked over and stood behind the chair she'd occupied, apparently about to dismiss him. Instead she spoke, "Alex loves the idea of politics. He can get very passionate about it all. That, combined with his youthful impatience, can be a fiery mixture. He wants people, all people, to be good now. He doesn't understand how someone could hear a good idea and not accept it immediately."

Jack took a chance. "What happened?"

She didn't seem hesitant to tell him. "You know he is taking an active part in the campaign. He was talking with a group of college students and several not only questioned what he said, but ridiculed him. The guard who was with him says it seemed like an orchestrated, pre-planned response. He says that Alex handled it very well, kept his cool, but was steaming underneath. By the time he got home he was furious."

"Has this happened before?"

"Yes, to me. We haven't been able to establish for sure if it is a concerted effort, or random protestors."

"I haven't heard of any more of the sort of protest that broke up your speech in Eugene a while back."

"Mostly it's been in smaller venues and more subtle."

"Heckling?"

"Not exactly. Usually it takes the form of three or four or five people scattered through the audience who will make a very loud sound such as 'hah' full of scorn after I've made some point or other. You should come sometime and see for yourself. It is strange and not something I can really complain about — and I probably wouldn't even mention it if it wasn't so consistent. After all, anyone has the right to disagree with me and express their dissatisfaction with what I stand for."

"Do the other, stronger threats continue also?"

"Yes. " Her answer was all the more potent for it's unspoken implications.

"I've asked around and it seems all the candidates have to deal with that."

"Yes, I know. That doesn't make it any more acceptable."

"Why do you think people do it?"

"You'd need a psychologist to give you a full answer. Maybe people just want to feel important and threatening a 'celebrity' gives them that feeling. But the kooks are not my biggest concern."

"What do you mean?"

"What I really have to worry about, if I'm going to worry about anything, is the vested interests. There are people out there who are scared of even the possibility that I might win. You'll be seeing more and more publicity in all forms attempting to belittle my ideas."

"You don't seem very upset." Jack wondered if she didn't put too much stock in the likelihood that others believed she'd win.

"Why should I be? What are they to me? I have confidence in the ability of the people to sort out fact from fiction if it is all laid out before them."

"Who do you consider to be your biggest critics?"

"Mr. Kelly, in the context of our conversation, an answer might convey a sense that I know, or at least suspect, who is responsible for the serious threats we have received."

"Fair enough. If I keep the information separate and don't imply a link, will you tell me?"

"It won't be hard to find them for yourself. Just stick around. One or another of them can pop out at any moment."

"You seem to take threats on your life and your sons' lives with very little concern. How can you do that?"

"Would you have me run and hide? Withdraw from the race, perhaps? That is exactly what they are hoping for. I will not be blackmailed."

"No, Mrs. Conner, somehow I don't think you would. And yet, is there nothing you'd give it up for?"

She looked at him for a moment before answering. "I have given up more than you can know to make this bid for the presidency, but I've done it with my eyes open. One of the things I've given up is my privacy. It's almost as if I have challenged thousands of investigative reporters and other such beings to examine every detail of my whole life. However I'm the one who decided to run. I can't begrudge them their jobs."

"...and other such beings? Have you something against investigative reporters?"

"No. Actually some of them are my very best friends."

Jack always enjoyed her quiet humor and thought it might serve well in the White House, but it made him get side-tracked and forget now and then that he was doing an interview.

"Mrs. Conner, there are those who say that you have no experience that will allow you to deal with foreign policy, if there is a terrorist threat or if there ever arose a need for military strength you'd really be out of touch. Do you think Americans are ready for a woman to be Commander-in-Chief?"

"Foreign policy. Terrorism. Military strength. Interesting that you lump them together in the same question. But in either case what is required is a sensible, integrated, firm policy. A woman is as capable of providing these necessities as is a man."

"You use the word 'firm'...?"

"Principled. America needs to have a plan, a goal first — an ethic if you will, on which we then base our foreign policy. If we perceive a need, then we must have a goal, a mission. That must be followed by a willingness to commit to whatever it takes to achieve that goal. If we are unwilling to do that, then we should keep out of it. We don't make threats. We either act or we don't act based on what is in the interest of America. We are not the world's policemen, nor are we the protectors of the world's morals. In one sense we are the largest and strongest participant in a fairly small global village. But that does not make us the arbiters of all the undercurrents of suppressed and blatant ethnic and tribal loyalties and passions. We can, and must, give to the rest of the world the right to work out their own problems. If their 'working out' collides with our interests, then we decide if we need to step in."

"You are prepared to go to war whenever our interest are at stake?"

"'Stepping in' can take many forms."

"Do you favor embargoes as a means of getting other countries to straighten up?"

"Embargoes are not my favorite form of encouragement to do better. If anything, the people in oppressed parts of the world need to see more of the good the West has to offer. I'm proud of western culture and achievements. How long do you think Castro could have remained in power if his people had free access to America? Remember, communist leaders – the former USSR, East Germany, North Korea – have always had to force their people to stay in their 'wonderful' countries.

"My dream is a network of satellites spread across the globe reaching out to all corners of the earth, providing internet access to all. A new take on the Radio Free Europe. Let everyone have their say — even the worst dictators. Let people have knowledge of all the sides and then let them decide for themselves."

"You have great confidence in 'the people'."

"Of course I do. Because there is no such thing as 'the people' — just many individuals who, when they have enough information, are capable of wise decisions on what affects their lives. Just as you and I are."

"Well. To get back to foreign policy. Do you think you will feel comfortable dealing with, say, the Chancellor of Germany, or the Prime Minister of Great Britain?"

"Yes."

"Is that bravado, or are you really so confident?"

"You made, I assume by chance, two interesting choices. I actually know both men."

The incredulity could not be kept out of Jack's voice as he exclaimed, "What?"

"Mr. Kelly, as I have told you before I have wide and diverse interests and contacts."

Feeling defensive and slightly off-balance, he blurted out, "The Chancellor is known to prefer not to speak English. How do you keep up this 'friendship'?"

"By the obvious expedient of speaking German."

"Oh, really? And in what other languages do you converse with various heads of state?"

"You think I have exaggerated — the on-going ill effect caused by your seeing me for the first time with cookies in my hand. I will not answer your question at this time. Just know this: I am qualified to be president in ways that no president or candidate in modern history has been."

It was said quietly, but for a moment, just one tiny moment, he had a glimpse of deep, barely restrained, power that could engulf him. He was at a loss for words. He stared at her for that moment and then recollected himself, glanced down at this notes, fumbling through them as if looking for something. Finally he said, "That just about covers everything for now. I trust we can do this again regularly. Is there anything you wish to add?"

"Its always a pleasure, Mr. Kelly. I look forward to our chats."

Was she making fun of him? She sounded sincere. "Thank you. One other thing, if you don't mind." She nodded. "A colleague from the paper, Sam Trowbridge, is going to ask you for an interview. I hope you will be willing to grant it."

"Call Mrs. Kramer about him. She'll arrange it."

"Thank you." He looked at his watch. "Once again you've been very generous with your time."

"Its my pleasure."

She showed him out. He waved to Chris and Alex who were in the living room playing chess, said goodbye to Mrs. Conner at the door, and made his way past the guards. On the way down the hill he told himself, it's never enough. I always go away feeling as though I don't know her at all. The doubts creep back in. What is it that I'm missing?

Chapter 14

When he ultimately got back to the office a day and a half later, Sam greeted him at the door and whisked him off to Walter's office. They talked about his articles and then Walter said, "We've got your interview with the Democratic candidate arranged. Jessie is all set, too. But we're having trouble with the Conner people."

"What kind of trouble?"

"They are inundated with requests, too many to fill all of them. It dawns on us that you get exclusive interviews with some regularity. Thank goodness I assigned you to that early interview. It seems to have given you an edge." Walter was conveniently forgetting the true purpose of that first interview. Well, let him think it was foresight on his part.

"Yes...?"

"The question is: Can you use your inside track to get Sam in? You are doing great stuff, but I want a different perspective."

"I can't guarantee anything," said Jack, wanting to make it sound difficult, "but let me see what I can do."

He went to his desk, called Mrs. Kramer, and in several minutes had Sam organized, as well as a tentative date for an interview with D'Arcy. Not wanting to give away too much, he waited several hours before he told Sam that his toils had finally managed to produce results.

Sam was still at Jack's desk talking about Mrs. Conner when Jack's phone rang. Sam excused himself and Jack answered.

"Is this Jack Kelly?" The voice was hushed and anxious.

"Yes. How can I help you?" Jack had calls like this with some regularity and had an idea of what to expect.

"You've been writing stories in the paper about interest groups and lobbies."

"Do you have some information that can help me?"

"I don't know. They'll find out. But...."

"But you want to tell. And you will remain completely anonymous if you wish. It's best to expose these things."

"It seems so innocent. They're so fine, such high...."

The line went dead. Had someone interrupted him, or had he chickened out? He? No, it could also have been a woman with a low voice. And whomever it was tried to mask his voice. There was nothing Jack could do except wait and see if the individual called back. He checked the number where the call originated and discovered, not to his surprise, that it was blocked. Occasionally these calls were useful — usually it was just cranks with nothing better to do.

The next few days Jack spent little time at home. He was either out on a story or at his desk writing. He could sense the stir in the very air of

Washington. The looming specter of Helen Conner had the political entities out scurrying here and there like squirrels in the middle of the road, not just one hundred percent sure which way they should go to be safe again. The problem was not just Helen Conner — it was all the people, ordinary everyday people, all over America who actually took her message to heart and decided to do something to fix what they had only complained about before. On every level of elective government there were new faces — even in races where the incumbent had for years run essentially unopposed. It didn't take very many people deciding to enter politics for a huge upheaval to take place. All over America politicians were looking over their shoulders to see if anyone was overtaking them.

It was not just elected officials taking on hunted looks. From Mrs. Conner on down, her followers talked of severe and definite civil service staff cuts — that there was no need for the majority of Americans to work hard so they could support the millions of often superfluous government employees. Mrs. Conner suggested that if many of these departments were legitimate and gave valuable service, they could and should be allowed to make their way in the free market. All candidates spoke of streamlining government. Mrs. Conner was the first one in a long time that people seemed to believe.

Mrs. Conner was still a long way from having enough supporters to win, but polls showed that while the Democrats and Republicans seemed to have more supporters, they tended to be wishy-washy. Mrs. Conner's followers were committed.

Jack lived and worked with these issues every waking moment. If nothing else he'd always be grateful to Mrs. Conner for spicing up the political process. Even if she lost, which seemed likely, she wouldn't necessarily go away. If she chose to, she could always be there stirring the stream — making the mud rise so it could wash away.

Sam caught up with Mrs. Conner in Houston. He called Jack after the interview.

"So, how'd it go?" asked Jack.

"Smooth. What a pro. I couldn't find anything for which she didn't have a well thought-out answer. Just for fun I asked her about an obscure country that I came across in some research I was doing a few days ago. I'd never heard of it before. I asked what she thought of the political situation there. She admitted that she wasn't familiar with that country, but to wait a minute. She picked up the phone, talked to one of her people for a moment, waited and then turned back to me. She said her people had no specific information about problems there, and then, can you believe it? She asked me to tell her what I knew. Of course, I knew of no 'political situation' there, so I was the one who ended up on the spot."

Jack chuckled. "What do you think of her personality?"

"Straightforward, businesslike, and the strangest thing — she came across as honest. I've seen her on T.V., heard her speak and she always seemed to have that persona, but I always assumed she was projecting an image as they all do. If anything, in person the effect is heightened. You've talked with her several times — what do you think?"

"I know what you mean, but I don't know how real it is. At this point I have no reason to believe she's ever lied to me. I find myself wanting to believe she is sincere."

"Yes. That's it. She makes me want to believe her. Something in me wants to believe that someone like her — like she seems to be, as unrealistic as it is — really exists and really might be president. Have we been in the business so long that we can see honesty staring us in the face and not even know it?"

"I hope not. Will you let me watch your tape? I'd be interested to see what she's like with someone else. Might give me some clues."

"Sure. I'll be back tomorrow. By the way, you should have been at her speech last night. I'll tell you about it when I see you."

"What?"

"I'll tell you tomorrow."

Sam handed Jack a disc. "This is a copy. You can keep it if you wish."

"Thanks. It'll be fun to compare with my interviews. So tell me about the action at Mrs. Conner's speech. I saw a bit about it on the news."

"The hall was packed. There were enthusiastic supporters, armed security guards, plainclothes secret service men that I recognized, so probably others I didn't, media people, lights, microphones, cameras — you know the routine. And also several contingents of protestors ready to explode as soon as Mrs. Conner appeared. She was introduced and as soon as she started to speak, the volcanoes erupted. They tried to drown out her speech yelling and screaming and chanting. It became clear very quickly that the loudest was a group of environmentalists. The security forces started to move toward the protestors. Mrs. Conner must have had the microphones rigged specially, because all of a sudden her voice boomed out louder than all the crowd noise. It was so startling that everyone became silent. She proceeded to address the protestors. Zeroing in on the environmentalists, she singled out one of the group, asked if all agreed that the young man was really one of them. They agreed he was, so she invited him up to the podium. The young man was clearly not prepared for this. Once he was up there, she asked him what he and his friends were complaining about — why they were afraid to listen or let others listen to her. She asked if he felt a loud voice was a sign of deep thought. The funny thing is, she was not condescending. She sounded as though she really wanted to know what the fellow thought. He got his courage back and seeing a good opportunity, started to spout his groups' rhetoric. She listened for a couple minutes and then asked him if he was sure of his facts. He said of course he was. She then challenged him to look at the documentation she had and to bring his own for her to read. It was so reasonable, he could hardly say no. And his people could hardly continue shouting her down. She went on with her talk and it was a rousing success. I kept stealing looks at the members of the environmental group — Green Eagles. Some looked thoughtful, but several were really steamed."

"What about the guy she had up on the podium with her?"

"She told the audience that the two of them would give a joint statement after they have a opportunity to study each other's sources. The young man was actually there at her hotel suite when I did my interview. He was in another room reading. You'll hear on the recording what she tells me about him."

"I appreciate you letting me hear the recording...." Jack knew it was a big favor. He himself almost never did such a thing — and then only for a very good reason and after editing. He felt that the finished story was for the world, but the interview itself was private.

"You owe me now," smiled Sam. "I know you have a special interest in Ms. Conner. Got a book in mind?"

Jack looked up, surprised. He hadn't mentioned the possibility to anyone. But then, of course, this was Sam. Jack grinned. "Thanks again," he said, holding up the disc and returning to his desk.

It took all of Jack's willpower to resist sticking the disc in his computer right then. He had work to do at the office and this recording didn't really fit into a legitimate work-related niche.

It was nearly eight p.m. when he finally got home and was able to stick the disc in his computer, sit back, and listen. The first part was familiar. Sam had the same habits as Jack. He had the recording going from the first minute so there was all the introductory chit-chat, and then there was a short interchange that sent a shock through Jack. He jumped up and replayed it. Yes. He'd understood correctly. Such a little thing.

Sam asked Mrs. Conner why she was also turning on a recorder. She replied that she always recorded interviews — also video-taped all public appearances. That way she never had to worry about misquotes — misinterpretations maybe — but at least there was a record to check back.

Jack didn't stop to analyze why it bothered him so much to think that she had been secretly taping all their interviews. He'd always been open about his recording, and would have understood if she'd just said something. In a rush of annoyance, he paused the disc, picked up the phone and dialed Mrs. Kramer's number. If she hadn't answered immediately he might have reconsidered and hung up. But there was Mrs. Kramer smartly and brightly saying, "Hello, Edith Kramer here."

Jack's emotion pushed him along and his voice showed his feelings as he spoke, "Mrs. Kramer, this is Jack Kelly. May I speak to Mrs. Conner?"

Mrs. Kramer was silent for a moment, clearly trying to sort out what seemed like an attack. She finally replied calmly and slowly, "I'm sorry, Mr. Kelly, Mrs. Conner is not available at the moment. May I take a message?"

Realizing there was no message he could give and beginning to regret his impetuous call, he just said, "No. No. I'm sorry to have bothered you."

She replied, "No bother. Are you sure there is no message?"

By now Jack was almost completely mortified and was beginning to hope he hadn't antagonized the woman who was his link to the biggest news story of the year.

"I'm sorry to have disturbed you, Mrs. Kramer. Good bye."

"Good bye, Mr. Kelly."

Jack set the phone down slowly, and with some chagrin started up the disc again. He sat in his chair and listened.

Sam did a good interview, and Mrs. Conner came across as she always did. There were no unfamiliar ideas. But there was something missing. When the interview was finished, Jack listened to random parts again. What was it? He got out a recording from one of his interviews and listened to parts of it. What he heard startled him. He got up and fingered through his videos, finding the one Nora gave him of her interview. Yes, it was missing there, too. He listened to another of his own tapes. Then he turned off the machine, sat down on the couch, and stared at a spot somewhere beyond his wall.

It came across so clearly on his tapes, now that he knew to listen for it. She spoke to him as if he were her friend. How could he have been so blind not to realize that Mrs. Conner treated him like a friend? A smile played across his face. It felt kind of good to think of her as a friend, but complicated things immensely. He'd have to think this through. The phone interrupted before he could get a handle on the problem. Absentmindedly, he reached over and picked it up.

"Hello," he said, half expecting it to be a computer generated sales pitch.

"Mr. Kelly, this is Helen Conner."

Jack was so surprised he could barely answer.

"Mrs. Conner. Hello. What can I do for you?"

"Mrs. Kramer said you called me."

"I did. I...mmmm." He couldn't think of a quick lie about why he'd called.

"Mr. Kelly, Mrs. Kramer said you sounded very upset, angry really. I value our relationship and wouldn't like to see any unnecessary hurdles put in the way." She spoke calmly with a matter-of-fact tone, but then Jack remembered what he'd figured out only moments before and suddenly it didn't seem so hard to tell her his reaction to hearing that she taped all of her interviews.

She listened to him and then was silent for a moment. When she spoke it was quietly, but Jack thought he heard some relief in her voice.

"When you first interviewed me, I hadn't started that practice. The second time I... well, I guess I didn't want to be so blatant — under the circumstances."

"It would have looked as though you didn't trust me at all, after my first article," interjected Jack.

"Yes, something like that."

"But surely, that was all the more reason to do so."

Jack sensed her smile as she said, "I decided to give you one more chance. After that it never seemed necessary."

He wanted to say something that would let her know he understood. All he could think of was, "I'm sorry. I should have known you would have done any taping openly, or not at all."

They chatted for several more minutes and then said goodbye.

Jack smiled as he put the down the phone and went to get himself a snack. As he was cutting into an apple, he remembered something she'd said once to the effect that if only she could get him to believe in her.... What if this was all part of a bigger game plan? What if she had 'special' relationships with a variety of journalists — winning favorable write-ups by the use of charm? He didn't doubt her ability to turn problems around and use them to her own advantage.

But Sam was his friend. Jack didn't analyze every word or action of Sam's to see if he had underlying motives. Why couldn't he just accept that he and Mrs. Conner got on well. Maybe because Sam wasn't running for president and it wasn't Jack's job to know and see through every action to whatever hidden agenda Sam might have.

For a few minutes Jack weighed on a delicate balance the difficulties arising from their newly discovered relationship and being in the middle of a hot, developing story. He could back out and let Sam, or someone else take over. Naw. He was going to follow it to the end.

Chapter 15

One of his first actions was to find the young environmentalist Mrs. Conner had invited up onto the podium. His name was Garth Wingate, and Jack tracked him to a hotel in Washington. He asked for and received permission for an interview that very afternoon. He was out of the office and into a taxi headed for the hotel in five minutes. Never give them a chance to change their minds was one of the secrets of his success.

Wingate's room was large and high priced — not in keeping with the image he projected. His lanky frame covered with rumpled jeans and an un-ironed canvas shirt looked as if it would never be caught wearing a gray suit. He was personable and friendly, if a bit dazed by his sudden celebrity.

"When are you and Helen Conner going to issue a joint statement?"

"I don't know if she truly meant that. You know politicians...."

Jack felt pretty confident when he said, "I'll bet she did." Then he asked, "Did you find anything new or thought-provoking in the documents she showed you?"

"I don't know. I wish she hadn't chosen me. She should have picked Jeanette or Paul or someone — anyone — else. They're the spokespeople for the group. I'm just a supporter."

"What do the Green Eagles believe in?" asked Jack, already knowing more about the group than he was willing to let on.

"That nature, the earth, is fragile and perfect and precious. That we must protect it as we would anything of great value. We must sacrifice to protect it, and not take chances."

"And someone like Mrs. Conner...?"

"She represents the worst sort of threat."

"How so?"

"She sounds so reasonable. People hear her and they think, 'Oh, things can't be so bad.' She talks and talks and calls for more information, more studies. Meanwhile destruction of the environment continues unabated."

"After speaking with her, do you still think she is evil?"

Wingate hesitated, his zeal temporarily confused by his experience. Zeal won the day. "She is very believable. When you are with her.... One on one she's hard to refute. She's so articulate. I wish Al had been there — he would have known what to say. Afterward he helped me see."

"So you do think she is evil?"

"Al says she's dangerous because she makes people believe her."

"Perhaps she is telling the truth?"

"No way, man. She doesn't care. She just wants power."

Jack was pretty sure he was hearing 'Al' speak and so tried to get Wingate's own impressions, if he had any of his own.

"How long have you been with the Green Eagles?"

"I've been involved with the environment since I was a little kid. When I was older, I was in different groups, but then I got to know the Green Eagles and joined them about a year ago."

"What makes them different?"

"Its like a family — a family that shares deep conviction and is willing to act on that conviction."

"How far, exactly, are you willing to go?"

"Whatever it takes, as Al says."

"Where does your group get its funding?"

"Uhh, donations, I guess. I'm not really involved in that."

"Nice hotel room. Are you on Green Eagle business or is this the way you always travel?"

Wingate looked slightly embarrassed. "This suite belongs to the Green Eagles. Various members have to spend time in Washington, lobbying and all that, you know. Al said I could stay here until I see Mrs. Conner tomorrow."

"She'll be in town?"

"She says we'll make our joint pronouncement from here."

"What will you say?"

"Same as I've been telling you."

"No change of heart, no new insights?"

Wingate's hesitation told Jack more than his words had.

"So Al wants you to follow the party line no matter what?"

"It's not like that and don't you say it in your paper. I probably shouldn't even be talking to you."

It seemed a bit late for him to be worrying about that now. Jack tried one more question, "Who is this Al that you refer to?"

But Wingate had clammed up and wasn't going to say anything else. Jack knew a stonewall when he saw one, so he thanked Wingate, said good bye, and left.

Back at the office Jack spent some time trying to find out where and when Mrs. Conner was to arrive in town. Apparently no announcement had been made. Not feeling that Wingate's word was enough to go on, he gave up and went back to work on his present article. His phone beeped let him know he had a text message and he glanced over to see who it was from. The Conner campaign. The text gave a time and place for the next Helen Conner news conference — tomorrow in Washington.

Later in the day Walter came out of his office and told Jack he'd just received word of a Conner news conference and thought Jack might be interested. Sure enough, the time and place were identical to those on the text. Jack said yes, he was going. He gave a passing thought to who might have send the text and assumed it was Mrs. Kramer, then he let it go.

Wanting to get a good seat, Jack left early for the news conference. Half the city had the same idea. It was clear that anything Mrs. Conner did from now on was 'news'.

The statements went smoothly in typical Conner campaign style, but Jack was somewhat taken aback by Wingate's assertion that, yes, he had studied Mrs. Conner's data and could see that there may be other ways to look at the issue than the one he had espoused. Most of the questions from the press focused on why exactly he'd changed his mind, hinting that there had been some subtle coercion taking place.

When Jack finally got a turn he addressed Wingate and asked him specifically about the interview they'd had. Wingate responded that he'd given the matter deep thought and come to his present stand. His expression held none of the tentativeness of the day before. In fact he seemed confident and in control. Jack tried to grasp the implications. Maybe he truly had changed his mind, or maybe this was what he always wanted to say had it not been for 'Al'. Perhaps the cameras, the rapt attention of the press, and, not least, Mrs. Conner herself had inspired him to the courage necessary to express his convictions. The motive was unclear, but one thing was sure — Jack would have to write a completely different story than the one he had half written on the computer back at the office. In all it was interesting campaign politics, but not really very significant. The Green Eagles, in a separate statement, repudiated Wingate, calling him a meaningless ex-member, who was not up to the standards of the group.

Jack called Mrs. Kramer to see if Mrs. Conner was free for an interview, but was told she was just in and out of Washington — but if there was another time that it was convenient? He said he'd call back.

Three days later a bomb went off outside the Conner campaign headquarters in Portland. Miraculously, the injuries were minor. No one claimed responsibility. The Conner headquarters may not even have been the target, as there were a variety of offices in the area. The type of bomb was simple, using components anyone could have procured with little difficulty. Although the circumstantial evidence pointed to amateurs, there were absolutely no clues, just lots of speculation ranging from protesters to terrorist. As a precaution security was enhanced for all three candidates and their V.P.s.

When he heard about the bombing, Jack called Mrs. Kramer and for the first time there was no answer. He'd come to expect that she would always be there for him. The call didn't go to an answering service, but there was also no message from the phone company that the number was disconnected. He tried again just to make sure he hadn't made a mistake. It rang and rang and finally he hung up.

Jack's reason told him that Mrs. Kramer must have times when she was away from the phone, but he'd pictured her with the cell phone in her pocket night and day. It also brought home to him how much he had come to depend on one source, an error he didn't often make.

The next morning Jack's phone was ringing as he got to his desk. "Hello, Jack Kelly."

The voice at the other end was breathless, scared, but muffled. "They shouldn't have done it. Someone might have been hurt."

"Done what?"

"I called before. But I think they are watching. They watch everything, everyone."

"I'd like to help you. Give me your name, some place where I can reach you. They won't know."

"They shouldn't have done it."

Jack knew how to be patient. This could be a crank call, or it might be a great lead to some story. He had just enough of those to make it worthwhile to listen — and he had an idea this was the second time this person had called. What was the first about? He asked quietly, "What have they done this time?"

"Conner's bomb. They said they just wanted to scare her."

Jack felt his throat go dry. "Helen Conner?"

"Of course. Who do you think I've been talking about? I *told* you. I told you before."

"The last time you called...."

"It's too much. It's too much." The caller was becoming panicky.

"No," said Jack willing her to be calm. "No, you can tell me everything. No one will know. You know that. That's why you called me."

"I have to think about it." The line went dead.

At least he had it all recorded. He checked his files and found the earlier recording that he thought was the same person. Sure enough — the voice was disguised, but there was a marked similarity. He listened several times and began to decide that it was a woman. He noted that the call once again originated from a blocked number. He thought about calling his friend, Lt. Zbornak, but decided that the police wouldn't be able to learn any more than he could. He'd have to wait for another call. Besides, this caller was shaping up to be a protected source.

Chapter 16

The first presidential debate was coming up in two weeks, and Jack wanted to get an interview with Mrs. Conner beforehand, if possible. He was almost afraid to try Mrs. Kramer's number and put it off for days. Finally, recognizing the procrastination for what it was, he picked up his phone and dialed. Once, twice, three times it rang. And then Mrs. Kramer answered.

Relief flooded through him, but Jack kept his voice businesslike and to the point. It was established that Mrs. Conner could fit him in if he would fly out to St. Louis on Saturday. Jack agreed immediately.

Jack got to St. Louis on Friday, because he wanted to hear her speech as well as do the interview. A portion of the Convention Center had been reserved for the talk. It was crammed full of spectators and journalists. It looked chaotic, but Jack began to pick out security people not only in uniform at the doors, but scattered throughout the auditorium in plain clothes. Everyone had to pass through a metal detector to get in. Jack noticed several people who were quietly asked to step into another room where he presumed they were given a more thorough search.

Taking his mind off security matters, Jack began to circulate through the crowd. It was still early and not many were sitting down. He asked person after person why they were supporting Mrs. Conner. There were a variety of answers, but through them all was the sense that these people trusted her in a way they had never trusted a politician. In fact, it seemed hard for them to even think of her as a 'politician' in the normal sense.

"What makes you trust her?" was Jack's question each time. And each time the answer was something along the lines of "just listen to her, just watch her, and you'll see." It was obvious that Mrs. Conner appealed to people on an emotional as well as a rational level.

When Jack asked what they liked about her ideas, there were also a variety of answers. Here they mostly centered around the fact that she inspired them.

"And will she make a good president?" he asked.

The replies were quick and unequivocal — it was time to have a truly new thought in American politics. The people are tired of politicians who say or do anything to get elected, who don't believe character matters, who think they are better than we are.

Jack knew from past experience that Mrs. Conner was always punctual so he found a seat in the back several minutes before she was scheduled to appear. And sure enough, precisely on the hour, she walked out onto the stage. A roar of applause and shouts of welcome filled the large room. Mrs. Conner stood smiling quietly, accepting the ovation. Then she began to speak. A hush filled the room immediately as her avid followers hung onto her every word. As in other speeches Jack had witnessed, the ideas were ones he'd heard before, and yet he felt himself swept up in the emotion. He had to fight the desire to shout 'yes!' or to applaud when the others did.

Ten minutes into the speech a man three seats away from Jack stood up. This must have been a signal because all over the hall others stood also — maybe fifty altogether. They began to chant, quietly at first, and then louder and louder. They were saying, "Never Helen Conner. Never Helen Conner." It was eerie and disquieting.

Mrs. Conner's supporters began to fidget. She herself remained calm. Apparently she had wonderful acoustics experts on her team, because her voice, while still sounding normal and well-modulated, rang out clear and crisp over the sound of the chanting.

"I see that we have with us, once again, some of those who are afraid of ideas, who have such disdain for American ideals, for the American people, that they want to silence anyone who does not conform to their agenda. Their ideas must not be legitimate or they would not be afraid to present them legitimately. I ask each of you in the audience gently, peacefully, quietly, and with compassion to turn and look at these people. See them for what they are."

There was a quiet shuffling as each person in the room turned to look at one or another of the protestors. Slowly, under the weight of hundreds of eyes, the chanting stopped. Only one tried to continue. Security guards materialized around him and using only the force of their numbers, carried him out of the hall. His shouts faded as the heavy doors closed behind them.

Mrs. Conner immediately called attention back to herself and continued with her speech, her only reference to the incident was a small apology to the crowd that they had to be subjected to the bad manners of a few who seemed unwilling to debate their ideas openly. Within minutes she had them once again interested in her vision of America.

Looking around the audience Jack saw rapt attentive faces. These people loved Mrs. Conner. Jack suddenly felt strangely oppressed. He got up from his chair and slipped out the door. He made his way to the restroom and splashed cold water on his face. He didn't understand his reaction, which made it all the worse.

He saw no reason to stay so he went back to his hotel room, where he lay down on the bed, put his hands behind his head, and stared at the ceiling. She was just one more in a long line of people who thought they could or should be president. That's all. He'd seen them before, he'd see them again. Eventually he fell into a fitful sleep.

His interview was scheduled for early the next morning before Mrs. Conner flew off to Kansas City. Jack suspected he looked as bad as he felt. But he prized professionalism so he gathered his paraphernalia and went to Mrs. Conner's suite. Annie had once again shown her superlative skills by booking him into the same hotel as Mrs. Conner.

When he stepped off the elevator on the top floor, a guard came to attention and asked for his I.D. Jack showed his credentials and was pointed in the right direction. At the door of the suite, two more guards asked again. One of them started to check him out with a hand-held metal detector, while a serious looking German shepherd sniffed around. Just then the door opened and Mrs. Kramer said to the guards, "No, no. Mr. Kelly is O.K."

They were not impressed and continued, Mrs. Kramer looking on with some embarrassment. Jack reassured her, "Thank you, Mrs. Kramer, but I don't mind."

"I'm sorry, " she said again.

Finally Jack was allowed into the suite. Just inside the door were two more guards. These had all the signs of being from the Secret Service. Their sense of duty and efficiency made the ones outside the door look like slackers. Jack had never seen Mrs. Kramer look so discomposed. Finally he was allowed into the room where Mrs. Conner waited. Mrs. Kramer turned and was gone, her duty done.

Mrs. Conner extended her hand and shook his. "I'm sorry about the guards. There was a threat and, well, they are only doing their job."

"Something serious?"

"It would seem so." She invited no elaboration, but Jack was not satisfied.

"Can you tell me any more about it?"

"I know that sensational stories sell newspapers, garners T.V. viewers, and titillates the social media. Terrorists of all sorts like the attention and would love to have the focus be on the harassment. I refuse to play their game, and I can only ask you as a responsible journalist to be unimpressed and refuse to play as well. It's easy to focus on what is evil. But the best, and really the only way to expose it for what it is, is for right-thinking, clear-thinking people to focus on what is meaningful, what builds rather than destroys, what achieves good rather than despair. I can do that and so can you."

"O.K., but bombings and death threats are news."

"Are they, Mr. Kelly? I wonder."

Turning the conversation slightly, Jack said, "I was at your talk last night. You handled the protestors very smoothly."

"They keep coming up with new tactics. We try to outguess them, and have so far. I hope we can keep coming up with ideas." She actually laughed.

"You find that behavior humorous?"

"No, but certainly a challenge to combat with dignity. I hope never to be hustled off the stage in ignominious retreat as happened in Eugene some time ago."

"I remember."

"Yes. Well, perhaps you have other topics to discuss."

"One more follow-up, please. What became of the man who was hustled out of the hall last night?"

"Oh, they let him go of course. He'd done nothing but make a nuisance of himself — easily forgiven and not against the law."

Letting that go for now, Jack said, "I see in many of your followers a very emotional response to your words, to you yourself. It could almost be described as worship."

"I try to understand that myself. I wish I appealed to them strictly on the grounds of reason and sound policy instead. The only explanation I have been able to come up with is that they have been hungering for someone to say the things I say. They are just very appreciative that their hunger is being satisfied."

"And you never play on that emotional response?"

"I try to give the same kind of speeches I did before I noticed the phenomena. The fact is, I don't know if it is good or bad, or whether I should change or not."

"Those people last night — well, the only way to put it is that they love you."

Mrs. Conner was sober and said in a quiet voice, "I wish they didn't."

"Why not? If you get enough to love you, you win."

"I don't want it to be me. I want them to love the ideas."

Jack wondered if maybe that was why they loved her. Perhaps her sincerity was so deep, so strong, that when exposed to it, people wanted more. Jack wasn't sure that was a safe sort of president to have.

Mrs. Conner was continuing, "I never saw this response before I began running for president. I have a large acquaintance and I never saw my friends acting this way. And yet I haven't changed." She seemed to be musing to herself, almost as if Jack wasn't in the room. And he was thinking that maybe she didn't fully appreciate the effect she had on people — even jaded, cynical reporters.

She came to herself and said with a big, self-effacing grin, "I'm sorry, Mr. Kelly, you didn't come here to listen to me ramble on in this way."

Was it sincerity, or was she manipulating him as easily as she did her supporters? Since there was no immediate way to find out, Jack obligingly changed the subject and asked about the up-coming debate.

"I look forward to it," replied Mrs. Conner. "It is the first time the American public will be able to judge us together."

"Do you have anything special planned?"

"If you mean some theatrical, political tricks, no. If you mean 'winning' the debate, why, yes, I do plan to do that."

The arrogance of her words was belied by the smile on her face and the tone of her voice, but still Jack asked, "What makes you so sure?"

"Confidence in one's ability to perform seems a prerequisite for this job."

"That kind of confidence can easily blind one to one's real performance," was Jack's rejoinder.

"Quite so. And, if, after this debate, I think I did extremely well while the rest of the nation sees me as a dreadful flop (most unlikely, mind you!), you may remind me of this conversation. But seriously, Mr. Kelly, have you observed any time during the campaign or in any of our interviews when my 'confidence' overstepped my achievement?"

"Well..."

"I hope you will always be willing to be honest with me. It is one of the biggest problems I see — the more it looks like I might actually be president, the more people want to stay on my 'good side'. Thank goodness for the boys. They still see me as 'Mom' and I can always trust them to be perfectly, impeccably straight with me about my faults, if not with their own. I treasure those who remain themselves, allowing me to do the same."

Jack took the compliment behind her words and smiled. "I'll try not to be dazzled by your presidency."

"You still don't think I have a chance, do you?"

"The polls indicate a slow, but strong and consistent trend upward for you."

"And you can hardly believe it."

"It is not my job to decide who is to be president."

"Just to be calm, clear, objective."

He wanted to be severe and disallow such teasing, but he laughed. "Time is short. I'd better continue with the interview," he said, wishing it were not so.

"Yes, of course, the interview," was Mrs. Conner's enigmatic reply. She composed herself very primly on the chair and looked at him expectantly. He wanted to laugh again, but didn't. Here he was being less and less substantive on issues. He'd have to work hard to get a normal article out of this interview. Friendship with this woman, if it was really beginning to grow and not just a masterful manipulation on her part, had to wait. He had work to do.

There was one thing he wanted to follow up before he forgot. "Is Garth Wingate still around?"

"Garth? Yes, he is with us quite a bit, I believe. I don't see him much myself, but Mrs. Kramer talks of him as if he were a stray puppy that she brought home. Why do you ask?"

"His conversion seemed rather dramatic and sudden. I talked with him the night before your joint press conference and he was still adamantly opposed to you."

Mrs. Conner's eyes narrowed slightly. She thought for a moment and then got up and walked across the room. She turned and stated rather than questioned, "You think he is insincere."

"Does he ever mention anyone named Al?"

"Not that I'm aware of. Al who?"

"I don't know, and couldn't find out. There are no Als listed among the active membership of the Green Eagles. But your friend Wingate hardly spoke a word to me that didn't sound as though it came out of this Al's mouth. I have to say that I was very surprised to hear what he said with you."

Mrs. Conner looked pensive. Finally she spoke, apparently it never entering her mind that Jack might suspect that she had coerced Wingate in any way, "Thank you, Mr. Kelly, I'm going to look into this." She sat down again. "Is there anything else you want to ask — or perhaps anything else that I should know?"

"Well, one thing has been bothering me...."

"Yes...?"

"Obviously, we've never had a woman as president before. America is such a sports-mad country, I was wondering — will you be able to throw out the first ball of the baseball season as so many past presidents have done?"

"Mr. Kelly, you are the first, can you believe it, the first person to ask me anything about my athletic ability and it's bearing on my fitness for president. My answer: don't worry, I can handle it."

She was always so elegant and graceful, so perfectly groomed. Jack couldn't picture her in old sweats, dripping with perspiration after a big game on the ball field. And yet why not? She moved with the strength and agility of an athlete. He never really thought of it in those terms before, but she was in very good shape....

"What sports do you take part in?"

"I've played most sports — remember I have two sons. My favorites are softball and volleyball."

"No kidding?" It was very coincidental. Had she checked to find out his favorites just to impress him? That was farfetched. What are you thinking, Jack asked himself. Maybe she would be a good president — anyone who liked those sports couldn't be all bad.

"Would you find it unusual," she challenged, "for the men who are running for president to be involved in some sport for recreation?"

"No, of course not. In fact it is common. I stand ashamed and beg your forgiveness."

"Granted."

"So, when do you find time to play?"

"I make time. After all, I am still at least partially my own boss."

They talked for a while longer on more substantial issues and then Mrs. Conner had to go.

"I'm sorry, my next speech beckons."

"I always appreciate your generosity with your time."

"But it is my pleasure."

Jack started for the door. Mrs. Conner stopped him.

"Just a minute, Mr. Kelly." She reached into a drawer and pulled out a small object that she tossed underhand at him. He managed to catch it. It was a campaign-style button, quite large — four or five inches across — tan colored with dark brown initials across the face. C.C.C.M.A.

"The latest group to importune me," Mrs. Conner explained. "Maybe you should look into them."

"What do the initials stand for?"

"You're the investigative reporter."

"But..."

"Good day, Mr. Kelly." She smiled and waved. He had no choice but to go. At least on the way out the guards didn't need to check him.

As he walked back to his room, he studied the C.C.C.M.A. button trying to think of any group he'd heard of that fit the letters. He opened his door, went in, put down his notes, and suddenly it hit him. Chocolate Chip Cookie Makers of America. He laughed out loud as he sat on the bed looking at the button.

His plane didn't leave until later in the afternoon, but Jack decided to go to the airport anyway. He was curious to see what kind of attention Mrs. Conner garnered when she was in a public place, but on essentially private business. She'd mentioned the general time of her flight and her destination — it would be easy to find out the flight number and airline. He packed quickly, checked out, and got a taxi to the airport.

It took him longer than he thought it would, but finally he narrowed the possibilities down to the most likely flight. He found the gate number, and was grateful it was the same concourse he needed to fly out of later. After passing through the security point, he stopped at the first gate. He mingled with the people there while keeping an eye out for the Conner party.

As it was, he almost missed them. It was one of the Secret Service agents whom he recognized and not Mrs. Conner. She had changed her normal tailored clothes for loose-fitting, bright, albeit expensive casual wear. And most striking of all, she'd let her hair hang loose in soft waves that fell well below her shoulders. Adding a pair of dark sunglasses made her virtually unrecognizable. Jack followed the group at a judicious distance. No one so much as glanced her way. The woman knew how to travel incognito.

They arrived at their gate with about ten minutes to spare. Mrs. Conner took a seat facing the concourse and the various agents Jack recognized lounged inconspicuously at her side. How many others there were around he didn't know. He stopped at the gate directly across from them and made an effort to appear involved in waiting for a plane. He got out a book and pretended to read. After a couple of minutes he glanced up and saw Mrs. Conner looking right at him. He felt himself blush, because, after all, what was he doing here?

Continuing to look at him, she raised her dark glasses and winked. At that moment one of the agents bent down and spoke in her ear. She shook her head in a negative response, but the agent spoke more emphatically. Jack was so intent watching them, he didn't even notice another agent until he appeared at his side and whispered in his ear, "No sudden moves, if you please."

Jack was startled, but remained calm. The agent steered him down the concourse, but stopped as Mrs. Conner stood up and came to intercept them. The agent was unprepared for her to step in. Jack marveled that it was all so calm, so completely unnoticed by anyone. They were all just several more in the hundreds of people swarming up and down the concourse.

Mrs. Conner reached them and said in no uncertain terms, but with a low voice, "Thank you for your diligence, Mr. Jenkins, but this won't be necessary."

Jenkins was apparently something of his own man. In an equally low, emphatic tone he said, "Kelly was following you. His flight leaves much later this afternoon."

Jack was too caught up in the events to wonder how Jenkins knew the time of his flight. Mrs. Conner was saying, "I'm sure he has a perfectly rational explanation that will satisfy you, don't you, Mr. Kelly?"

Jack hoped so. Jenkins had not loosened his grip on Jack's arm. Nevertheless, Jack was not one to be intimidated. "I'd hoped to have a discussion with Mrs. Conner about the activities of the C.C.C.M.A. Now there's a group to watch out for, Jenkins."

Mrs. Conner was barely able to suppress a smile and Jenkins looked confused. Meanwhile, another agent joined the small party. "Mrs. Conner, it's time for you to board now. "

"Thank you, Mr. Smith, I'll be there momentarily." In a smooth, but irresistible move, she extricated Jack's arm from Jenkins' grip and lead him several steps away — enough to be 'alone' but not really out of the sphere of the agents.

"Why are you here?" she asked.

Feeling foolish, Jack quickly explained his reasons. Mrs. Conner's only comment was, "Fair enough."

The agents were looking decidedly anxious to board the plane. Before she turned to go, she said, "Jenkins and Smith are very good at their jobs. They don't trust anyone."

Jack started to be flippant, but realized he meant it when he said, "Good for them."

Then they were gone. Jack went to find a restaurant where he could have some lunch and spend time writing until his plane left.

Chapter 17

The first presidential debate went well for Mrs. Conner. She held her own and certainly didn't look out of place with the old pros. They, in turn, were not sure how to treat her, so they choose to err on the side of caution. Essentially, they pretended that she was not there. Their well-worn, often-heard words did not have the resonance of Mrs. Conner's call for each citizen to take responsibility for himself and his actions. Her specific plans sounded reasonable — even possible. Jack felt the power, the emotion, wakened by her words as he watched the debate on T.V. It wasn't necessary to see her in person to feel the charisma.

Next morning the polls showed a 4-5 point leap upward for Mrs. Conner. The Republicans and Democrats weren't panicking yet, but growing apprehension was behind the spin control that took up much of the next day or so.

To Jack's knowledge the Conner camp had never used spin control. For example, when asked about the debate by a breathless, intense network reporter, a top Conner aide replied, "Didn't you see it?"

"Yes, of course." the reporter said.

"Well then, I'm sure that you and every other American are capable of knowing and judging what you saw and heard. You don't need me to tell you."

It was so out of character with most political pronouncements that the reporter hardly knew what to say next. Jack chuckled to himself, knowing the challenges of the Conner style.

The days that followed were busy and full. He kept working on his series about special interests and he delved deeply into every aspect of Helen Conner's past and present. It was disconcerting to come to the conclusion over and over again that she was what she seemed to be. He felt that he knew every detail of her life from the time she was a child. There was nothing there to question. She was intelligent, well-rounded, kind to dogs and children, had always paid her taxes, faithfully married to one man (who also seemed to be a fine person), successful in all her pursuits. She seemed to be good. And it scared Jack. Was it possible to be so wealthy and so clever and yet so clean? The scariest part of all was that he continued to grow in his liking and respect for her.

Every now and then he continued to get unsigned text messages stating a time and place and the word 'Conner'. He followed up and each time the event proved to be a speech in which Mrs. Conner brought out a new point. Jack assumed it was Mrs. Kramer looking after him as usual.

Jack didn't have any face-to-face interviews with Mrs. Conner, but he occasionally called Mrs. Kramer's number and was able to get a statement over the phone.

The protests continued — but all the candidates shared in the bother.

It was after the vice-presidential debate that things really began to heat up. Thomas D'Arcy came across as so suave, so sophisticated, so intelligent, and yet so likeable that he won the debate easily. The swords that had been rattling were now drawn in earnest. The Republican and Democratic candidates themselves acted as if above the fray, claiming no knowledge of such things, but rumors swirled and grew. One of the dirtiest was that D'Arcy and Mrs. Conner had been lovers for many years and that there were two children hidden away. The names were not revealed to protect the innocent children.

Mrs. Conner's total comment when asked about it by an intrepid reporter was, "An absurdity deserving no comment."

Through it all Mrs. Conner kept campaigning her way. She didn't even get near the mud. She simply went another way, continuing to invite Americans to be more than they thought they could be and offering them practical, reasonable ways to achieve so lofty a goal.

Her T.V. ads were equally different. In thirty or sixty second slots, she didn't use sound bites. Instead she said something along the lines that "such spots were not adequate to share any important policy issues with you. Go to your news sources — magazines, newspapers, T.V., the internet — become knowledgeable. Insist on getting the information you need to make sound decisions. You get what you deserve. Make sure you deserve the best." That was followed by the words "Conner for President." All in all they were judged to be some of the most effective ads of all time by those who made it their job to decide such things. As she seemed to have endless supplies of money, she also bought thirty minute time slots during prime time. These were expertly produced, slick programs that entertained and enlightened.

Her IT people were of the highest caliber and her presence on the social media was consistently adept and extremely popular. She knew what she was doing and did not hesitate to exploit any advantage.

Jack wasn't surprised as the weeks closed in on November that Mrs. Conner was only slightly behind in the polls.

In hopes of getting a rounded picture of Mrs. Conner, Jack asked for, and to his surprise, received permission to interview Alex Conner. The young man greeted him with the same coolness Jack felt on previous occasions, but he seemed willing to cooperate.

"Has the campaign lived up to your expectations?" Jack asked.

"Its one thing to read and study about this — another to be in the very middle."

"Do I detect a note of having had enough in your voice?"

"Its harder than I thought it would be, but worth it."

"Harder in what ways?"

"You know about the on-going threats?"

"Yes."

"Mom makes us be careful all the time."

Jack pictured the scene of Mom lecturing the boys and their assigned Secret Service agents on taking care — the boys hating the restrictions, the agents figuring they knew their job, thank you very much.

"And frankly," continued Alex, "I am surprised that Mom isn't far ahead by now. She is so superior to the other two. But putting all that aside, I wouldn't be missing this for the world."

"What about Chris? I never see him out campaigning."

"No. And you won't. Chris' interests lie in other directions. Just leave him alone. There is nothing there that need interest you." Alex spoke politely, but Jack sensed — what, anger perhaps? — underneath the smooth words.

"If there is something to hide, it's best to state it frankly. Everything comes out eventually."

Alex let his guard slip a little. "What is it with you people? You've met Chris. He just doesn't want to be any more in the public eye than he has to be. Is it a crime to have other interests?"

Jack let him spout off, but then said calmly, quietly, "I neither know nor have heard of anything that is other than positive about your brother. I also suspect that he doesn't need to be defended by you."

Alex let that sink in and then said, "O.K., I see that I was being overly defensive. Chris just... Reporters are not fair. You can't trust them." Then he seemed to remember who he was talking to and his cheeks colored a little, but he didn't back down. "Mom says that I am too impatient with the faults of others, but look at Mom, the best qualified candidate to run for president, maybe ever, and the news media can't see it and won't report it." He looked at Jack, a challenge blazing from his eyes.

Jack just smiled and said, "You will admit to a certain prejudice on the matter...."

The reply came grudgingly. "Some prejudice, but only a little. And it is not just me, Mom has a huge following. Let me ask you, if you're not afraid to answer, where do you stand?"

"You are not completely unjustified in distrusting the press. I can only speak for myself in this, but I have to say that my job is not to judge whether or not your Mom is fit to be president. I just try to lay out the facts about her for my readers. They'll make the final decision."

"I read your articles. There are always implied questions, reservations."

"Perhaps you will be willing to chalk it up to the difference of you growing up with her and thinking you know her, and my short, intense attempt to learn everything I can and then chose what is useful for my readership. There are always questions."

"Are there, Mr. Kelly, or does there come a time to put aside the questions and accept what you know, what your heart tells you is true?"

Jack was disconcerted to find himself in the middle of the same kind of interview with Alex that he was forever having with Mrs. Conner. What was it about this family? Where did he stray and let the interview get so out of hand? What kind of article would come from a boy's philosophizing? Sternly deciding to get control back he said, "On the day I vote, I'll 'decide', in the meantime I have a different job to do." Then they continued to talk about the campaign and Alex's role in it. The young man was able to curb his passion and continued the interview with relative good grace. In the end Jack marveled at such self-possession in one so relatively young.

The second debate took place in mid-October. This time the Democrat and Republican came out with no holds barred. They had been checked the first time by the knowledge that certain attacks might backfire on them because she was a woman, but this had disappeared in the subsequent weeks of campaigning. The second debate had them treating her as they would any man in the same position, trying to belittle her by references to her inexperience, and party-less status.

Since each of the men thought Mrs. Conner was the biggest threat, they pounded away more at her than at each other — while at the same time trying to incorporate as much of her clearly popular message as they could into their respective platforms. They came across as faintly confused bullies. Next morning Mrs. Conner showed another gain in the polls. Apparently unable to learn from their mistakes, the Democrats and Republicans continued their attacks on Mrs. Conner. Their campaigns took on a frenzied air – more "against" her rather than "for" something of substance. Meanwhile the ponderous, hulking mass of vested interests and preservers of the status quo began to mobilize as if it had finally sunk into that collective consciousness that quite possibly neither a Democrat nor a Republican was going to be the next president. And if such a momentous event occurred — what then?

Jack was fascinated as he watched the tactics unfold. Some used a frontal attack, joining in to belittle and criticize Mrs. Conner's message. Others made a strong effort to draw her within their circle of influence. Mrs. Conner told Jack over the phone that her biggest problem was keeping them from making her into one of them simply by defining her as such. She was plied with offers of contributions, and other perks, that were unmistakable efforts to 'buy into' her campaign, and hence her presidency. She expressed gratitude that her workers had the experience all along in dealing with this so they were able to meet the challenges and see through the ploys.

In several of her half hour television spots she explained, to the discomfiture of several prominent groups, exactly what they were trying to do. She said if they were treating her this way, imagine what they had been doing for years with the Democrats and Republicans. She looked America in the eye and asked, "Are they smarter than you? Do they know what is best for you? Are you going to let them win? I'm not asking you to give up anything of value. I'm inviting you to be yourselves, free from the endless meddling of powerbrokers, bureaucrats, and politicians who think they know more about what is best for you than you do yourselves. Show them who is right — those who have confidence in you, or those who want to control you."

Chapter 18

The election was on Tuesday. The Sunday two days before was the last debate. The race was too close to call.

The debate was to be held in Washington, and Jack was asked to be one of three panelists who were to ask the candidates questions. It was a great honor and Jack wondered why he was chosen. Walter took it in stride — wasn't Jack one of the best? The week beforehand Jack immersed himself in the ideas and positions of all three candidates. Mrs. Conner was easy, but the other two required more work. Sam and Jessie were his constant companions, helpers, and research assistants. By Saturday he felt ready. On Sunday he was nearly to the debate venue when his phone rang. It was Walter.

"Look at your email right now. I've sent you something."

"What is it? I don't have time. I just at the door of the conference center."

"Just look. Now."

"This had better be good."

He opened the email from Walter as he walked toward the security station. There were photos – clear, bright photos. As he thumbed through them, felt as though someone had slugged him in the stomach, and he had to lean against the wall of the hall. After a moment, he made himself look at the photos again. He couldn't stand it.

Taking a deep breath, Jack called Walter back. He drew on some tiny reserves and asked Walter. "Where did you get these?"

"They popped up on email moments before I called you."

"Who has them?"

"Far as I can tell every major newspaper and T.V. station has received them, too. The Democrats and Republicans have them, also. Everyone is going to wait until the debate and see what happens. She's going to be crucified. What a story. If only she hadn't come across as so fine — so above this sort of thing." Walter seemed to be talking just to give Jack a chance to recover. "I wonder if even the men candidates could survive this sort of thing? I wonder who the man is?"

Jack made himself think of the photos again. He'd seen pictures like this before. They weren't even all that smutty — just pictures of two people making love, shown in crisp, clear black and white. They were smiling, they were quite naked, and they were Helen Conner and Will Camden. Jack wanted to erase it, make it go away somehow -- put them back in the camera and delete the images. How could she? How could she? Will Camden, of all people. Maybe there were others. Maybe there were others and Camden was the only one to take pictures. Walter was talking again. "What do you want to do with these? I don't want to use them, but there is going to be a huge story here."

"I've got to go. Thanks, Walter."

"What are you going to do?"

Jack didn't answer because he was already hung up on him and was speed dialing Mrs. Kramer's number.

Jack was so taken aback when it was Mrs. Conner herself who answered that he could barely speak. In a strained voice he said, "I have something you need to see. Now."

"Mr. Kelly, is that you? Are you all right?"

"I have something you need to see. Let me email it to a private box where you can look at it right now. Right now."

She hesitated and then gave him an address. He forwarded the photos immediately

"Mr. Kelly, what is it?"

"Just check this email now." He paused and then said quietly, "Good bye."

The next minutes were hell. He went through the procedure necessary to get ready for the debate, but every time he tried to calm down and sort out his thoughts, the image of Helen Conner and Will Camden intruded, blocking out all rational thought. Part of him wanted to leave the hall, miss the debate, and put all of this behind him. The other part knew he was in the middle of a breaking story and he had to be there to see it out.

What an ending to the book he was planning to write! But somehow the thought of his book left him empty and chilled him more than the winter wind. There were other things to write about. The heart had gone out of this idea. And yet hadn't he always suspected? Hadn't he always wondered? A tiny thought crept in — no, he hadn't always suspected, he hadn't always wondered. He tried to remember Mrs. Conner as he knew her, and the photos just did not fit. Was he being fair? Anyone could be tempted. She wasn't married. It wasn't as if she were an adulteress.

Jack was 'fixed-up' for the cameras and was outwardly ready for the debate. If he wasn't nervous going on live in front of America before, he sure was now. Maybe Mrs. Conner simply won't show up. She had such innate poise — she might bow out gracefully and slip back into oblivion.

In the hall several moods prevailed. There was the excitement of the public who had the privilege of being there in person as spectators, the harried, but competent, air of the technicians wanting everything ready for the live broadcast, and the thinly veiled intensity of those who, like hunters, were closing in for the kill. The last were those who knew about the photos.

Jack wondered if Mrs. Conner was there, but didn't want to ask, hoping to stave off the inevitable. The format of the debate included five minutes at the beginning for each candidate to give a statement. Earlier, lots had been drawn, and Mrs. Conner was to be the first. As the minutes ticked down, the tension in the room grew. Even those who didn't know anything began to catch the mood.

Jack and the other two reporters took their places, and the moderator did his introductions – first the three journalists, then the Democrat and Republican. They were trying to look normal, but both had a smugness just below the surface. Finally, Mrs. Conner was introduced. The room hushed as she walked out and a small ripple went through parts of the

crowd. In her hand Helen Conner carried a large manila envelope.
Jack's throat went dry and he was grateful for the water in front of him and
that he didn't have to speak yet. The moderator explained the format and
invited Mrs. Conner to speak first.

Jack saw a bit of strain about the corners of her eyes, but generally she
didn't look like someone whose world was about to crumble around her.
She paused as she reached the podium. She looked at the audience, the
panelist and finally at the camera. When she spoke it was calmly and
quietly, but with confidence.

"I had a speech prepared to deliver here today. There was nothing new
or startling in it, but I was planning to be honest and straightforward with
you all. Circumstances have forced me to change the speech, but I trust you
will believe the honesty is still there.

"Today through the bravery and kindness of one individual, some
photos that I was not meant to see until it was too late, have come into my
possession. These same photos have been distributed to most of the major
media outlets in the United States."

Mrs. Conner began taking the photos out and Jack's mind was
screaming, "No!"

Mrs. Conner continued, "These photos show a man and a woman in
the act of making love. I know the man — he worked for my campaign
for a time. The woman I do not know."

Jack — as well as nearly everyone else — was dumbfounded, but
Mrs. Conner wasn't finished. "Whoever fabricated these photos chose a
woman whose body was similar to mine. My experts tell me that she
probably also had hair like mine. It was fairly simple for them to take

photos of my face and put them into the image. When I say simple, I do not mean unsophisticated. It requires specialized skills, but any number of people have the skills necessary. Every one of us has seen what special effects can be achieved with film when we have gone to the movies. Who hasn't heard of Photoshop?"

Mrs. Conner then held up one of the photos so the camera could zoom in on it. She had her hand placed casually over the parts unsuitable for broadcast over prime time national television. She spoke very matter-of-factly. "As you can see this looks exactly as if it were me. I am told that the face probably is mine. The people who performed this hoax may well have taken pictures of me in various public places — choosing from them what would work in their counterfeit images.

"Think of the timing. This is clearly the work of people who are afraid. Who is behind it? And what do they fear? I hope the journalists of this great country will concentrate on these questions and not be fooled by such a clever, malevolent conspiracy."

There was a stirring in the crowd. Mrs. Conner addressed the obvious question. "You are saying to yourselves right now - what is there to make me believe this woman? Is she just a desperate politician trying to salvage a campaign that is suddenly hanging in tatters about her? I would ask the same question except I know that is not me in these photos. And there is one critical fact that the fabricators don't know — couldn't know. One fact that allows me to prove irrefutably that this is not me."

"They did a fairly good job of finding a body double." Here she actually laughed a bit. "They were kind to me here and there. But what they didn't know is that I have a birthmark on my body that would have showed up clearly and unmistakably in these photos. Due to the nature of its placement I cannot show it to you. I trust you will understand."

She held up the photo again, pointed, and said emphatically with that quiet power Jack had come to recognize, "This is not me."

A hush covered the room and Mrs. Conner didn't break it for a moment. Then she smiled and said, "I hope that this will be the end of it and we can get on with what really matters — choosing a president of the United States of America. I am sure my distinguished colleagues representing the Democrats and the Republicans have nothing to do with this terrible lie and disgusting, deliberate attempt to destroy my reputation." She smiled at each of them in turn while the camera panned across their confused, slightly guilty, faces. "So let's get on with the debate and show the voters the three candidates they have to chose from. Let Americans decide the direction they want their country to go and who they want to be at the head of the federal government."

No one spoke. Even the moderator seemed stunned. Mrs. Conner was all poise, perfectly in control. She was...presidential. When no one spoke, she took command and indicated the Democrat who was to speak next. She invited him to the podium and then went to sit on her stool.

The Democrat finally recovered himself and got up to speak. His opening remarks were slightly disjointed as he tried to present his planned speech, but also disavow any knowledge or complicity in the photos. The Republican was only slightly better because he had five minutes to recover. After that the debate followed its course more or less smoothly. The panelists asked questions, the candidates answered. But the questions about the photos did not go away. The formal debate had to end before the journalists could allow the smoldering embers to erupt into flame.

Finally, the cameras were off and the hall was inundated with reporters. They must have been gathering outside throughout the debate. Jack saw Jenkins and Smith and several other agents trying to hustle Mrs. Conner away. This time she would not allow it. Instead she advanced toward the horde and offered herself up. A feeding frenzy followed, but no one could shake her calm or her story. Some even insisted that she show her birthmark as 'proof, but Mrs. Conner drew the line there.

"What about the man?"

Already Camden's name was beginning to whisper its way through the super-charged atmosphere, but no one spoke it out loud yet.

"I hope he is as innocent as I am," answered Mrs. Conner. "If he was party to it, I hope he will come forward and name those responsible. They are the ones who need to be exposed."

"What would you have done if you hadn't had the birthmark?"

"Stood in front of you and told the truth. I will not be blackmailed."

"Is there anyone else who can verify this alleged birthmark?"

"My husband is dead. My physician has been informed that he will be questioned on this issue. What he says will be up to him. All I asked of him was to tell the truth. There is no one else in my life who would know."

Jack couldn't bring himself to leave, but he couldn't join the seething mass, so he hovered on the edges listening, but asking no questions.

The journalists kept on and on, asking the same questions using slightly different words over and over again. Mrs. Conner patiently and persistently answered them all.

Eventually as the journalists became satiated and calmness once again prevailed, Mrs. Conner left with her entourage. The reporters scurried off to write their stories. Jack went home to bed.

But sleep didn't come, and he lay awake staring at the ceiling. He kept trying to organize his thoughts. He'd just witnessed one of the most extraordinary political events in his career as a journalist. He should be out there right now — even if it was the middle of the night — working the story, contacting sources, finding experts, questioning the doctor, looking for Will Camden. Walter would be expecting it. Instead he traced patterns in the wood above his head.

The ringing of his phone disturbed him only slightly — he almost didn't answer, but after five rings, he reached over for it. Grudgingly he said, "Hello."

"Mr. Kelly, I'm glad you answered. I thought you might be working. This is Helen Conner."

By now Jack was sitting upright on his bed, his feet on the floor.

"I came home," he said. Jack had never heard Mrs. Conner sound so hesitant.

"Oh. Good. Good. I…I want to thank you for sending me the photos."

Jack took a deep breath and said, "I'm sorry. I thought it was you."

"I know. What else could you have thought?"

"Perhaps I could have given you the tiniest benefit of the doubt."

"Maybe you did without realizing it. You were the only one who brought them to my attention. Whatever your motives were, it allowed me to salvage my campaign. The boys had planned to be there. Can you imagine what it would have been like...? Thank you for sparing them that."

"It's really not you in the pictures?"

"It's really not me."

"Why did he do it?"

"Will?"

"Yes."

"If we knew that we'd know a lot."

"I suspect it will all come out."

"I hope so. I have to go now, Mr. Kelly. Thank you again."

"Well... good bye, and good luck on Tuesday."

"Thanks."

After she hung up, Jack sat absentmindedly holding the phone to his chest as if he didn't want to break the contact yet. It was crazy to be a reporter and have a person in the White House that he liked, who was almost a friend. He wondered if she was able to disarm all journalists this way.

He wasn't too old to change his profession. Maybe he could

concentrate on finishing one of the several books he had started. Hey, maybe he could be an expatriate, go to France, lie on the beach and watch attractive women walk by. Why not go back to college and get a degree in engineering? He fell asleep imagining other lives, yet knowing in the morning he'd go to the office and maybe even write one more pre-election piece.

Next morning Walter was understandably miffed at Jack for not bringing in a story the night before. And when he asked about the photos, Jack said nothing.

A gleam of realization grew in Walter's eyes. "It was you! You sent her the photos. Hell of a way to get a story. But now I want something written, on my desk. I trust that isn't asking too much."

Jack was surprised at how easy it was to get back to work. His story was short but good and made it in time for the deadline. The day went by in a haze. Talk buzzed all around him. Everybody knew Mrs. Conner was the focus of his attention, so they all thought he'd want to talk about the debate and the photos. He humored them in a distracted way, but was grateful when he was finally able to slip away and go home.

He hadn't thought so much about Carrie lately, but tonight he missed her terribly. He wanted someone to be there when he got home. Someone to smile and welcome him. Someone he could talk with, laugh with.

Chapter 19

Tuesday morning found him awake early and ready to vote when the polls opened. He had a plane to catch. He was going to Oregon to cover the election night with the Conner contingent.

Once inside the voting booth, Jack could no longer avoid thinking about who he was going to vote for. He stood inside the curtained cubicle hidden from the world, but not from his own thoughts. He voted for everyone and everything else first and then only the presidential choice was left.

He looked at the three names and considered everything he knew about each one. Why did he hesitate? There was only one choice he could make. He punched in next to Helen Conner's name. He didn't really think she would win, but he didn't want his vote to get in the way of such an outcome. Maybe that one vote might make a difference. If enough people made the choice he did perhaps a message would go out and reach the Democrats and Republicans. Maybe. Just maybe. For the first time in days Jack was smiling as he went back to his apartment.

At home he picked up his suitcase and took a taxi to the airport, his travelling companions a light heart and the expectancy that he would actually enjoy the next hours. How amazing to think that it was less than a year ago he'd first headed out to Portland to interview the unknown Helen Conner. Whatever happened tonight, he was proud to have known her.

The election night party was held in one of the ballrooms of the downtown Portland Hilton. The Conners were privately awaiting the results at an undisclosed location, but planned to make a showing later in the evening. Jack mingled with the party. All around the room were large T.V. monitors and a large electronic tallyboard showed the constantly updated returns. It was still too early to project a winner. The networks news coverage was mostly limited to local results across the country. It promised to be a long night.

Jack talked with a variety of Conner people, more for the sake of having something to do than the expectation of getting any meaningful information. After a while he decided to prowl around the hotel. The rumor was that the inner circle was at the Conner home, but Jack thought it more likely they'd be in the hotel somewhere. He took an elevator to the top floor and then, using the stairs, worked his way down, looking for secret service personnel in the hallways. He didn't find anything unusual, so he rejoined the party.

Hour after hour it remained too close to call. Even the most intrepid T.V. anchors were unwilling to make a definitive statement. With so many hours to fill, the talk became increasingly vapid. They had expert after expert telling what was likely to happen and why, if this or that candidate were to win. Jack paid little attention, finding such reports boring at best and foolish the rest of the time.

Occasionally he'd listen — as when a group who generally claimed to be spokespersons for women and minorities tried to explain how this woman and this black man running for high office was a bad idea. They seemed offended that this had happened and that it wasn't their people who brought it about. And then there was the man who represented a massive agri-business conglomerate that had tentacles throughout the government. He said that if Mrs. Conner won and was able to reduce farm subsidies as she promised, that small farmers, 'the backbone of the nation', would suffer. A member of Green Eagles said there would be 'war' if Mrs. Conner won. Their people and all caring citizens would have to mobilize to stop the 'invasion' of dangerous ideas. A senator who discovered he'd lost what he assumed to be a secure seat to a Connerite upstart, suggested that the people in his district had been seduced or maybe hypnotized, and were now going to get what they deserved. He said that this was going to be the end of America.

There were also interviews with Conner supporters, but the media bias toward the status quo was clear. The Democrats and the Republicans were 'normal', 'mainstream' Americans. The Conner followers were 'radical', 'unlikely', 'untried', and just plain different. The media were endlessly annoyed that Mrs. Conner had adamantly refused to have a 'party' with a name. Ignoring history, they even suggested that a two-party system was American and third parties should be banned or know how to keep their place as minor, meaningless irritants. Whenever the Democrat or the Republican surged ahead the announcement was made with relief and confidence. When Mrs. Conner seemed to be gaining, the announcements were laced with incredulity.

At a quarter past midnight, even though the race was still too close to call, Mrs. Conner made an appearance at the ballroom. A hush went through the crowd as she made her way to the podium, flanked by Chris, Alex, and any number of secret Service agents. She looked out over a crowd of quiet, breathless faithful. And then she smiled. Her supporters burst into thunderous unending cheers and applause.

When the noise finally began to abate, Mrs. Conner spoke. Her speech was short, simple and heartfelt. She thanked each of them for their support and hard work. She finished with, "They say we can't win; that we shouldn't win. But they have never really known you. And what it means to you to take back control and responsibility for your lives. It's not over."

The roar from the crowd was even greater than before.

It wasn't until morning that a clear, unequivocal winner could be named. In a vote that included the largest voter turn-out in many decades, the Democrat received 28%, the Republican got 33%, and Mrs. Conner, 39%. There was no question, no mistake. It was no landslide victory, or clear mandate, but Helen Conner was to be the next president of the United States.

There was some talk of how this or that could be finagled in the electoral college, but try as they might, amazed as they were, the powers that be had to admit in the end that because of Mrs. Conner, America no longer had politics as usual. The earthquake epicentered in the status quo was bad enough, but no one knew how long the after shocks might continue and just what damage they would do. All over the country on that Wednesday you could almost hear the sound of complacency being rent asunder. In Washington it was a virtual roar.

Jack had returned to his hotel room in the wee hours of Wednesday morning to wash and grab a quick nap. As unbelievable as it is, he overslept. Seeing the daylight outside, he turned on the T.V. and learned of Mrs. Conner's victory as she herself was shown, gracious as ever, thanking those who had voted for her and reassuring those who did not.

Since he'd already missed the excitement of the celebration party, he took his time getting ready. He wanted to look good, because he had an interview today with the president-elect. Two weeks earlier he'd asked to interview her the day after the election and she had agreed. At the time he assumed it would be a 'how-do-you-feel-after-all-that-hard-work-with-no-success' interview. As usual she'd smiled and suggested that he was going to have the honor of the first exclusive interview with the new president. She'd been right again.

He wondered if the interview was still on, but he wasn't going to check — just show up and take his chances. He drove up to the Conner home, but had to park the car nearly a quarter mile away. The quiet streets near her home were clogged with journalists, well-wishers, and protesters. Sound trucks jockeyed for position around the entrance to her driveway. Her beautiful landscaping was being trampled by people trying to get ever closer, and by the police and Secret Service agents who were forming a nearly impenetrable wall. Her home was not built with such security problems in mind.

Jack joined the melee and tried to squeeze his way through. At least he wasn't hampered by cameras or placards. In the section he passed through he saw Pro-life, Pro-choice, Save the Earth, Ban Smoking, Death to Infidels, Animal Rights, Gun Control, Save Our Guns, Gay and Lesbian Rights, and The End is Near. What else there was he couldn't guess, but it was clear that those who had something to say were ready and eager to say it.

Jack was near his goal when he heard a voice behind him only just audible over the din. "Mr. Kelly." He turned and recognized Jenkins. He wondered if the man was ever off duty. The agent took his arm and guided him through the crowd and past the security forces. As they reached the house, Jack said, "Thank you."

Jenkins only reply was, "You are expected."

Once inside the foyer, Jack had to submit to a thorough search. Finally he was lead on into the house. The living room was also a beehive of activity. Jack saw Alex in deep conversation with several men three times his age. Mrs. Kramer was on the phone and at the same time talking with another Conner aide. D'Arcy and his wife were there. Others whom Jack recognized were scattered about. Most of the people there Jack knew or had seen before. Chris was over in a corner looking slightly overwhelmed, but keeping his cool.

Jenkins lead him on back to the study. The door closed behind him and there was blessed silence — all the voices inside and out were only a distant hum. He went to the fire, giving it a poke or two. He heard a small noise and turned to see Mrs. Conner enter the room.

Hello, Mr. Kelly."

"Mrs. Conner...er...Madame President."

"Not quite yet. Mrs. Conner will do for now." All of a sudden she laughed. It was a merry, engaging laugh and Jack was drawn into it, too. Finally, he regained control.

"You won."

"Yes, I did. Although I prefer to think that it was the ideas that won. If I won, it could have been my personality. If the ideas won, there is wonderful reason for hope that much good will come from this presidency."

"You never doubted you'd win?"

"Not for a single moment." But then she couldn't keep a straight face and they laughed again.

"What now?" Jack asked when he could.

"A short vacation away from it all."

"By yourself?"

"With the boys and my ever-present guardian angels."

"Jenkins and crew?"

"Yes. It's part of the job, but I wonder if I'll ever get used to it."

"Where are you going?"

"It's a big secret."

"After seeing your front drive, I can understand why. It is good of you to see me in the midst of all this."

"I want to maintain a good relationship with the press during my time in office."

"Maybe you should go out and talk with them."

"Later."

"O.K., you take a vacation. Then what?"

"My transition team is already gearing up. I had them briefed and ready. Come January we expect an easy and fruitful transfer of power."

"What will be your first act as President?"

"The very first? I'm not sure. But we have lots of plans."

They talked on for more than a half hour. She gave him the names of several key appointees, allowing him to get the scoop on everyone else. Jack knew she must be very busy and pressed for time and access from all sides, yet she never offered less than her full attention to him. There was no glancing at her watch or checking toward the door. He thanked her for seeing him, and she replied by thanking him.

"What for?" he wondered.

"You've helped me more than you can know during these months of campaigning."

"Me?"

"Don't try to analyze it or find hidden meaning. Just know that it is true. I don't know what it will be like for me between now and January, but Mrs. Kramer's number is still good."

"Thank you."

"Oh, and Mr. Kelly, will you take this with you, please?" She handed him a smallish brown paper bag. He started to look inside, but she said, "Take care of it later."

So without looking inside, he bid farewell and was escorted back out to the road. Several people tried to talk to him, thinking he must be someone important, but he ignored them all.

Once free of the crowds, he opened the bag. Against all sense, all logic, all that was reasonable, the sack contained fresh, homemade chocolate chip cookies. Jack didn't even want to try to guess who made them and why. People heading up the street to join the throng in front of the Conner's, wondered for a moment about the lone man going the other way, a brown paper bag in his hand, laughing out loud.

Chapter 20

For the next two months, Jack kept daily watch over the Conner transition team — he and half the journalists in America. His stories continued to have the extra depth that he was able to achieve by judicious use of Mrs. Kramer's number. The rest of the time he concentrated on the shift that was taking place through the whole fabric of American political life. He watched and documented as the special interests began to adapt, each fighting for a place in the new order. He followed the labyrinth of money and influence, saving much of what he found for later stories. He wanted to see the actual results in the new government.

Some were trying to change themselves. Others worked overtly or covertly to obstruct the new administration, hoping to make it fail miserably, or, worse, to be meaningless. In some quarters a grudging admiration began to grow as Mrs. Conner announced her proposed cabinet and other high officials. On the whole they were well-respected men and women from various walks of life including government. On the political spectrum, most tended to be moderates, although, as far as Jack could tell, none were timid, yes-men. During a phone interview, Jack asked Mrs. Conner why she didn't have more radicals among her staff.

She replied, "I'm not out to frighten people. My presidency was never intended to include wild, untried ideas, or pre-defined ideologies. I'm sure what appealed to the voters was the logic, the common sense, the normalcy of my agenda. What is radical about expecting people to be their best? What is radical about wanting people to be responsible adults — rather than victims? What is radical about wanting the government to serve the citizens only in those areas where there is no other option, and otherwise staying out of our lives? What is radical about stopping government programs that are wasteful or redundant or can be better run by the private sector? These ideas strike to the very heart of most people, and they know it is the right way to go."

"Perhaps what is radical is your notion that a) people really do want to be responsible, b) these projects of yours can be carried out."

"My job for the next four years is to do just that."

"There is so much opposition gearing up to fight you."

"My plan is to take each important issue to the American people, let them see all the sides. Educated public opinion makes for a very big bulldozer that can plow through even the strongest special interest."

"There are some volatile forces in ferment right now. Do you feel threatened personally?"

Mrs. Conner did not answer immediately. Jack imagined her at the other end of the line, weighing what she was going to say. When she finally responded, she didn't really answer. "We have very good people who spend all their time on security so that we can go about our business without having that uppermost in our thoughts."

"Be careful." The words came out before Jack really thought them through.

Mrs. Conner laughed quietly, "I will."

In early December two independent research teams confirmed that the photos of Mrs. Conner and Will Camden were forgeries. Jack was there to listen to the detailed description. The proofs were technical, but conclusive. Those who had claimed all along that Mrs. Conner was simply very glib and able to lie well, explained that these findings were a cover-up and that the researchers had been paid off. But the general populace had believed her the night of the debate and hence were not surprised at the outcome.

Over a hasty lunch, the day after the photo results came out, Sam asked Jack, "What do you think?"

"I'm glad for the objective proof."

"You didn't believe her?"

"I saw the photos. They were very...graphic."

"Early in the campaign you voiced doubts about her sincerity. But as the months went by, I could see that changing. What happened? Have you decided, along with 39% of the voting public that she is simply what she says she is?"

"The questions are always there below the surface ready to spring out again. On the other hand, isn't it just possible that someone like Helen Conner can not only exist, but be selfless enough to run for president?"

"Selfless? You really are taken with her. There is a woman who has just managed to gain for herself power and prestige that only a handful of people have ever gained."

"Maybe I have bought her line. Maybe she is just an incredible actress, with deep ulterior motives, but I don't believe it. For all my doubts, for all my willingness to find the holes in her fabric, I think she is real." Jack was on the verge of telling Sam that, in fact, he considered her almost a friend, but an unfamiliar reticence stopped him. Sam noticed the hesitation.

"And...?" he queried suggestively.

"Nothing."

"Don't feel you have to tell me anything. I'm just your best friend."

Jack got out of it by grinning and then saying in mock seriousness, "And don't you forget it." Then he looked at his watch and grimaced. "I've got to get back."

Sam gulped down his Coke and said, "I'll come with you."

As they walked back they talked about Sam's story dealing with a minor scandal in the SEC.

During the last weeks before the inauguration, an uneasy calm settled over the capitol. The old administration was quietly folding up its flawed eight years in hopes of slinking away unnoticed. The new administration waited with vigor and impatience to begin. Both Republicans and Democrats tried to understand what they were going to do without one or the other in the White House.

Jack, anything but calm, worked on a surprising lead about the Green

Eagles. Garth Wingate had continued to be with the Conner team where Jack ran across him more than once. Efforts to find 'Al' had proved fruitless until one day, while at the coffee machine, Jack's attention was drawn to the T.V. monitor. Albert Quinlain, described as a international financier, was talking about business and its role in caring for the environment. Not only his ideas, but his word usage reminded Jack of Wingate's rhetoric when they first met. Albert — Al. It was a long shot but sometimes long shots paid off.

Jack gathered all the information about Quinlain that he could, but it was precious little. Curiously, even the web held little substantive information. His great wealth was self-made. He was secretive, using his wealth to keep himself insulated from public view. And he was very concerned about environmental issues. Jack scoured back issues of major newspapers and magazines. The few pieces he found were innocuous. He printed out one of the photographs of Quinlain at a large corporate gathering and stuck it in a file for later reference. Finally, he asked for and received permission for an interview, not being 100% straight when he indicated that he wanted to do an article about the relation of big business to the environment.

Quinlain was a younger man than Jack had expected, within a year or two of Jack's own forty-five. He was tall and solidly built. Jack had certainly learned through the years to respect first impressions, and that meant he had to struggle to put down the feeling of dislike that arose unbidden as he began talking with Quinlain. Trying to analyze it quickly so he could put it behind him, he could find no obvious reason. Surely it wasn't just envy of Quinlain's wealth and position. The man wore his wealth like a mantle; it affected his every move, his every word. Then Jack realized what is was — Quinlain was too sure of himself, of the impression he was making, of the inevitable superiority of his words and actions. Jack had never liked overt arrogance, and Quinlain only served to reinforce that prejudice. And yet Quinlain was all charm. Jack imagined that he had the capacity to get his own way when he wished.

Jack had been given only fifteen minutes of Quinlain's time so he started off asking straightforward questions of Quinlain: Are big business and environmental concerns mutually exclusive?

"I used to think so when I first started out, but in the last few years I have come to see that the Earth is the only thing that matters and that my job is to use my resources to care for and nurture the environment."

"In spite of any losses?"

Quinlain was warming to his topic, and Jack saw the zeal of a fanatic glow behind the cool exterior. "That is one of the best parts. When the public is educated, they are willing to buy safe products, even if the cost is slightly higher. Education is the thing. The children must be taught from infancy to cherish the Earth above all else. There are some wonderful programs in place, and more are being started as we speak."

"How did you come to change your mind?"

"I looked around me one day, and began to see, really see, for the first time. How could anyone with eyes not know?"

"What about the new President, and her less than enthusiastic response to ideas such as children being taught to cherish the earth above all else?"

Such distaste crossed Quinlain's face, that for a moment, Jack thought he was going to spit, but then he controlled his emotions and smiled ruefully, "I have not hidden the fact that I dislike her stated policies on this issue. However, she is always talking about her willingness to change if shown the truth, so I will make it my job to help her see the light."

"And if she doesn't?"

"She will."

Time was up and Quinlain showed no willingness to go overtime, so Jack gathered his things and got up. He turned to the door, and then turned back, "One more thing — do you know Garth Wingate?"

"Wingate? No, should I?"

"No. Thank you for your time."

Had he been taken aback by the question? Jack was watching, looking for a connection, but Quinlain had been on his guard ever since the Conner question and Jack was unable to judge his reaction to the mention of Wingate. Anyway, it was just an interesting footnote to his special interest stories. He'd enjoy following Quinlain's attempts to get President Conner on his side.

For now the events surrounding and leading up to the inauguration and transfer of power pushed all that to the background, but not completely out of thought.

Jack was at the swearing-in ceremony and had access to several of the balls that night. He wasn't normally interested in this whole scene, but enjoyed trying to get a feel for the mood of the old Washington hands -- the bureaucrats who'd been here forever and seen a lot of presidents come and go. There seemed to be no consensus except that President Conner looked smashing in a formal gown. Beyond that, it was anybody's guess.

Chapter 21

It was one of those February mornings when you wish Spring would come. Today the sun was shining, but the weather service said another cold snap was on its way. Jack was willing to enjoy this day, and not let tomorrow's possible storm clouds get in his way. President Conner was going to be giving her first major speech later in the day. Jack was actually excited, looking forward to hearing what she was going to say. In her short two weeks in office so much had already happened.

Jack took a leisurely lunch and returned reluctantly to work. He was tempted to go for a walk, but chose responsibility over frivolity. Even before he got to the building, he could see unusual activity. He hurried inside. Everywhere stricken faces greeted him. He raced up the stairs not waiting for the elevator. He nearly collided with Sam as he came out of the stair well.

"My God, Jack, have you heard?"

"What? Heard what?"

"It's Chris. Of all people. They've kidnapped Chris."

"Chris who?" asked Jack, not wanting it to be what he suspected.

"The president's son."

"What's known?"

"Go to Walter's office. He's got it all."

Jack pushed into Walter's office without knocking. "Fill me in."

"Its so sketchy right now. We're trying to confirm. But watch this."

Walter picked up the remote control and pushed 'play'. "I recorded this twenty minutes ago. It was broadcast over all the major networks, internet, satellite."

The image was of a man, his head covered with a large cloth bag, wearing nondescript clothes and gloves. Tied in a chair next to him was Chris Conner. The boy looked dazed, but not panicked. There was little fear in Chris's voice when the masked man made him read a message.

"I will be killed if their demands are not met. Take your time. Consider the consequences. And be ready. You will hear from us."

Then for no apparent reason other than intimidation, the masked man struck Chris a hard blow across the mouth. The man grabbed him by his hair and forced him to look straight back at the camera. A trickle of blood ran slowly down from the corner of his mouth. The screen went blank.

Before Jack could speak, the door to Walter's office burst open and a despondent Annie said, "There is confirmation from the White House. Chris was taken from outside his school. Two Secret Service agents were injured. They don't say how severely. Nothing more." Annie went back out, leaving a silence behind her.

Jack felt numb. He spoke his thoughts out loud. "Why Chris? Of all people, why Chris?"

"I know," Walter said quietly. "I know. He's the boy we all wish was our own son. Maybe that's why. Terrorism aimed at the most innocent."

Jack was barely listening. He got up and went out the door having just enough presence of mind to say, "I'm going to the White House," and then he was gone.

His press pass got him through the growing crowd outside the gates, but once inside he began to wonder if this was the place to be. He'd had the crazy notion that somehow he'd be the one who got in to see the President. Right. He joined every other journalist who had access to the White House. They were all thoroughly searched and treated with impatience by White House security — typical of closing the barn door after the horses were loose.

They were isolated in one room and had only each other for company. Jack was tempted to leave, but couldn't bring himself to do so. After about two hours a harried minor spokesperson arrived at the briefing room and said, "The President will be making a formal statement at 8:00 pm. There will be nothing until then, if you wish to leave now. The President requests that her remarks be broadcast as widely as possible. Thank you." The spokesperson turned and fled as unanswered and unanswerable questions bombarded her back.

Jack looked at his watch, considered the trouble of going out and then getting back in, and decided to wait it out here. Some left, but most agreed with Jack.

The time dragged by, but 8:00 came. The cameras were ready. The podium was prepared. Journalists were crammed into the room. At 8:00 President Conner entered. Jack had never seen her look so grim. The press corps sensed this was not the time to shout out questions. The room was unnervingly still.

The President stood behind the microphones and for several seconds stared into the camera. Then she spoke:

"This message is for the thugs, the meaningless, mindless criminals who kidnapped Chris Conner. I am not interested in their demands and I will not hear them. They have only one option. The boy must be set free immediately. No conditions. No terms. The Presidency of the United States of America will not be blackmailed or extorted in anyway, for any purpose." She paused. "Nor will I. I, Helen Elizabeth Conner, suggest that you let my son go unharmed and every mother and father, every sister and brother, every child, every cousin of the kidnappers had better pray that he is well and safe. If Chris is harmed in any way, you will wish you had never been born. I speak now to make it clear and unequivocal. I will not speak on this subject again. You have no other option. If Chris Conner is returned whole, the kidnappers will be found and punished to the full extent of the law. If he is injured or dies...."

She stared fiercely into the camera and then got up and walked out of the room. Stunned silence followed her. The press secretary, looking a bit dazed himself, stepped up to the podium.

"I have a message for the press, written by President Conner. She has asked me to read it. 'Any journalist, or any media outlet which in any way gives aid or air time, press space or platform, to the kidnappers will give up the right of access to this White House. These criminals deserve no attention. Make your choice. Thank you. That will be all." The press secretary hurried to the door.

The journalists sat still for a moment and then leapt to their feet and pushed their way out of the room, rushing to file their stories, talking amongst themselves as they went out.

"Is it possible? Did she threaten to kill every relative of the kidnappers?"

"My God! She won't negotiate for her son's life."

"Seems to me she right. You can't deal with scum."

"But her son..."

"Have you ever seen anything like it?"

Jack stayed seated in his chair, wrapped in a confusion as deep as any he'd ever known. Who exactly was that woman who just made such a pronouncement? Was it a gigantic bluff? Of all the things he knew of her, the love she had for her sons was something he'd never questioned.

Suddenly he realized he was completely alone. What a story! He'd better report in. But he sat for a few minutes more. He was roused as he heard a side door open. Standing in the doorway was Jenkins. Jack stood up and started to go.

"Sorry. I was just going."

"One moment, please."

Jack stopped.

"Will you follow me?" Jenkins was polite, although it seemed to gall him slightly.

Mystified, Jack followed him into the inner reaches of the White house. They stopped in a small comfortable room.

"Do you need to file a story?"

"I was planning to."

"You may use this room. When you are done I'll be outside the door."

Jack sat down and wondered what was going on and what he was going to do. First things first. So he called the paper and filed his story over the phone. He didn't mention his unusual circumstances, and when Walter broke in on the line and asked if he was coming in, he said, "I don't know. I'm not sure."

"The woman is full of surprises. Follow up as you see fit."

"Right, Walter. Good night."

Jack hesitantly opened the door to the hall and sure enough Jenkins was right there waiting. All he said was, "Follow me."
Jack followed him.

They got into an elevator and went down several floors. Jack couldn't imagine where he was going. Wherever it was, it was a part of the White House he'd never seen before.

While the elevator door was still closed, Jenkins mumbled something into a hidden mike, listening for the answer through the wire to his ear. When satisfied, he opened the elevator and led Jack across the hall into another room. This room was large, but had a cozy feel to it. There was a beautiful full-sized pool table in the middle and President Conner stood at one end with a pool cue in her hand. Jenkins closed the door behind himself as he went back out. Jack and the President were alone.

She didn't smile. In fact her face was set like a mask in a

noncommittal expression.

"Do you play pool?" she asked in an ordinary voice, as if her son were not in the hands of terrorists and she had not moments ago seemed to threaten to destroy whole families. Jack could play this game, whatever it was, because it sure wasn't pool.

"Yes, I do."

"Choose a cue," she said, gesturing to a wall rack. He picked one that was straight and true and turned back toward the table.

President Conner said, "What game do you prefer?"

"Straight pool?"

"Very well. You may break."

The only light was over the table so the corners of the room faded into shadows. The only reality was right there at that table. They played hard and well. She was good, but then so was he. The score remained close.

As they played she asked him questions about himself. He knew that if he said one word that so much as referred to Chris or the kidnapping he'd be sent away. So he talked. Much more than was normal for him. She made great pool shots and drew him out on many subjects. They talked about movies and books they'd read. He even told her about Carrie.

It seemed so normal, but the whole thing was surreal — like a dream that seems so reasonable and ordinary as you dream it, but upon waking you can't imagine where it came from.

Jack lost all track of time. As inexplicably as it began, it was over. President Conner put down her cue and said, "Jenkins will show you out." She headed for another door at the far end of the room. He watched her and then started toward Jenkins' door. The President stopped and started to turn back, "Mr. Kelly...." Her voice was not as controlled as it had been. Jack thought she was going to say something more, but then she just said, "Good night," and went out, closing the door behind her. Jack went out to find Jenkins.

Without a word Jenkins led him out a different way to the private entrance of the White House. A car was waiting. Jenkins opened the back door for Jack and then went around and got in the driver's seat. Without saying a word or asking for directions, he drove Jack to his front door, waited until he was inside and then drove away.

Once inside Jack was amazed to see the hall clock indicate that it was after 3:00 am. As he got ready for bed, Jack finally had the leisure to think through the events of the last hours. What was his part in it all? One thing he was sure of — he could not speak of the time alone with President Conner. She was trusting him in a way that he hoped he deserved. But, again, what did it mean?

Chapter 22

Next day the office had a forced sense of business as usual. There was a paper to get out, world, local and national news to be found, written up and printed. There was no word from the White house, but the kidnappers were trying to get someone — anyone — to pass on to the public their outrage at the President's statement. No legitimate media outlets would accommodate them. Sadly, there were plenty of outlets willing to broadcast anything, and, of course, the internet buzzed with rumor, innuendo, and speculation.

Ignoring the kidnappers was terrible — their threats were graphic and extensive — but Jack agreed that this was the best course. That didn't make it any easier, and Jack had to consciously keep his thought away from any consideration or wonder as to Chris's plight.

Jack wanted to be available if the situation changed, but it was hard to concentrate on anything really important, so he decided to find out some more about Albert Quinlain. He got out the file with the notes he'd taken and the photo clippings. He had it all spread out in front of him, but his mind wandered again and he found himself thinking of Chris. His gaze fell on the top photo. A sudden jolt of recognition hit him, and he nearly fell out of his chair trying to get his magnifying glass out of the top drawer. There in the background, could it be? Yes. How had he missed it before? Slightly blurred, but unmistakable, Garth Wingate had been photographed behind Albert Quinlain. AL. Jack knew where to find Wingate and he was already dialing.

Wingate answered, and after reminding him who he was, Jack asked, "Have you and Albert Quinlain been getting together much lately?"

Wingate's tone belied his words, "Quinlain, you say? Albert Quinlain? Don't think I know him. Say, man, I got to go. "

He hung up fast.

Jack thought, won't Mrs. Kramer be interested to hear about her little 'stray dog'. Maybe he really had changed his convictions. On the other hand, maybe he was a spy for the Green Eagles. That concept would give a nice twist to special interest stories — spying and infiltration as forms of influence peddling. Jack smiled, and then remembered. For two whole minutes he'd forgotten about Chris.

He was tempted to follow-up on Wingate and Quinlain, but decided to let it rest a day or two until...until what? Aagh. He'd do it in a day or two.

Jack went by the White House before going home. Journalists were keeping a constant vigil. They reported that the President and White House officials and staff had all gone about their normal schedule as if nothing was out of the ordinary. Security was as tight as they'd ever seen it, but that was all that hinted it wasn't a typical day — that and the expressions of despair on every face.

By he time Jack got home it was very cold. The storm that had been forecast was well on its way. Freezing rain and sleet were expected. Oh, for spring to arrive!

Next morning the worst was upon them. Jack considered staying home until he got an enigmatic call from Walter. All he said was, "You'd better come down." Jack was beginning to dread such calls.

It was miserable out, but he managed to find a cab that was able to get him to the office with only minor difficulties and one close call on the slippery road. He went straight to Walter's office.

"What now?"

"Watch this."

Walter started the file on his computer. It was the masked kidnapper again.

"You all think you are so clever. Chris Conner lives. He is in front of you, but you will not see him. And so he may die. Let it be on your heads."

Walter added, "The White House got one, all the media outlets, internet sites. What do you make of it?"

"I don't know, but I'm going to the White House."

"The streets are murder. Be careful."

"Yeah."

"I've got a car and driver waiting down below. I've got to go see the publisher, if you can believe it. If you want to wait ten minutes, I can drop you."

"Thanks, but I think I'll go down and see if I can get a cab."

Jack was just outside the building turning up his collar and checking for taxis, when Sam came in huddled against the cold and greeted him, "Cold day to be out."

"I'm heading for the White House. What's your excuse?"

"Love of the job."

Jack laughed.

"They're getting younger every day." Sam gestured toward a bum lying on the sidewalk, not even in the protection of the doorway. His clothes were thin and certainly insufficient to protect him. Jack felt the familiar pang of compassion combined with the sense that there was little he could do. He started to walk by. Then he stopped Sam who was just going in the door. "Let's help him out of the wind at least."

Sam turned back. "Shall I give him my coat, too?"

Jack was already at the bum's side and was lifting his head to see if he was awake. Incomprehensibly, the face was that of Chris Conner. He heard Sam say, "I was only kidding," as Jack pulled off his coat and wrapped it around the boy.

"Sam, help me," he called.

Sam seemed to catch his urgency, though still not understanding it. "Is the guy all right?"

Jack looked around and saw Walter's car and driver. "Take his legs," he ordered Sam.

Jack caught Chris under the shoulders. Sam said, "Where to?" and then stopped dead when Jack said, "To Walter's car."

He still didn't move, but for another reason, when Jack said in a low voice, "This is Chris Conner. I've got to get him to a hospital."

Recognition dawned on Sam's face. He continued carrying the boy toward the car, whispering, "What do you want me to do?"

"Keep this quiet. Go to Walter's office. Tell him, but no one else. And give me your coat, too. I'll call the White House from the car."

They had Chris in the back of the car, before the driver could more than sputter out a protest. Jack cut him off, saying, "Get us to the hospital — fast as you can without danger."

"The roads are bad. I'm here for..."

"Just move out. This may be one of the most important drives of your life. Go."

Jack had his coat and Sam's wrapped around Chris and was cradling the boy in his arms. He was terribly cold, but at least alive. He seemed drugged rather than unconscious.

Jack pulled out his phone and accessed Mrs. Kramer's number. It rang and rang. Be there, Jack whispered. Be there. Who else could he call? He was about to hang up and try someone else when a woman answered. "Who is this?" Jack demanded.

"I might ask the same thing. This is a private line."

"Is Mrs. Kramer there?"

"Who is this?"

"I need Mrs. Kramer, or President Conner or Jenkins of the Secret Service will do. I need one of them now." Jack kept his voice low, but the message finally seemed to sink in at the other end.

"Just a minute." He'd been put on hold. Thirty seconds went by. Forty five. A minute. It seemed an hour. Had the person gone off and forgotten him?

With a rush of gratitude, Jack recognized the voice that said, "Jenkins here."

"This is Jack Kelly. I have Chris Conner with me. We are on the way to...."

"Hold on. Not so fast. What are you trying to pull?"

"Chris was left outside the newspaper building in the cold. He seems drugged, but alive. I saw him and am getting him to help as quickly as possible."

"What vehicle are you in?"

Jack gave the make and color and asked the driver for the license number.

"Where are you now?"

Jack gave the streets.

"Carry on."

Jack disconnected and was able to concentrate on Chris.

The driver said in a tentative vice, "I couldn't help overhearing. Is that really Chris Conner, the President's son?"

"Yes."

"Oh, man!"

"Just drive."

About a minute later one police car pulled in front of them and another slid in place behind. No sirens. No lights. The roads were too slick for high speed driving, but their very presence allowed Jack to drop a level or two of anxiety.

Doctors and nurses were already outside the emergency entrance when they drove up. Gentle, competent hands got Chris onto the gurney and began to run with him down the passageway. Jack ran, too. A plainclothes officer of some sort tried to stop him.

"We'll take it from here."

Jack didn't even break stride. "I'm staying with him until someone shows up that I know." He dodged around another officer and was running beside the gurney. They all turned into a treatment room and the door was closed behind them.

One of the doctors looked at Jack. "You found him?"

Jack explained. The doctor thanked him and then asked him to stand back as they began their testing, probing and treating. Jack sat down on a chair by the door, closed his eyes and leaned his head against the wall. The vision of Chris's deathly pale face didn't disappear.

The door next to him swung open slowly. Jack tensed and then relaxed as he recognized Smith of the Secret Service. The doctors didn't even look up. Smith surveyed the room and then faced Jack.

"Come with me."

Jack hesitated. Smith seemed to understand. "The area is sealed off. He's safe now. Our best agents are here."

Jack followed him down the hall to a room that appeared to be a visitor's waiting room. "Wait here," was Smith's terse command.

Wait for what, Jack wondered. He paced around the small room and then sat down and thumbed through some magazines. After about ten minutes, Jenkins came in. He wasted no time in idle conversation. He just flipped on a small recorder and said, "Tell me everything."

Jack was trained to see, to remember and report, so he was able to give a full description and remain concise at the same time. Jenkins just nodded now and then, not interrupting. Finally Jack said, "That's all I can think of now. Talk to Sam. He'll have a different perspective."

"You saw nobody, nothing suspicious, when you came into work earlier, or as you were going out before you saw him?"

"I've tried to remember, but there is nothing. I don't even know if Chris was there or not when I first went into work. I'll go back and walk through it. Maybe that'll jog my memory."

"We'd like you to stay here for awhile."

"Sure. Whatever I can do to help."

"The fact is, we are checking into your activities over the past three days. Very convenient, finding Chris."

Jack was incredulous, but too drained to be angry at the implication. He just looked at Jenkins and shook his head. With an unconscious wave of his hand he dismissed the agent and his suspicions. As long as they took care of Chris that was all that mattered. The rest would sort itself out. Jenkins left.

Alone with his thoughts Jack went over the whole thing again and again. He thought of the last message of the kidnappers. They'd intended to leave him on the street. Maybe they didn't realize how cold it was. Maybe they just wanted him to lie there mistaken for an addict or a homeless person until he regained consciousness. Maybe they had been there watching. No. They were going to let him die on the pavement and then blame the uncaring, unseeing populace. They would have said, "We let him go alive. You let him die." If one of the kidnappers had walked in the room that moment, Jack would have killed him with his bare hands.

Curtains had been drawn across the windows of the waiting room and Jack hadn't bothered to try to look out. Now he heard voices just outside the door, speaking low but imperatively — a quiet argument. The door opened and Jenkins entered first, followed by the President. In a dismissing tone of voice, she said, "Thank you, Jenkins."

He stared straight ahead and didn't budge. Jack thought, Good for you Jenkins. Guard her even if she doesn't want it, or in this case, need it. The President seemed able to recognize an immovable object when she saw one, so she ignored him and turned to Jack. Her eyes were shining, but she maintained an outward sense of control and dignity.

"Chris is going to be fine. The doctors say you saved his life. A little longer in the cold and...."

"Thank God it worked out the way it did."

"Yes. Thank God. And thank you. You continue to bless me and my family."

Jack had no time to respond because she turned and was gone — Jenkins two steps behind, caught off guard by her sudden departure.

Jack sat down slowly with a whole new set of sensations to consider. So much he could have — should have — asked her. His instincts as a reporter were continually being sabotaged by his feelings for her. If only he didn't like her so much. He wondered if he had any value left as a White House reporter.

As far as Jack could tell everyone had forgotten him — at least no one came in to check on him. He waited for awhile and then walked out. Jack smiled at the guard outside his door who started to speak. Jack cut him off with a pleasant, "Tell Jenkins I'm going down to the office. He can find me there."

At that moment Jenkins himself appeared, taking the decision of whether or not to detain Jack forcibly out of the guard's hands.

"And where might you be going?"

"Thought I'd go to work. I can't do any good here."

Jenkins seemed about to protest and then thought better of it. "I'll show you how to get out quietly."

First they took an elevator up several floors, switched elevators, and went down to the basement. As they were going down Jenkins found his voice, "I'm to tell you that there will be a press conference at the White House at six o'clock." He hesitated, "The President said to trust you. She's my boss. But my job is to keep her safe."

"She has nothing to fear from me," Jack said quietly as he stepped out of the elevator. Jenkins remained inside. Jack turned and the two men stared at each other as the elevator doors closed.

Chapter 23

As he walked out of the hospital garage Jack thought, if I go back to the office before the press conference, I'll be inundated with questions. He didn't relish the idea of being the news rather than reporting it. He decided to get something to eat instead, but first he called and checked in with Walter.

"Where have you been? Why haven't you been in touch?" were his first words.

Not exactly answering, Jack replied, "What's the story so far?"

"You ask me? You're the one who knows the most. In fact the White House contacted Sam who told me they want to keep everything under wraps. There is no official word about the return of Chris — only an announced press conference at 6:00. Can you make it?"

"Sure, I'll be there," not telling Walter that he already knew about the press conference. "There has been nothing about Chris?"

"All I know is that Sam came up here saying to keep quiet and that you found Chris and took him for help. I called the hospital and they played dumb. Why aren't you in here writing this up?"

"I'll come in after the press conference, if I can."

"If you can? If you can?" Walter sputtered.

"Don't worry. Whatever story is there, the paper will have."

As an afterthought, Walter remembered to ask, "What about Chris? Is he all right?"

"I'll see you later, Walter, and tell you what I know."

Jack picked a booth in the restaurant, sat down, and ordered. As he waited, he looked through a newspaper an earlier patron had left. It was full of national and international news, most of which touched not at all, or only peripherally, on the present administration. He'd become so focused on the surprising new president that his horizon had become severely limited — as if the new administration were the sum and center of all activity. He really needed to get out more.

Buried about ten pages back was a short piece he skimmed through, one more in countless such stories — car accident kills driver. Then he went back and looked again. The name of the deceased was Garth Wingate. Of all the rotten luck — sure, for Wingate — but also for Jack's story. He was all poised to discover the connection between Wingate and Albert Quinlain and the Green Eagles. Quinlain symbolized money, power and influence. Green Eagles represented over-zealous, passionately-held ideas. Did they come together? After this business with Chris calmed down, Jack planned to look up Paul Sutcliffe, the Green Eagles' spokesperson, and follow from that angle.

He still had time when he finished eating so he checked his phone messages. They were the normal, standard stuff, except one that sent his ideas off in another direction completely.

"You're not there. Where are you? I've tried and tried. The other was bad enough, but the boy and now Garth. He never hurt a soul in his life. I want out. I want out. But I don't know how. Will you help me if I come? How can I ever hide from them? Meet me at Rosselli's at five o'clock. Help me."

Jack looked at his watch. He could make it. He knew Rosselli's, a trendy restaurant, was only about fifteen minutes away. He could go there and still get back to the White House by six.

In the taxi Jack tried to sort it all out. The caller was surely the same one who had called twice before. She — Jack decided it was definitely a woman — seemed to be implying foul play of some sort. Garth? Could that be Garth Wingate? Maybe his accident wasn't an accident. Who was 'the boy'?

Traffic was bad and he got to Rosselli's at eight past five. Outside the restaurant four police cars and one ambulance had their lights on, and a large crowd milled about just outside the flimsy police barrier. Near the entrance of the restaurant was a figure lying on the ground covered with a tablecloth. Jack was about to tell the driver to go on to the White House when he saw Det. Zbornak. He got out and walked over.

"What's happening?"

"Taken up ambulance chasing?" Zbornak chuckled.

"Just coming for a bite to eat. What's Homicide doing here?" replied Jack.

"Hit and run supposedly. Probably some fool who went out of control and then panicked. Got to check it out."

"Don't think I'll eat here after all. See ya 'round."

Jack got in the waiting taxi and headed for the White House. If the caller had been at the restaurant, it seemed highly unlikely she would have hung around. He certainly didn't have time to wait and see.

Security was tight for the press conference. Jack had an idea what to expect, but the others apparently did not. The press secretary came in three minutes late and stepped behind the podium. He took a deep breath and began. "I have a prepared statement for you regarding Chris Conner. It should cover all the information you need to know, but I will consider some questions afterwards." Emotion caused his voice to waver as he went on. "Chris Conner is alive and well and being given the best of care in an undisclosed location. His kidnappers set him free this morning. The FBI has no one in custody yet, but several very positive leads are being followed. We expect results shortly."

The atmosphere of the pressroom was electric. The journalists were bursting with questions that they began to throw at the press secretary. He fielded them calmly and quietly, giving absolutely no substantial information. "No, we have nothing to say about where he was dropped off."

"No, we cannot disclose his present location." "Yes, he is very well — just needing to rest." "No, he is not injured." "Yes, the President is pleased and grateful."

It went on and on like this and Jack just sat back and smiled to himself. He'd write the same innocuous story as every other reporter in the room and be done with it. He was grateful they'd left his name out. What he wanted now was to go home, have a hot shower and go to bed — a day well ended.

Terminating the briefing, the press secretary reiterated the Administration's stand — any publicity for the kidnappers meant an end to White House access. When asked to define 'publicity', he said, "Use your own judgment — and we will use ours." And then he was gone and the journalists scrambled out to spread the story abroad, good news for once.

Jack imagined that all over America, T.V. programs were being interrupted for special bulletins: Chris Conner, beloved son of the President, was safe. Sanity was temporarily restored.

Jack walked out slowly, letting the others get to their stories first. They'd know down at the paper already because of the T.V. coverage. He had time to write the story later. Behind him a voice spoke quietly, "Mr. Kelly, excuse me."

Jack turned slightly and saw a young man. "Yes?"

"Can you come with me, please?"

Jack didn't know the young man, but figured him for part of the White House staff. He followed him to the side of the hallway, away from the push of the reporters making their way out.

The aide said quietly, "Go back into the conference room as though you have forgotten something." Then in a regular tone, he said, "Thank you," and walked off.

Now what, thought Jack. He started on out, reached into his pocket, patted his other pockets, turned and went back into the conference room. A door stood ajar at the other end. A figure appeared briefly, beckoned him, and disappeared.

Jack went through the door and closed it behind himself. The same person waved him over to the elevator. The aide pressed a button and then before the door closed stepped out. Jack was alone, going down. So much for a day well ended.

The elevator stopped and Jack was met by the ubiquitous Jenkins, who, as usual, said as little as possible. He just turned and walked down the hall. Jack, ready for anything, followed.

They went into a large, bright room. Jack had the sensation that someone had just left the room by a far door, but more to the point, in a large bed, his shoulders and head propped up with pillows, lay a grinning Chris Conner. Jenkins stayed back as Jack walked up.

"How are you, Chris?"

"A lot better than I would have been if it weren't for you. I asked them to bring you down here so I could thank you."

"No need for thanks. I'm just grateful it worked out this way."

"Never-the-less, I do thank you. Have a seat." Chris indicated a chair by the bed. "There's something I'd like to do for you, if you are interested, I mean."

"For me? Truly, all the thanks I need are to see you here — safe and well."

"Mom says I have to tell my story to the press eventually and I thought, well, maybe you'd be willing to listen. You could write it up and then I wouldn't have to talk to so many reporters."

An exclusive of Chris Conner's ordeal with the kidnappers?
Yeah, Jack would be willing to listen.

"I'd be honored. Let me know when."

"Right now."

"Isn't it a bit soon? I mean, you've been through a lot."

"I'm not a child. None of this," he made a motion that seemed to indicate the White House and all that it stood for, "is my first choice of what I want my life to become. Alex loves it and, of course, Mom belongs here now. But I *am* here and I have no desire to shy away from the responsibilities. There will be time later for myself."

Jack was thinking that he sounded too old for his years.

"So you want the whole thing told and done with," ventured Jack.

Grateful for Jack's understanding, Chris nodded.

"Fair enough. You talk. I'll listen. If you get tired or want to stop for any reason, just tell me. If I need to, I'll ask questions at the end."

Jack pulled out his recorder and turned it on. He suspected that somewhere just beyond the walls others were also listening. In fact, he was surprised that this was being allowed. As if reading his mind, Chris said, "I asked to be able to do this. They agreed on the condition they could listen in. Here's the microphone." Chris pointed out an unobtrusive mike that Jack would never have noticed. Chris was grinning again and Jack could help chuckling, "I think I get the picture."

Chris began his story. He told, in a shaky voice of his capture, of seeing two Secret Service men down, not knowing at the time if they were dead or alive.

"From the first Alex and I have thought it was a game. We'd try to ditch the agents — you know — stupid kid's stuff."

Apparently Chris knew nothing about the kidnappers, how many there were all together, although he'd seen six, he never saw them unmasked, or had any idea where they took him. He was certainly knocked around, but not seriously injured. He was mostly ignored, except when videos were made. He said he told them from the first that his mom would never deal with them.

He explained to Jack, "Mom sat us down and talked to us about this very thing before the campaign even began to heat up. She said we had to recognize all the dangers as well as the possibilities. No matter how much she loved us, there could be no dealing with blackmailers or extortionists of any sort, if she became President. She would do every thing in her power to protect or save us, but not give in. She made us promise that if anything happened in our lives that was grounds for blackmail that we would come to her, no matter what it was, no matter how bad.

"Anyway, they played Mom's message for me and taunted me with the idea that I was meaningless and unloved. 'What kind of mother was she?' Mom's ultimatum sounded just the opposite to me, and I told them the wrath that was about to descend on them was going to be like nothing they'd ever imagined, that their only hope was to set me free. I figured I might as well act brave." Here Chris chuckled quietly. "I didn't feel very brave." He was silent for a few moments staring at the bed covers. Then he roused himself. "Well, after that there were several who wanted to kill me on the spot and others who wanted to let me go. Their confused state of mind was evidenced when they let me hear them argue. Before that they'd kept me isolated. Finally, they realized what they were doing and left the room. The only thing I know after that is that one came in with a hypodermic needle and shot something into my arm. I woke in the hospital. And then was brought here."

It was a story that cried out for elaboration — details of the agony he went through, details about the kidnappers themselves and everything they'd said. But if Jack believed anything, it was that President Conner was deadly serious that anyone who gave publicity to the kidnappers would be banned from the White House. As it was he'd be walking on a razor edge as he wrote up Chris's tale. Jack pictured the story and saw it as simple, straightforward and probably better for it. The FBI would, no doubt, get all the details necessary for an arrest. Right now, although he was trying to hide it, Chris was looking done in.

"That's enough for now," said Jack. "We can talk some more another time, if you like."

Chris nodded and his eyes drooped, almost closing. Jack stood and Chris came fully awake again. He put out his hand and Jack took it. They shook.

"Mr. Kelly," Chris hesitated, rethought what he'd been about to say, and then said, "You're pretty cool."

Jack thought that Chris was 'pretty cool', too.

The door opened and Jenkins appeared, ready to take Jack out. They had a car for him and he asked to be dropped off at the paper. There was just time to catch the deadline.

As Jack walked into Walter's office, the editor started to speak, "Nice of you to show up...," but Jack stopped any long harangues with the news of his interview. Walter immediately leapt into action — organizing all the necessary components to get the story out for the paper edition. An hour later the work was done, the presses rolling, the world scooped as the electronic update went out immediately, and relaxation was possible for a few minutes. The gang was all in Walter's office content with a job well done, another edition with an exclusive on the front page. So what if in several hours it all stared again and today's news counted for almost nothing.

Jessie spoke the thought on everyone's mind, "Come on, Jack, 'fess up. How did you get in to see Chris Conner?"

In the last hour Jack had come to realize that Sam and Walter had kept his part in Chris's discovery and subsequent rush to the hospital completely quiet. That suited Jack, but did make his access to Chris seem extraordinary. Oh well, let them wonder. Besides, he wanted to go home and sleep. Putting on his most sincere face he said, "After years of hard work, dedication, and toil you become famous and well-respected and sought out..."

The others were beginning to pelt him with wadded up paper and erasers, so he ducked out the door and went home.

Chapter 24

The days that followed seemed peaceful. The kidnapping faded out of the collective thought. Chris was safe. The FBI was on the case. At the next few press briefings questions were asked. The answers were always the same and invited no elaboration.

"Chris is perfectly recovered."

"He will not be going back to school at this time."

"Security for the First Family has always been top notch."

"The FBI is following several promising leads."

It didn't take long for the whole thing to become a non-story. And Jack was grateful, but found it surprising that no one ever discovered his part.

Jack didn't get out of town much for stories these days. He found it endlessly fascinating to watch and document the ongoing dance between the President and the Congress. The famous few months of 'honeymoon' never took place. In spite of many new faces, Congress and the bureaucracy that fed each other were unwilling, or unable, to pull themselves out of the inbred, extensive lethargy that lay under the bustle of daily life. There was lots of talk, lots of seeming to act. And yet nothing of substance, nothing that struck at the heart of the status quo, had been faced. President Conner had no party backing her so it was a continual uphill battle to get legislation dealt with.

Yet slowly, with incremental steps, she began to show her strength. True to her campaign promises, she managed to get all sides of an issue out to the public — even those ideas she fiercely opposed. Her trust in the people returned in the form of extremely high approval ratings and constant pressure on Congress by their constituents. As the months passed there was a slight but unmistakable shift in the congressional mindset. From ignoring or stonewalling the President while paying her lip service, they began to consider and sometimes even go along with her ideas. There, of course, remained plenty of those who were unendingly critical and sought to destroy or disrupt her value as President.

While focusing on Washington politics, Jack did continue to follow other stories of interest. He saw that Paul Sutcliffe of the Green Eagles was going to be in town so he arranged an interview.

Sutcliffe was an ideal spokesperson for his cause. He was articulate and good-looking. He dressed conservatively and had an engaging smile. More than once he found his picture on the cover of this or that news magazine. The Green Eagles was a radical group, but Sutcliffe, while pulling no punches, made them seem reasonable, gave them a charming human face.

Jack met him for lunch. They made small talk as they ordered and then Jack asked, "Was it a disappointment to you when Garth Wingate changed over to the other side?"

"As our new president is so fond of saying, we are each responsible for our own actions. He made a choice and I have to respect that."

"Did you ever talk to him after his disaffection?"

"Oh, a few times, but inevitably, we drifted apart."

"He died recently."

"Yes. A car accident. Very sad."

"Tell me about Al Quinlain."

Sutcliffe was very smooth. His hesitation was slight and if not looking for it, Jack would have missed it.

"Al Quinlain? What about him?"

"His connection with the Green Eagles."

"He's given us some money. Believes in our cause. That's about all."

"Where do the Green Eagles stand as regards the new President?"

"If you know anything about our group you know that we do not support her. While she 'looks into' issues, the world is being destroyed before our eyes. She is an egotistical, self-righteous, foolish, and hence dangerous, woman."

"Dangerous?"

"When a terrible tragedy is in progress, those who stand in the way of those trying to help are adding to the tragedy and need to be removed."

"How do you plan to do that?"

"Naturally, we continue to work within the political process. For example, we are joining with many other thoughtful, concerned individuals and groups from all over the world in support of Earth Initiative II. We also work to make her ineffectual so we can concentrate on Congress. And we will strive to make sure she does not have a second term."

Sutcliffe's voice was beautifully modulated, his words seemed so calm, so normal. "Only political opposition?" Jack asked. "Alleged members of the Green Eagles have been arrested in various parts of the world because of overt, illegal acts of eco-terrorism that go beyond protest and endanger human life. Is such activity condoned and encouraged by you and the Green Eagle leadership?"

"Individuals occasionally overstep the bounds of civilized behavior. On the other hand, very little of value has been achieved by sitting back and waiting for others to act."

"So you do agree that criminal action is legitimate to 'save the earth'?"

"What is defined as criminal depends on who you are and where you live. I raise the philosophical question: May it not be true that the real criminals are those who take the only world we have to live in and systematically destroy it? And should not they be stopped at all costs? Serial murderers are hunted down until they are captured and punished. What about murderers of the earth?"

"What form of punishment do you advocate for those who do not share your view of 'saving the earth'? Injury and death as has happened?"

"Good heavens, no. I was simply raising a philosophic point."

"So you do distance yourself from those who break the law in the name of the Green Eagles?"

"We are a large, loose-knit organization. People may evoke our name without checking with us. We are hardly responsible for what individuals do."

"And yet if you talk...'philosophically"... about these things, are you not in a sense, encouraging people to follow through with action?"

"Again — individuals, as President Conner says, are responsible for their own actions. Neither I, nor my organization, would dream of suggesting otherwise."

Yes, Jack thought to himself, you are also unwilling to renounce violence although you talk around it a lot.

When lunch was over and Jack was headed back to the office, he couldn't decide if Paul Sutcliffe was a simple zealot or an unstable fanatic. One thing was sure, Jack hadn't added to his store of information about Albert Quinlain. His instinct told that there was something there, hidden just under the surface. All he needed to do is dig in the right spot.

Jack made efforts to see Quinlain again himself but was always rebuffed with a polite refusal that left no suggestion of possible relenting. One time he did manage to get Quinlain on the phone only to have him hang up when Quinlain recognized the direction the questions were going. So Jack looked for his answers in the labyrinth of financial trails left in the world's computers. Mostly he found dead ends.

Congress had been in session long enough for the storehouse of data that Jack had accumulated about special interest money to be useful. He continued with his series on who had paid or given what to whom and with what results. President Conner had been advocating sincere campaign finance reform. Everyone agreed something should be done, but somehow, the congressmen and senators just never seemed to get around to addressing this with serious, hard-hitting laws. It was too much, apparently, to ask Congress to limit itself. It was such wonderful, rich fodder for Jack's articles.

Meanwhile the President continued to win the battle for the hearts and minds of the people. And even Congressional leaders had to admit to a grudging admiration for President Conner's handling of foreign policy. She was gaining the respect of the leaders of many foreign countries, even if they didn't always agree with her. She was hated by petty tyrants and dictators whom she treated with the disdain they deserved, or ignored completely.

World-wide environmental groups had been planning Earth Initiative II ever since Earth Initiative I had not lived up to their expectations. Early planning rumors suggested that it would be held somewhere in Africa and take place in the latter part of the President's second year. It was a long way off still, but enthusiasm was growing in the environmental community. They had a vision of true world consensus and reform. When asked about it, President Conner said she preferred to have information on a subject first before commenting on it. And she reminded people that consensus on an issue is not the same as fact.

As the months went by, Jack had no real personal contact with any of the Conners. Oh, the President always smiled a greeting at press conferences, but that was what she did for every journalist she knew. President Conner and Chris had each sent notes thanking him again for his part in helping the boy. Neither note was on official White House stationery, which Jack found strangely pleasing. Now and again when there was a big story, Jack made judicious use of Mrs. Kramer's phone number — on several occasions the President herself came on the line and gave him insights and exclusive quotes. Walter liked having a reporter with inside sources so he never pried. Sam was not so reticent. It was a quiet family dinner with Sam and Carol.

"Hey, I can appreciate as well as the next guy the importance of having and maintaining good sources," said Sam in mock exasperation, "but don't years of friendship count for anything?"

Jack laughed, "Sorry. You'll just have to wait until I write my memoirs."

Changing the subject, Sam said, "Those are some strong implications you made in your last article."

"About seemingly benign special interests that let money flow to unlikely recipients?"

"Yeah. Have you more of the same? Your article seemed to suggest a follow-up coming soon."

"I can't tell you how fascinating this subject is. When I got involved back during the campaign, I thought it would be the basis for just a short series. But the scramble for power, influence and the quiet unheralded ability to affect or even make policy, is a vast quagmire. There are times when I have to fight to keep sight of the big picture. But, yes, there is plenty more to come."

"So do you name specific names in the next article?"

"There are several groups that have the outward impression of being 'worthy', yet are questionable in their tactics or use of money. I'm rechecking my facts and then I'll be writing it up."

"Into the lion's den once again."

"Ah, let them sue. I've got the fact to back me up."

But not all the facts. In one case, that of the Green Eagles, Jack could see the money, see it's effects, but never trace it back to the original source. Every time he thought he was near, he'd find it was another blind alley. Instinct told him it was Albert Quinlain at the end, but he had no hard facts.

Chapter 25

That night as he was heading back to his apartment, he received an extraordinary text message. All it said was, "This is Mrs. K. Call me at my number. Be discreet."

This was different. Was there a breaking news story? But why 'be discreet'? He picked up his phone and as his finger hovered over speed dial he stopped. 'Be discreet.' Did Mrs. Kramer suspect that Jack's phone was somehow tapped? Why else was she being so cryptic?

He grabbed his jacket off the back of the chair and headed for the nearby mall. He bought a cheap, throwaway phone and dialed Mrs. Kramer, feeling as though he had over-reacted. She picked up the phone after the first ring.

"Where are you calling from?"

"I'm on a throwaway phone that I just bought."

"One moment please."

He waited and then it was President Conner on the line.

"Mr. Kelly, I know this seems strange, but will you please call through regular channels and ask for an interview?"

"Madame President...."

"Will you? Tomorrow?"

"Yes, of course, but..."

"Thank you."

The line went dead as she hung up. What in the world was that about? Guess the President just couldn't live without him. The flippancy didn't work even in the privacy of his own thoughts. He kept thinking of her voice trying to sound normal, but not completely able to hide an undercurrent of strain.

First thing the next morning he called. Yes, came the reply, it seemed the President was free at 3:30 if Mr. Kelly was able to come then.

He told Walter, "I'll be over at the White House this afternoon."

"Have they called a press conference?"

"Actually, I felt it was time for another interview with the President."

"And what does the President think?"

"She's agreed."

"I don't know how you do it, Jack, but whatever it is, keep it up."

As he walked out of Walter's office, it dawned on him that he'd better prepare for the interview. It was clear the President had something to tell him, but he ought to be ready with subjects of his own.

At the White House everything seemed perfectly normal. He had to go through all the normal security checks and was ushered along all the normal channels. He was taken to the Oval Office where the President held many of her interviews. She was sitting behind her desk when he was shown in, and rose to greet him.

"Mr. Kelly, what can I do for you today?"

He was willing to play along and was grateful he'd prepared a real interview.

"It's been awhile since the paper has run an exclusive and the time seemed right. I know you are busy. Shall we begin?"

"Yes. But it is such a lovely day and I'd enjoy a break. Shall we walk in the garden?"

"Certainly, Madame President. After you."

Never in all their encounters had Helen Conner been so formal, so impersonal. She obviously was up to something. Outside the Oval Office several Secret Service agents flanked the President completely cutting off the possibility for talk. The President seemed to accept this and left him to follow as best he could. Jack had a fleeting thought that maybe the power was starting to dull her humanity.

Once outside the agents moved away slightly and allowed Jack to walk alongside the President. Among the roses they came to a graceful little gazebo that had been built shortly after the President took office.

"Shall we sit down here?" The President indicated seats in the rose-covered structure.

Once they were seated Jack began, "Madame President..."

She cut him off saying, "Will you turn off your recorder, please."

Jack's feelings must have been expressed on his face, because she softened her voice and added, "I need to talk to you privately, completely privately."

Jack couldn't help glancing at the open gazebo and the space beyond. Surely inside was more private.

She smiled, "What looks to you like an innocent garden structure, is really a sophisticated electronic marvel. We are safe from all forms of eavesdropping here. I use it regularly for important and unimportant meetings. No one will see anything strange about an interview with you here."

"But why the elaborate secrecy?"

Her smile faded. She looked sad, "I'm not sure who to trust right now." Then with more animation she said, "But that is not why I asked you here today. It's about the direction your special interest series is going."

"I beg your pardon?"

"I want to ask you to stop."

"Madame President, I'm dumbfounded. I'm sorry if what I write will end up having some negative consequences that reflect badly on you. I don't see any such connection now, but, of course, you know more about that than I do. If you asked me here to get me to stop digging, you've sadly misjudged me."

She sat so calmly letting his indignation boil itself dry, that finally he thought to ask her, "Why?"

"The White House, in conjunction with the FBI and CIA is carrying out an investigation of certain individuals and groups. You are beginning to touch on the edges."

"Forgive me for being so blunt, but that is hardly a reason to give up my series. If anything it encourages me."

"You see, these people are very sensitive about being investigated. We keep getting close and then they fade away like mist on a summer's morning. There is no doubt in my mind that someone here in the White

House is working for them."

"Who are you talking about? Why are they under investigation?"

"I know I'm being obscure. The fact is I don't want to tell you too much, give you a clue that will get you in deeper. But the fact is, we are not sure who we are looking for. We just see the results of this person's or group's actions. We are trying to work backwards to find the source."

"What actions?"

"A variety of crimes including Chris's kidnapping and several deaths."

"Deaths?"

"I can't tell you who. Just believe me — these people do not hesitate to kill anyone who causes them trouble."

"But Chris?"

"The actual kidnappers operated under someone else's bidding. I don't think Chris was ever meant to go free. But the kidnappers panicked." Did Jack see a tiny smile flicker across her face? "We know where they are and have placed an agent amongst them to glean what we can."

"Why haven't they been arrested?"

"They will be when we are sure they are no longer any use to us free."

"If you suspect someone close to you, won't that person tip off the kidnappers?"

"There is an element of the investigation that I carry on privately, shall we say."

"But getting back to my series..."

"I am only asking you to slow down."

"Which part of it is touchy?"

"Mr. Kelly, people have died. One of my most trusted agents has gone missing. Chris was lucky."

"I've done dangerous work many times before."

"Please. Just for a while. That's all I'm asking."

"A while?"

Several weeks. A month. Surely there are other stories to do in the meantime."

"Madame President, do you know what you are asking me to do?"

She took a deep breath and when she answered her voice was low and he could barely hear.

"Yes, I know. I'm asking you to stay alive."

Whatever answer he'd expected, that wasn't it. She was telling him all this because she was worried about him? Or had she kept an emotional appeal ready in case he didn't listen to 'reason'? He wouldn't look at her. He wasn't sure which would be worse — to find sincerity or insincerity in her face. The silence between them grew and finally he said, grudgingly, "I'll think about it."

"Thank you."

"I'd better go."

"Yes. I think I'll stay a while. One of the men will walk you back."

He started to leave, but she called him back. "One moment, Mr. Kelly." She handed him an envelope. "For your piece about this 'interview'." As he looked in her face he saw a woman more troubled than he'd ever seen her — more troubled than he'd ever imagined she could be. As he watched she consciously put the troubling thoughts away and smiled gently at him.

"Thank you for coming and for listening. Good bye."

In the taxi on the way back to the office, he scanned the contents of the letter. It was great stuff. She'd given him advance word on the stand she was going to take regarding Earth Initiative II. It was going to make a powerful article. Her stand seemed calm and reasonable, fraught with common sense, but many environmental groups would, no doubt, be furious. She had no intention of sending anyone as a representative of the USA, let alone go herself, until it was made completely clear by the organizers that the participants were not expected to rubber stamp anything environmentalists said. The environmentalists needed to understand that they represented one of the many areas of legitimate concern among thoughtful people worldwide, but not the only or premier one.

Groups like the Green Eagles wanted to claim the high moral ground. President Conner wasn't willing to concede them that position. "Convince me," she often said. And in several instances so far, she had changed her stand when presented with unequivocal evidence, backed by independent research. Curiously enough, that tended to enrage some activists even more.

The article almost wrote itself what with the material the President had given him and the comments he gathered from the opposition. It wasn't until he was leaving the office that Jack remembered the real interview with the President. His professionalism rebelled against being told what or what not to write. His feelings told him to respect the President's request. Several weeks? He hadn't planned to do the next article much sooner than that anyway. For the next few weeks he was covering the build-up to and actual meeting of the President with the heads of other major powers. And then the President was going to address the United Nations.

Thinking back Jack smiled as he remembered President Conner's first meeting with the Chinese Premier. They were scheduled to talk about the sensitive negotiations going on between China and several of the countries in the region. China had been claiming the need to 'interfere' in the region, claiming 'national security' interests. With Russia behaving badly and now China, it was the cause of much distress around the world and the previous administration had exacerbated the problem by waving a big stick, but having no coherent policy, just talk and more talk. Empty rhetoric. The threat of a return to another Cold War had the military calling for an arms build-up. Tension mounted world-wide. Elements of the population including some 'un-named' sources in the military, didn't believe a woman was capable of handling such a problem. Some of the members of women's groups, in disarray after Mrs. Conner's election, said a woman could handle it, but only the right kind of woman. The rest of the population waited and watched.

President Conner's policy remained the same for all nations — free exchange of goods and information — particularly information. One of her earliest acts had been the establishment of Internet Free World. It was a rousing success — airing ideas that covered the spectrum. It was a paragon of fairness on the theory that given information, individuals could and would make sound decisions. The President considered IFW to be a success because all sides complained that the other side was getting too much exposure.

It was known that the Chinese Premier was planning to try to pressure

President Conner into cutting back on broadcasts to his part of the world. It had been a beautiful day when the Chinese delegation arrived. The two presidents, flanked by interpreters and aides, strolled through the garden. And then to the amazement of all, President Conner dismissed the interpreters and invited the Chinese premier to sit with her in the gazebo. They were seen to be in animated discussion. No one had ever asked and President Conner had never mentioned that she spoke fluent Chinese.

The Premier came out of the meeting thoughtful and slightly subdued. At one point later in the day Jack saw him look at President Conner while her attention was elsewhere. The expression that flitted across his face was one of puzzlement. Jack wondered what threats or promises were made. No one was told of the content of their private conversation among the roses, but the Chinese, while continuing to talk the same line, were seen to be backing off from all blatant aggression.

Later President Conner was asked how many languages she knew. She smiled and replied simply, "A number. I've been blessed with a facility and an ear." And she never told exactly how many languages she understood. The psychological advantage this gave her in her dealings with foreign visitors was inestimable.

And now the leaders of most of the world were to gather in New York. Jack decided to put off thinking about President Conner's 'request' that he stop his special interest series. The next several weeks were going to be filled with enough to interest him and his readers. No one was going to notice if he put off the next installment. He knew he was justifying, but he didn't care. He was glad he could come up with a fairly legitimate reason to do what the President wished.

Had he completely capitulated and become her lackey? Was this the way good and honest men were corrupted? Well, he promised himself to spend the next day doing nothing but research. After all, she had only asked him not to write; there was nothing about stopping the research. The key was there. He wanted to find it, put it in the lock, open the door, and find Albert Quinlain.

Chapter 26

Mrs. Lowrey from the apartment down the hall rode up the elevator with him. As they got out, she said, "I hope you aren't having problems with mice or rats."

"What do you mean?"

"I hate mice and rats. You'd think we'd be free of them in a place like this."

"I'm sorry, I don't understand."

"I saw the exterminator coming out of your place."

"What time was this?"

"Oh, let's see. I was on my way out to have my hair done. He'd just left your apartment. I called for him to hold the elevator, but he must not have heard me. Had those earphones on. "

"What time was it?" Jack asked with more patience than he felt.

"4:00 or thereabouts."

"Do you remember what he looked like?"

"What's the matter? Didn't you request an

exterminator?"

"I'm sure nothing's the matter. Did you get a look at him?"

"No. Not really. He didn't look in my direction. The name on the overalls was Bush, or Rush, Pest Control, something like that. Is it important?"

"I doubt it, but thank you."

He waited outside his door until Mrs. Lowrey was inside her apartment. Even then he hesitated. The President had spoken of unknown men who would kill those who got in their way. On the other hand, the President also had known at what precise time he was sure to be away from the apartment.

That was a ridiculous thought. He started to put the key in and suddenly caution got the better part of valor. He went back down to the lobby and called Zbornak at the station and explained. Fortunately Zbornak was an old friend and only scoffed a little at Jack's concerns. He said he was just getting off work and would come by on his way home. Jack waited in the lobby.

Zbornak poked fun at Jack all the way up to his apartment. He even took Jack's key and opened the door. The force of the blast blew him back against Jack and knocked them both over. Neither was seriously hurt, only shaken, as they stood up and looked inside. There was no fire and surprisingly little damage, except in his office.

The experts came, sifted through the rubble, and went. The neighbors gawked and finally went back behind closed doors. Mrs. Lowrey was suddenly unsure if she'd seen anything at all. Zbornak said he'd be more inclined to trust Jack's instincts in the future and certainly was not going to open any more doors for him. The bomb experts found remnants of a small, highly sophisticated bomb, but nothing else — no fingerprints or other hard evidence. Everything pointed to a professional.

"Do you have any enemies?" a detective asked him.

"No one specific."

"But you have some ideas?"

"In my business it's easy to offend people."

"Offend?" The detective glanced at the destroyed office. "Something a little stronger than that I suspect. And this looks like a warning to me. If they'd wanted you dead, they could have rigged the bomb to go off when you started the computer instead of when you opened the door."

Jack stood with his back against the closed, locked door listening to the elevator take away the last policemen. Years ago Jack had developed the habit of backing up everything he did on the computer and then sticking the disks in a fireproof box he kept in the bedroom. So his loss was only in the hardware that could be replaced. That was small comfort to him as he looked at the devastated room.

So. Everyone thought he was close to something. Everyone wanted to warn him off. They'd all misjudged their man.

He decided to spend the night in a hotel because of the mess, but before he left he got out and cleaned the snub-nosed .45 he purchased four years ago after he'd received some credible death threats. Since then he'd kept his permit current, although he never really thought about the gun except when it was time to go down to the range for target practice. Finally, feeling secure in a cookie-cutter hotel room, he slept, the gun within easy reach on the side table.

Next morning at the office Jack expected to be inundated with questions — even to find himself the subject of a front page story. But there was nothing. He called Zbornak and asked what was going on.

"I don't know exactly where it came down from, but the lid was slammed tight on this one. It was taken out of our hands completely. I don't even know who to tell you to contact. I guess they'll be in touch with you if they need more information. I suppose the chief will know. I can try to find out for you if you want."

"No. No thanks. I'll find out if I need to."

Jack felt like a blindfolded man in the middle of a bunch of hungry chained tigers. Which way should he move, could he move, and be safe? The solution seemed to be finding a way to get rid of the blindfold.

Chapter 27

Jack had never seen such tight security. Secret Service agents literally swarmed about the President. At the meeting there was an undercurrent of tension that was noticeable to everyone but the most insensitive. Speculation flowed in muttered waves whenever journalists gathered. The President's people smiled false smiles, sending furtive glances over their shoulders, and saying that all was well.

Apparently they were right. Or all the security paid off. The conference went smoothly. The final photo session included all the heads of state shaking hands and nodding good-naturedly to the cameras. As for accords, they would all go home and do whatever was in their own national and political interest.

Back in Washington the Secret Service heaved a collective sigh of relief and returned to normal levels of care for the President. Apparently, the latest danger, real or imagined, was past.

Two days later Jack was at an address the President gave to sum up the accomplishments of the just finished conference. She spoke of the value of getting together even if there was disagreement. There remained in the world a large number of different concepts as to the best economic policies, the role of environmentalism, what place the electronic revolution had in developing countries, the threat of terrorism, how to deal with wayward nations. She said there didn't have to be one answer to fit all nations and situations, but the leaders of each nation had to be responsible for the decisions they made, and ideally stay as much out of individual citizen's lives as possible.

The speech was well done as was typical of the President, although it didn't add anything new to Jack's understanding. He didn't like to join the milling crowd that always tried to mob the President as she moved from one place to another. So he had already drifted out of the building and was down the block watching as the President emerged, all smiles and waves for her public.

The door of the limo was held open, the President turned back toward the crowd to answer one more reporter's question. Jack was leaning against the building enjoying the scene that had been repeated so many times through the years.

The shots rang out loud and clear over the sound of the crowd. As if in slow motion Jack saw the bullets hit the President once, twice, knocking her backward. The third shot hit the body that leapt in front of her, pushing her on into the limousine. The fourth and fifth shots left an agent on the ground where the limo had been. People were screaming and trying to run, pushing and shoving. The limo was accelerating away, the back door swinging shut by the momentum.

Jack was poised, ready to leap into action, but there was no place to go, nothing to do. His eyes searched the crowd looking for someone with a gun. He saw many Secret Service agents with guns frantically casting about, but not the 'one'.

A lone shot stunned the crowd into a moment of silence and then the screaming intensified and the panic doubled. Jack saw a number of agents pulled as if by a magnet toward one spot. Their dead calm once they arrived there, rippled out quieting and giving a false calm to more and more of the crowd. Like a tsunami that first sucks away and then rushes back into shore, the crowd, led first by journalists, then joined by the morbid curiosity of the public, began to converge on that spot. Agents had to stand fast and try to push back those who wanted to stare at the body, clearly dead, splayed out on the sidewalk, a gun still clutched in the lifeless fingers.

Jack was standing on precisely the same spot that he'd been when the President walked out of the building. He tried to concentrate, make a decision as to his next move, but his mind just replayed over and over the sight of bullets striking Helen Conner in the chest. His back slid down the rough granite of the building and he sat, separate from the commotion, his face in his hands. He didn't even notice the tears rolling down his cheek.

He didn't know how long he sat there, but he stayed until a police officer came up, took his name and told him to move on. This called him back to his senses and he hurried to the hospital. In what he assumed was ridiculous optimism, he held out the hope that she was not dead.

Other journalist had been quicker than Jack. He joined the throng outside the hospital and asked the first person he came to if there had been any news. The reply was negative. He made his way to the door and was refused entrance as all the other journalists before him had been.

Fifteen minutes passed. Half an hour. An hour. At least she must still be alive. Jack allowed a tiny hope to creep in. Two hours after Jack arrived a presidential aide came to the door. He was immediately bombarded by questions.

"Please. Please, I have a statement to make. Please quiet down."

The journalists finally realized they weren't going to get anywhere by shouting, so they quieted down and let him speak. He had a paper in his hand from which he read, unsuccessfully attempting to hold the quivering out of his voice, "President Helen Conner has just gone through surgery, the result of two bullet wounds. She is in critical condition, but the surgeons have every reason to believe she will make a full and speedy recovery. Two Secret Service agents were also wounded and have gone through surgery. The doctors are guarded in their prognosis. Dead at the scene of the shooting from what appears to be a self-inflicted wound, is the suspected assassin. No identity is known at this time. You will be given another up-date when there is something else to report."

The aide ducked back inside the hospital. Determined reporters who tried to follow were stopped by guards. Some of the journalists dashed off to file stories. Camera crews from every channel filmed live reports. Cell phones were at nearly every ear. Jack knew he had a story to tell; he had been an eyewitness after all, but he didn't want to leave the hospital and couldn't seem to stir up the will necessary to call in the story. About fifty feet away Jack caught sight of Sam. He edged his way over to him. Maybe Sam could do the story. As he approached Sam looked up and saw him. A look of concern came over his face.

"Geez, Jack, what happened to you?"

"What...?"

"You look like hell."

"I was there. I saw it."

"The assassination attempt? You were there?"

"I watched it all. I've got to file a story."

"What you got to do is get a grip on yourself. Come over here and sit down." Sam led him over to a chair.

"I tried....""

"Just sit down. Take it easy. We'll get the story out." Sam took his recorder out of his pocket and clicked it on. "Start from the beginning."

Jack began to talk, slowly at first, his thoughts disjointed, but then the professional in him took over of it's own accord and he ended up giving a precise and powerful record of his impressions. When he finished he felt calmer, more in control. Sam let out his breath in a half whistle. "This is great stuff. Let's get back to the paper and write it up."

"You go. It can be your story. I want to stay here."

The tone of Jack's voice left no room for argument, so Sam just nodded and got up. "Call in if there is any news."

Jack stayed seated on the wall, nodding to Sam. Sam hesitated a moment, not sure he should leave Jack. But he waved a hand and said, "Go. Go. I'm fine. Really." So Sam turned and with one more glance back over his shoulder, headed for the office.

Ten minutes later the same aide appeared at the door. This time Jack was caught at the back of the journalistic surge forward. The aide said, "I've been asked to tell you, to assure you, that there will be an update in three hours. There will be nothing until then."

Throughout the crowd, eyes were glancing at wrists and calculating whether to leave or stay. Jack decided to go find something to eat — not because he felt hungry, but because he knew he'd better take advantage of this opportunity. He found a nearby restaurant and ordered a meal.

He was beginning to feel more like himself and the horror of those several seconds was not filling every corner of his thought. Several other reporters that he knew came in, and space being at a premium, invited themselves to join him. He didn't really mind, but he didn't join in their speculations about the shooting, and when he was done eating, he excused himself and walked back to the hospital.

He'd long ago decided that one of the essential skills required by anyone who wanted to be a successful journalist was the ability to worm one's way through a crowd of like-minded journalists. He did pretty well and ended up only three deep away from the door. Since he was tall enough to see over almost everyone there, that seemed good enough.

At the appointed time the aide showed up once more. But this time the press secretary was there also. Jack assumed that various critical officials had been arriving by the helicopters that were coming and going from the roof of the hospital.

The press secretary spoke: "We have an update on the attempted assassination of President Conner. The President remains in stable condition. She was awake for a few minutes and was able to speak with her sons. Barring complications there is expectation of swift, complete recovery. Two bullets struck the President in the chest. Both just missed vital organs. There will be detailed information on this later. A third bullet was stopped by Secret Service agent Stuart Jenkins who threw himself in front of the President. Agent Jenkins remains in critical condition at this time. We regret to inform you that agent Kerry Wilhelm was pronounced dead of gunshot wounds one hour ago. There is no further word yet on the identity of the deceased individual who at this time is considered the prime suspect in the assassination attempt. We will update you in the morning as to the President's condition. There will be no more this evening. Thank you."

Chapter 28

It went on this way for two more days and then on the third word went out that several journalists would be able to see the President for a few minutes first thing in the morning. The chosen journalists would be expected to share with those not allowed in. Jack said a quiet thank you to the lovely Mrs. Kramer when he was chosen to represent the newspaper reporters.

Altogether four journalists and a cameraman were escorted through the intense security to President Conner's big, bright, airy room. It was heart-rending to see the President in bed, for the first time looking small and frail. There were files on the bedside table that showed that she was apparently well enough to be doing some work. Jack had seen her in many different situations and recognized the smile she gave them to be genuine. But there was a pitiful tiredness behind it that she tried and very nearly succeeded in hiding.

The reporters were allowed to ask several questions each. When it was Jack's turn, the first words out of his mouth were not those he'd planned to say. Instead it was a quiet, very personal, "How are you?"

She smiled ever so slightly, and said, "I've been better."

The other journalists had questions more to the point. President Conner was able to reply to them all with grace and precision except to note that, no, they still knew nothing about the assassin. They were all shooed out after 7 or 8 minutes and Jack knew that the President had accomplished her mission — the reports would show that, yes, she had been badly injured, but that she was recovering and would soon be fully capable of returning to her duties.

On his way out of the building a man he'd never seen before came up to him and said, "Jack? Jack Kelly, is that you? What have you been doing with yourself?" The man grabbed his hand and vigorously pumped up and down. Jack felt the paper the man had passed to him and calmly slipped it into his pocket, willingly going along with this man's ridiculous story. Finally the stranger said, "Good to see you, Jack. Let's do lunch real soon."

Jack waited until he was in the taxi before retrieving the paper. The note instructed him, please, to be just inside the west entrance to a nearby mall at 10:30 am. It was signed, "Discreetly yours, Mrs. K."

Trusting it really was Mrs. Kramer he was dealing with, he went to the mall after turning in his story, wandered in and out of shops, and just happened to be at the west entrance at ten thirty.

Another man he didn't know brushed by him and whispered, "Follow me."

Jack wasn't sure if this was over-reaction by Mrs. Kramer or if there truly was some danger to be avoided. Either way he was willing to find out what it was all about, so he followed, discreetly. Outside, when they reached the curb, a car with darkened windows drove up, the door opened, and Mrs. Kramer asked him to get in. The other man just kept walking.

Mrs. Kramer's succinct, if incomplete, explanation was, "The President would like to see you privately." She left no room for questions. Jack, thinking he ought to at least respond, said, "O.K.", and they drove silently to the hospital, taking a guarded entrance into the underground parking lot.

Mrs. Kramer went up the elevator with Jack and took him to the President's room. None of the guards stopped or checked them in any way. She opened the President's door, Jack walked in, and the door was closed behind him. He was once again alone with the President. She smiled and indicated a chair by the bed. He sat down and waited for her to speak.

"I hope you don't mind coming."

"Not at all," was Jack's wildly understated reply.

"It's just that everyone hovers over me so much. I wanted someone I could just talk with."

"You can hardly blame them for 'hovering'."

"I know. But I end up using all my strength trying to make them believe I am more well than I feel. I wish they'd just tell themselves — yes, she is in pain, unwell, but she will recover. And there's no doubt that I will. Jenkins saved my life, you know. He's the one I'm worried about."

"I was there. I saw him jump in front of you and push you into the car."

"You were there?"

"Off to the side. I just stood there and watched it happen."

"Poor you." She said it with such sincerity that Jack was finally jolted out of his melancholy. He laughed.

"Poor me, indeed. I suppose there is a slight chance that you actually went through a worse time than I did."

She started to laugh, but then a wave of pain went through her and showed itself on her face. Her hand went out and up toward him. He took it in his own two hands and held it tight. At that second it was as though a bright light illumined the room. Part of his mind was wondering how he could not have been aware that he loved this woman completely, unreservedly, probably from the first day he'd met her. The knowledge of his love filled him with unspeakable joy, and great sorrow that he could never tell her. But he was here now and it was her fragile hand in his.

The pain passed, but she left her hand where it was and he certainly had no intention of letting go until he had to.

"Should I call someone?"

"No. Please don't. I don't want to take painkillers any more than I have to. If it becomes unbearable, I let them give me a little, but I don't want to be drugged up."

"You really meant what you said during the campaign about legal drug use."

"I always meant what I said during the campaign. What was the point otherwise? But I'm not going to run again. First Chris, and now...." She couldn't finish.

"You're not going to run again?" Incredible hope surged through Jack. If she didn't run again, she'd be safe and she'd be a private citizen again — an individual who an ordinary man, say a newspaper reporter, could maybe even ask out....

Then her words broke through his imagining. "Let them win. Four years is enough. Who was I to think I could make a difference?"

Jack took all his wild speculations and put them aside. With her hand ever so gently still encased in his, he looked at her and said, "No. You won't let them win. It's not in you to give up. You're tired and sore and maybe even afraid, but you won't give up. Not you. Don't tell anyone you're quitting. Wait until you are well first, then decide. Everything will seem different when you are out of here."

"I don't know." She sounded so defeated.

"I know," smiled Jack. "I know that you are an extraordinary woman. And I know that you will make a sound decision once all this is behind you."

She stared at the ceiling for a moment or two, and then made an obvious mental shift, sighed and said, "I'm feeling tired. Will you read to me?" She looked over at a book that was lying open face down on the table. It was an adventure novel.

"Of course," Jack replied, but he had to let go of her hand so he could stand and get the book. He placed her hand down gently as if it were a separate object and went to pick up the book. She seemed unconcerned one way or the other about where her hand was.

"I'll probably fall asleep as you read. I'll mean no disrespect." She managed a ghost of her charming smile.

"I'll read until you do."

"Thank you, Mr. Kelly." And he knew it wasn't because he was going to read to her. For his part, he was grateful that she considered him among her friends. He knew also that he'd never burden her with declarations of his love. To be the friend of such a woman was a treasure too great to be spoiled.

He read the words of the book as well as he could, under the circumstances, since his thought was otherwise engaged in review of his entire relationship with Helen Conner. He knew they had a special relationship, but try as he might, he couldn't in all conscience find any time when she treated him as anything more than a friend. He had never believed one could really fall in love with someone who did not return that love. Guess he'd have to rethink that concept.

After about half a chapter, Jack could tell the President had fallen asleep. Reluctantly he got up and quietly set the book back on the table. A mad impulse made him want to stoop down and kiss the tiny furrows in her brow that even sleep had not smoothed. Instead, he touched his fingers to his lips and ever so gently, placed them on the back of her hand. He let the touch linger and then turned to go.

The agent outside the door told Jack to go to the elevator. As Jack got there it opened. Chris and Alex Conner stepped out, followed by Secret Service agents. Alex's face formed into a scowl, but Chris seemed genuinely happy to see Jack.

"Been to see Mom?" he asked.

"Yes. She's just fallen asleep."

"Listen, Mr. Kelly, if you don't mind, could we talk to you for a few minutes. There are empty rooms down the hall," Chris said.

Alex was trying to hush him up. Chris turned to Alex, "He might know something."

To which Alex replied in a short, scornful, "Right."

"You know what Mom said."

"But did she know what she was saying?"

"She's not often wrong."

"All right. All right. Since Mom's asleep now anyway."

Jack listened to this exchange, wondering at its meaning. He waited until they'd finished and then Chris asked him again if he would join them. Jack agreed and Chris led the way, dismissing the agents to wait by the elevators. The whole floor was sealed off by security people so they had no trouble finding an empty room.

To Alex's obvious discomfort, Chris told Jack, "Mom always said that you were someone we could trust." Jack felt a warm glow inside himself at the thought of such a compliment.

Alex broke in. "Yeah. The great Jack Kelly, incisive, dedicated reporter. He gets this close," he held his fingers a fraction of an inch apart, "to exposing the whole thing and then a bomb blast, and who knows what other threats, cause him to back off so fast you can smell the fear."

"Mom asked him to stop." Chris's statement was quiet, meant to calm Alex.

"Oh, well, then that really shows something about his character, doesn't it? Best to do what she says and let her be killed."

Jack had had enough of this bickering and wanted to get to the bottom of what the young men were talking about. "Excuse me, I don't know what's going on exactly, but I'm willing to find out if you two can stop arguing long enough to tell me."

Alex and Chris looked at each other, scowling, but then the antagonism melted from their eyes and they smiled with the private understanding of brothers who love each other deeply in spite of squabbles.

Alex spoke first, "I'm sorry, Chris, I just want to get those guys."

"Me, too," replied Chris. And then he spoke to Jack. "Alex and I think we can figure out who's behind the attack on Mom." Jack must have looked a bit incredulous. "First of all it wasn't the guy who shot himself afterwards. There are questions as to whether he really did shoot himself or was 'helped' to commit suicide. Regardless of whether he pulled the trigger or not, there is a presence in the background. We think the same person or persons are behind my kidnapping, Mom's shooting, the pre-election photos, to name a few things. Some of this is hunch, some of it fact. We think you may have information that can help."

"If I do, I will, but why do you think I know something?"

"Your series on special interests. One of the groups you talk about keeps coming up in our investigations."

Jack knew what they were going to say. "The Green Eagles." He made it a statement, not a question.

"So you have been suspicious of them, too," said Chris.

"Not in regard to this."

Alex broke in, "Let's not talk here any more. I think we should do this back at the House."

"I agree. Let me just go and check to see if Mom is still asleep. I'll be right back." Chris slipped out the door and Jack was left with Alex.

"There are too many unanswered questions hanging about in the air here," said Jack. "I don't mean to sound condescending, but why do you think you can find someone who every law enforcement officer in America is looking for right now?"

"There is something you need to know about Chris. His IQ goes off the chart. He's probably one of the most brilliant people you'll ever meet. Oh, he always went to school at his normal grade, did enough work to seem like a normal kid. The fact is he could breeze through college work when he was about six. My parents helped him see how to be a 'boy'. They gave him whatever it took to challenge him and keep him always striving while showing him how not to be a 'freak'. He can do things with a computer that you and I can't even imagine. I might feel left out except that I have tons more common sense than he does." Looking guiltily at Jack he added, "About most things."

"But how do you have access to the necessary data?" Alex didn't quite meet Jack's eye. "Chris can get into any computer anywhere. He can sneak in, find what he needs, and leave — no one ever knowing he's been there. Mom caught him once a few years ago. She was really mad. Forbad him to do it again. He said he never caused trouble, it was just interesting to see what he could do. Kind of like doodling would be for the rest of us. Mom wasn't impressed. But he can access any data."

"But where do I come in, and why aren't you talking to the authorities?"

"First, Mom is pretty sure there is a big leak in White House security. Jenkins she trusts completely, but we can't turn to him until he's better. You may have some missing pieces — Chris thinks it's possible."

Chris came back in and said, "Let's go." Jack's dealings with the Conners were always unusual, but seldom boring. He followed the boys, deciding it wasn't out of line to ask, "Where are we going?"

"To my room," was Chris's enigmatic reply.

Alex chuckled, "Be patient. You'll see why when we get there."

"I should go to the office and get the files I need," Jack told the boys.

"I wish there was another way. They might be watching for you."

Jack didn't want to think of the implications of that as he said, "You can't access my files from your computer."

"You don't know Chris."

"What I mean is, the computer I do this sort of work on is not hooked up to any modems or other outside sources. I even turn it off when I'm not using it. I know right where the backup disks are. It'll just take a sec."

At the elevator the boys' agents fell back into place. In the garage they stepped right into a high-tech, state of the art, bulletproof limo with darkened windows.

They stopped in the No Parking zone in front of the office and Jack ran upstairs. He gathered the necessary disks and files and tried to slip out, but Walter saw him.

"Well, Jack nice to see you taking the time to check in."

"I'm not. I can't tell you what's up. But if I can later, well, 'big scoop' only begins to hint at the potential. I've got to go."

"But, Jack...."

He was already in the elevator and waved goodbye to Walter as the door closed.

Chapter 29

Chris's 'room' turned out to be a suite. The first section was a traditional boy's bedroom. Next to this was a room that could be reached only through the bedroom. With the door closed, it gave the impression of being the closet. But inside it was at least as big as the bedroom and packed with computer hardware. Jack couldn't even begin to guess the function of three fourths of the equipment. There were two comfortable chairs in front of several, what seemed to Jack, ordinary-looking personal computers. Alex pulled in one more chair from the bedroom.

Chris, who had always seemed so shy, was completely at home and had a confidence born of the conviction that here he was in charge. "Where do we start?" asked Jack.

"So far, we've only scratched the surface," replied Chris. His voice went quiet and his eyes seemed more moist than usual. "It's been hard to concentrate." He looked up at Jack. "She's going to be all right, isn't she?"

"Yes," Jack said, wondering if saying it out loud made it true.

"When we visit she always acts so...brave."

"Maybe if you didn't show how worried you are, she wouldn't have to be so brave. I imagine she'll go to great lengths to spare you."

Chris thought about it and then smiled. "Yeah. That makes sense. Thanks, Mr. Kelly." The smile turned into a big grin. He looked at Alex. "Let's catch us a murderer."

Alex grinned back at him and they gave each other a high five. Gad, thought Jack, are they brilliant, talented young men, or boys playing at boys' games?

Alex suggested, "Let's get an overview of what we have to offer each other."

Jack told of the paper trail he'd been following, the myriad of blinds and dead ends, but also of his conviction that Albert Quinlain was behind the big money he was trying to trace.

"Albert Quinlain? I remember him. He tried to take over Mom and Dad's company. When the company proved to be too strong for a take-over and they didn't want to sell he tried to seduce Mom. Boy, did he misjudge her. He thought he could charm her, disarm her, and sneak in the back door.

"I can remember Mom and Dad at dinner one night, laughing. She found a lesson in it for us. 'Boys', she said, 'His ambition rules his common sense. He actually believes that anything he wants, he can have. If its not given, he thinks he has the right to take.'

"Mom and Dad shared a look and they both laughed. Dad said, 'He never met your Mom before.' And they laughed again. I guess he's not so funny after all."

"So it could be more than just the radical environmental angle. He might even have a personal vendetta against your Mom. But this is all speculation. I have no proof of any sort that it is him — just a gut instinct. And proof is what we need."

Chris's fingers flew over the keyboard and Jack saw FBI, police, Interpol, CIA, and heaven only knows what other files being scanned for the name Quinlain. What little there was seemed innocuous.

"Let's come at it from a different angle," Chris said. "Knowing the assassin's mind-set, Alex came up with the idea of making a list of everyone in the Washington area, or who was connected with Washington, and died in the last several years. We wanted to see if there were any 'eliminations' that would give us a clue."

"That's a good idea. What did you come up with?"

"A very long list of dead people," said Alex with some resignation.

Chris was more upbeat. "It's a matter of going through to see which of the dead had any, even the remotest contact, with the administration or other government agency."

"You've done that already?"

"Yes, but we couldn't see anything significant."

"Let me look through it."

Chris handed Jack a print-out. "As you see, the list gives the name, cause of death, and connection with the government."

Jack went slowly through the list. He made a mark by the name Garth Wingate. He knew some of the other people on the list, but he didn't stop until he got to the name Rose Hyland. Where did he know that name from? Cause of death: hit and run. Yes. At the restaurant to meet the woman informant who never called back.

Trying to hold back his excitement, Jack said to Chris, "This one. Rose

Hyland. Do you have more information on her?"

Without asking why, Chris began to search.

Rose Hyland: executive secretary to one of the top men in the FBI; impeccable security clearance; killed by an out of control driver who was never found; before coming to the FBI worked at Jones, Limited, American subsidiary of a multi-national company based in the Bahamas.

"That's it!" cried Jack, his finger jabbing at the screen. "That's it. We'll find him now. Somehow. We'll find him now."

The other two looked slightly bewildered.

"You say that you think the business with the photos was related to the kidnapping and shooting?" Jack's mind was racing.

"Yes," replied Alex.

"Chris, can you find the name of the person or company that tried to donate a large sum of money to your Mom's campaign? It came through Will Camden. Your Mom made him give it back."

While Chris dug into computer files that looked private and Presidential, Jack got out his disks, put them in the computer next to Chris's and called up the data he wanted. Chris had the name of a corporation on his screen. He looked over at Jack's monitor and instantly made the connection. Alex was still unsure what the excitement was about, but Chris was whooping and laughing. "We've got him, haven't we? We've got him." Jack was grinning and nodding.

In exasperation Alex said, "Would you two be so kind as to explain to this poor ignorant soul just what's happened, and who we've got?"

Chris stood back and bowed to Jack. "Mr. Kelly, if you'll be so kind.'

Jack bowed back. "Why certainly. I'd be delighted. Each of these companies is a front for what I've come to call Albert Quinlain, Inc."

"I can see how Will Camden fits in, but Rose Hyland?"

"And Garth Wingate," said Jack. "Those three take it beyond coincidence." Jack went on to explain first his suspicions about Wingate: that he never really stopped working for and supporting the Green Eagles, that he spoke of 'Al' with such reverence, and then how later Jack sprung the name Quinlain on him. Jack figured that he panicked and called Quinlain. Quinlain couldn't accept weak links. Next thing you know, Wingate's dead in an automobile crash.

"But what about Rose Hyland?"

Jack told of the anonymous calls — one about the bomb at campaign headquarters and then the message to meet with reference to 'Garth' and 'the boy'. "I think she meant your kidnapping," Jack said to Chris. Then he told of getting to the restaurant late and finding the aftermath of a terrible accident. "I didn't put it together then, just thought the commotion scared the informant away. Now I believe Rose Hyland was the one who was going to meet me. She was in over her head and hoped she could get out. Unfortunately, she was stopped in a very convincing manner."

"You know, Will Camden's completely disappeared, too. Do you suppose he's dead, too?"

"I wouldn't be surprised."

"Chris, go deeper, using the information Mr. Kelly has, and find the real Albert Quinlain," suggested Alex. Chris was already at it.

The picture that began to appear was that of an extremely wealthy, self-made man with a fanatical passion for environmentalism. He was the early driving force behind the militant Green Eagles, but as his wealth grew he faded out of the limelight while continuing to support it through his various real and dummy corporations. He seemed to be a man obsessed with the view that nature had to be cared for and nurtured and kept pure, and that no individual human life should be allowed to stand in the way of that goal. On balance, saving the earth outweighed almost any number of human lives. He was a man used to getting his own way. From his first contact with Helen Conner he'd been thwarted over and over.

Jack's research into Quinlain had always been based on the assumption that he used his money to get influence, not an uncommon occurrence. Now he saw a man obsessed beyond the point of reason. He watched in fascination as Chris sent electronic probes that stole silently and stealthily into every corner of Albert Quinlain's life. He molded and sculpted a detailed picture that stripped away all the safety and security Quinlain thought he had built into his life. Bank records, Swiss accounts, offshore holdings, credit card transactions, phone records, tax records — nothing was hidden from Chris. Jack realized that the digging he'd done looked pitiful compared to this.

When he was done, Chris said, "Look here, and here, and here. It's the phone calls, I think, and those payments, that convince me."

"But legally, we've got nothing. I agree that he's our man, but he'd hire a good attorney and laugh at any charges from this evidence, even if arrived at through legal channels," Jack said, putting a damper on Chris's enthusiasm. "And I don't even want to think about how you did that

Chris."

"But surely the FBI or some agency can start watching him now, and hope he makes a mistake," said Alex in frustration.

"Yet who can we ask? Who can we trust? Jenkins will not be up for a while." In a flat voice Chris continued. "But I know a way to start getting to him now."

He looked over at Alex, a tiny mischievous smile at the corner of his mouth. Comprehension began to dawn in Alex's eyes. "Oh, yes," He said. "Yes! NLE."

"You got it."

"What's your plan?"

"Slow beginnings, but then more and more rumor. Never lying, just suggestion. Subtle. Quiet. Inexorable."

"Do it."

"If I may ask what you two are talking about...?" Jack interjected.

It was Alex who answered, pride for Chris only thinly veiled, "Are you familiar with NL Econonet?"

"Yes. The internet newsletter assumed by many to be the anonymous writings and musings of various Nobel Laureates," replied Jack.

"It's Chris."

"What do you mean?"

"NLE is Chris. He's the founder and he writes all the articles, constructs all the dialogue between the major 'contributors' — the whole thing. Naturally, other people join in the conversation, but they are like letters to the editor in a normal magazine. Using the magazine analogy, Chris is editor, publisher, all contributors."

Chris was blushing a little. "It started out as fun, but I find I really enjoy thinking from a variety of perspectives and then trying to articulate those perspectives."

"But the Nobel Laureates...?" mused Jack, trying to get a grip on the idea that *Chris* could be the NLE.

"Nobel winners who when asked all pretty much deny taking part, don't they?" asked Chris with mock innocence.

"Sure, but everyone assumed..."

"That they were lying?" finished Alex.

"Well, yes."

"The ones we find to be humorous are the one who don't deny it."

Convinced, Jack said, "I tried to get an interview with you — with NLE — during the campaign."

"I remember."

"I'd ask how you remained hidden from all the serious and casual hackers who have made it a mission to break into NLE, but I doubt I'd understand your answer. I will ask why you don't let yourself be known?"

Chris answered, "Think for a minute, Mr. Kelly, and you'll know the answer."

Jack looked around this extraordinary room and then back at Chris. The answer was obvious. "People who are willing to listen to a conversation between supposed Nobel Laureates might not be so interested in listening to a teenager, no matter how brilliant."

"And I started when I was twelve. I can assure you, I was not a figure to inspire anyone then."

"But when will you tell?"

"I don't know. Maybe when I'm old enough to look the part — if I'm still carrying on at that point. By then I may have found something else to do as a hobby." He grinned at Jack who had no choice but to grin back.

"Does your Mom know?"

Chris and Alex looked guiltily at each other. Chris answered, "I've been meaning to tell her."

"You'll have to. The sooner the better."

"I know."

"What are your plans about Quinlain?"

Chris's eyes turned hard. "I'll plant ideas, rumors, throughout the internet about him. I can even mess with his money. The rumors will grow. Eventually NLE will feel compelled to discuss the rumors. No matter what Quinlain does to stop them, to challenge them, they'll grow and slowly but surely everything he holds important — money, reputation, influence — will begin to crumble around him. Maybe the authorities will get him first, but one way or the other, he's finished."

"What will your Mom think of this?"

Chris looked to Alex for help. He just shrugged. "We'll find out when we tell her, after she's better."

Chris looked back at Jack, "Don't you think we should do this?"

The vision of bullets tearing into Helen Conner's body rose up unbidden in Jack's thought. "When you do it, do it well. I'd offer to help, but you are way out of my league."

"You brought us the name. It's hard to think of a greater help than that."

"Chris. Alex. Thanks for inviting me to the party."

They all laughed and shook hands.

"I should go now. Why don't you copy off anything you need from my disc. I won't be aiming at Quinlain in my series for a while. I'll wait until rumors start. When it seems right, I'll add fuel to the flame."

Chris stayed and Alex walked Jack out, finding an agent to drive him home. Alex was quiet as they walked down the hall, but then at the door, he stopped and said, "I haven't liked you very much. I misjudged you and your intentions, and I'm sorry."

"I'm glad to know you and your whole family."

Alex nodded and grinned.

Jack lay on his bed unable to sleep as he contemplated this day. So much had happened — Alex and Chris and the computers, the NLE, Quinlain on the road to ruin, and the realization that he loved Helen Conner. In one day his life had become very complicated. Once she recovered and was back at the White House he would have to quit the Washington beat.

How could he ever write again with any impartiality? For that matter, he may have been way off base for a long time — his sub-conscious being able to recognize what he'd only now admitted to himself. No. Walter or Sam would have been quick to tell him if he strayed too far.

He'd been wanting to work seriously on his book. Or maybe he could be a foreign correspondent again. Or a free-lancer. When she was well, he'd decide. Somewhere on the fringe of his thought was the knowledge that if he quit reporting from the White House he might never see her again. A noble gesture, but was it really necessary? And she valued his friendship — that was clear. Eventually he fell into a restless sleep, having resolved nothing.

Next morning when Jack arrived at his desk there was a note stuck to the computer. Walter was asking for his presence the moment he arrived. What now? thought Jack as he walked across. The door was open so he knocked on the sill and walked in. Walter, his expression unreadable, indicated that he should sit down.

"What's up?" asked Jack.

"Just what I'd like to ask you." replied Walter.

"What do you mean?"

"Don't act coy with me. I'm your editor. You can tell me what's going on. Start with the 'big scoop' from yesterday."

"Sorry, boss, nothing there after all."

"You were seen leaving here in a car that had 'White House' written all over it. We know you have close ties with sources inside."

Jack stood up. "There's nothing to tell, Walter. Sorry to disappoint you."

"We've known each other for a long time and I know something happened," said Walter with the true journalist's unwillingness to let a story go until he got to the bottom of it.

Wouldn't you like to know, thought Jack. And I can imagine how you'd react if I told you I was in love with the President of the United States. Put that way it seemed ridiculous even to him.

Completely ignoring Walter's questions, Jack walked out of his office. At the door he stopped, turned back, and said with a hint of mischief he couldn't hide, "I've got to get back to work. There's a big world of news out there and a deadline coming closer every moment."

Walter just groaned and said, "If you can tell me sometime, I'd love to hear it."

Chapter 30

The next weeks were anticlimactic. Everything was so...normal. Jack wrote stories. He went to the hospital each day for the Presidential medical updates. She continued to improve and returned to the White House to finish her recovery. She had several other interviews with small groups of reporters. Jack was not included again. In fact, he didn't see the President or her boys. In spite of his various resolutions, he began to think he should try to get another exclusive interview as soon as the President was well enough, and to that end he called Mrs. Kramer.

To his dismay, she put him off saying the White House would let it be known when the President was ready for such activities again. Two days later the first interview with the almost completely recovered President aired on CNN. Whatever influence he'd had, whatever special treatment, was gone. Jack knew it with no doubt.

What had gone wrong? Perhaps the President had learned about his part in helping Alex and Chris. Maybe she disapproved. Or maybe Jack had been fooling himself all along — seeing what he wanted to see, not what was really there.

To top everything off, Jack was worried that he was developing a case of paranoia. He occasionally had the sensation that he was being followed. He never really saw anyone he could identify. Once or twice he tried sudden maneuvers to get rid of the unknown watchers. He decided it was futile. He had to go to work. He returned to his apartment at night. They could just wait for him there. "They". If they existed.

He also was fascinated with the drama that was slowly unfolding across the electronic networks. Quinlain's name was slowly being brought up, subtle questions asked, allegation piled on top of innuendo. Quinlain must be starting to sweat, because none of the denials that showed up were heeded.

Jack had never gone so long having no direct contact with President Conner. When the message came, he wasn't sure if he was happy or miffed. Regardless, when the President asks for your presence, you go. The appointment was for six pm. He left work early, feeling strangely nervous. He showered, shaved, and put on clean clothes.

As he came out of his apartment he was surprised to see Agent Smith get out of a nondescript sedan, hold the door, and invite him to get in. Having gotten used to strange occurrences, Jack complied. Although he fully expected to be taken to the White House, he couldn't help wondering if he was being kidnapped by turncoat agents. In line with common sense, he was taken straight to the private entrance to the White House.

Smith escorted him down an unfamiliar passageway to a door that was guarded by Jenkins. Although Jack had tried he'd been unable to get word on the agent's recovery. He was truly happy to see the man well and back on duty. He wasn't sure what to say to him, so he just smiled and nodded and stuck out his hand. For the first time Jack saw Jenkins unprepared. But he recovered quickly and took Jack's hand. His grip was solid and sure. And Jack was almost positive he saw the agent smile somewhere in the vicinity of his eyes. The moment passed and Jenkins opened the door and gestured for Jack to go in. Jenkins and Smith remained out in the hallway.

The door was the back entrance to one of the White House kitchens — no doubt the scene of much hustle and bustle on banquet nights — now quiet and still except for President Conner who seemed to be in the middle of making a sandwich. No cookies in sight.

She greeted Jack.

"It's good to see you, Mr. Kelly."

"The pleasure is mine."

"Can I make you a sandwich?"

"No, thanks."

The President, always so confident, so in control, seemed almost nervous.

"I wanted to see you, let you know, you were right that day in the hospital."

"What do you mean?"

"To make no decision about running again until I was well."

"Are you well now? Truly well?"

"It's surprising what a body can take and then recover from. I'd like to say it was my excellent constitution. The fact is I was very lucky. Lucky the shooter was a fraction off. Lucky that Jenkins was there. It's hard to even think about Kerry Wilhelm."

"I can't imagine."

"But this is not really why I asked you here today. The first thing is that, yes, I will run for a second term. You have the first official word." She paused for his comment. He had none. He just nodded. "I couldn't let them win, you know."

Jack wondered if the boys had told her what they were up to. Should he say something? He couldn't think about that now, because the President was still talking.

"But there is one problem about running again. And I need your help, your advice as a friend and, well, as a man, on a touchy matter."

"Of course, I'll help in any way I can."

"I'm in an odd position as President. In many ways I am very unapproachable. I don't complain. That's how it must be." She blushed a little. "This is so awkward. Forgive me. How can I explain?"

Jack waited patiently, not really sure he wanted to hear.

"Something has happened to me that I never counted on. I know running again is the right thing to do, but it complicates another matter that is close to my heart. You see, Mr. Kelly, I have become acquainted with a man, perhaps I should say, I find myself loving a man, who I am sure will never presume to make advances to me. Apparently, one doesn't call up the President of the United States and ask her out for dinner and a movie."

Jack was feeling sick. He wanted to get out of the room, but couldn't be so rude. He wanted to scream at her to shut up. Couldn't she see how she was torturing him? Be fair, he told himself. Get a grip. She's turning to a friend for advice. Hell. He didn't want to be a friend. What was she saying?

"....You see my problem. How would you feel, as a strong, independent man, if a woman made advances to you, declared herself? Do you think I should tell this man how I feel? Mr. Kelly, where are you going?"

Jack had had enough. There were limits. President or no, he didn't need to be party to this. Summoning what calm he could muster, he said quietly, "I'm sorry, Madame President, I can't help you with this problem. I think I will go now."

"Mr. Kelly, please, why can't you?"

"If you'll excuse me..."

"All I ask is some simple advice. Why won't you help me?"

"Why? O.K., if you must know. I will not help you figure out how to tell another man that you love him, because, fool that I am, I find that I'm in love with you myself."

Jack was already halfway to the door when the President spoke, "Jack. You're the man. It's you I love."

He stopped and stood with his back toward her, trying to sort out what she'd said.

Her voice was quiet and compelling. "Truly. I love you."

He turned and somehow they were in each other's arms and nothing else mattered.

"What are we going to do, Helen? I want to be with you...."

"Before you say anything else, make any promises, will you do me a favor?"

"Name it."

"Be patient. Go now, and think, really think about all the implications of our love. On Saturday I'll be at Camp David. Come then after you've thought it through."

Jack began to protest that he loved her and didn't need to think about it at all.

"Please," she begged, "on Saturday."

"You ask me to do the one thing I never want to do again — leave you."

"But will you?"

"Yes. But if I walk out into the passage now, they, Smith and Jenkins, will know. It'll be written in bold letters on my face, in my very walk. They'll say, 'Jack Kelly loves the President'".

"Jenkins won't be surprised. I'm sure he suspects already."

"How do you know what Jenkins thinks?"

"We talk some times."

"Jenkins carries on a conversation?"

"I'll admit he's no overly wordy, but he doesn't miss much. He has a great respect for you."

Jack laughed, unbelieving, and then was thoughtful for a moment. "I'm glad."

Reluctantly, the Helen said, "You have to go now. Will you come Saturday?"

"Yes, I'll go now and come Saturday. Until then..." Jack enveloped her in his arms and gently kissed her.

As he went out the door he avoided Jenkins eyes, and then realizing that was foolish, looked up and grinned. Smith took him out and Jenkins remained behind. Had Jack seen him wink?

Four days until Saturday. Four days. Four days to make sense of his life turned on end. He was in love again, a condition he had not thought possible. And then instead of finding just any ol' woman, he loves the President of the United States. And she loves him. Once he began to come down from the first intense initial amazement and wonder, he thought more soberly about the implications.

He couldn't see dating her for an extended period. Surely the only solution was marriage. But what about her political career? No, that part wasn't for him to decide. He'd ask her. She would know how best to answer. She trusted him to think it through, he could do the same for her.

O.K., what about his own career? It wasn't realistic to think he could continue as a reporter. Rather than distressing him, that was a freeing thought. He knew he wrote good articles — was his writing equal to the several books he always planned? He'd find out.

But who would he be as the husband of the President? It was uncharted territory, at least in America. Would he even be 'allowed' to be her husband? He thought back — was there anything in his life that he'd always assumed would remain hidden? How would various of his activities be construed? Wait. He was a good man and an honest man, if not a perfect one. No matter what anyone found in their gleeful sifting through his life, if it was true he'd not deny it. He always thought it was so stupid to lie, to cover-up, then have to scramble and back-track.

Jack got a jolt as he realized that if the President was going to marry some other man and he was not involved, he would consider it his duty as a conscientious investigative reporter to find everything. The people had a right to know. He believed that whole-heartedly. But, damn it, he'd lived an honorable life, by and large. It was nobody's business to poke and pry and try to make perfectly innocent actions seem otherwise by an ideologically governed choice of which 'facts' to present. He'd thought of these things before and tried to be fair when he delved into people's lives. Somehow he'd never really understood. The thought of his life being spread out for all the world to poke through like satiated vultures was, frankly, scary.

So how would he handle it? The answer was clear and he hoped he could manage it. He'd be honest, impersonalize any unwarranted attacks, and, most important, keep his sense of humor. If he can laugh at himself, there is very little that he cannot face.

He didn't spend all his time thinking about the problems. At one point he got out the tapes of his most recent interviews with President Conner... with Helen. Had she been trying to tell him all along, subtly, that she cared for him? He listened and wondered.

He daydreamed about their life together, the things they'd share, the political arguments they'd get into, the places they'd go.... It hit him like wave of hot, humid air on an August afternoon. He could barely breathe. The Secret Service. They'd always be there. He'd have his own guards to follow him wherever he went and to die for him if some crazed fanatic got a notion to achieve fame as the one who did in the First Husband. No going for walks together or out to a show. Every move they'd make would be a major production. It seemed dreadful, stifling. And yet it was only for a few years. The Secret Service would still be around after her presidency, but not so completely. She lived with it. He could learn.

Jack didn't go to the office the rest of the week. He wasn't sure he could function normally and he didn't really want to try. Walter attempted to get a reason from him, but had no success. Sam was more persistent and came knocking at Jack's door. Jack contemplated not acknowledging that he was home, but knew Sam well enough to know that he'd probably stake himself out in front of the door and wait.

Sam wasted no time after Jack let him in. "What's going on?"

"Nothing," was Jack's unsatisfactory reply.

"Do I have to pry it out of you — resort to devious ploys?"

Deciding to be at least partially honest, Jack replied, "I'll admit something is going on. But I promise you it is nothing to worry about. I wish I could tell you. And as soon as I can, I will. Do you want to go out for dinner?" Jack realized this may be one of the last times he'd be able to do such a spontaneous activity.

"Sure. Carol's visiting her mom and I'm at loose ends until Friday. Let's go, but I haven't given up trying to find out what's happening."

Jack laughed, filled with the warmth of good companionship and the secret of love. "If I told you, you wouldn't believe it anyway. So just be patient. All in good time. All in good time."

Chapter 31

Saturday seemed far away. At the same time it bore down swiftly
upon him. Finally, Saturday morning found Jack awake too early feeling
like a school boy preparing for his first date. He was up and ready, but it
was not time to go yet, so he tried to read, but couldn't concentrate. Finally,
he got out his car and headed off, suddenly worried that now he'd be late.

Ultimately he arrived at about the right time and was admitted. He
was shown into the living room of the President's cabin. He stood looking
out the window at the trees swaying slightly in a gentle breeze. A door
opened at the other end of the room. Jack turned and saw her. She was so
beautiful. All his well-thought out speeches vanished. The first words out
of his mouth were, "Will you marry me?"

From across the room she smiled and replied, "Yes."

It was too wonderful, too perfect, too silly to be on the other side of the
room from the woman you'd just asked to marry you. Jack began to smile
and then to laugh. Helen began laughing, too. He walked to her, and both
still laughing, they embraced.

After a time of delicious closeness, Jack said, "When do you want it to be?"

"As far as I'm concerned, the sooner the better."

Jack looked around the room. "Do you keep any resident preachers in residence here?"

"At least I'd like to have the boys here. How about tomorrow?"

Jack laughed, but then saw that she was serious. "Do you mean it?"

"If it suits you."

"The moment you said you loved me, my life spun off in a new, marvelous, unpredictable direction. I'm committed wholeheartedly."

They sat on the sofa, the President snuggled in the reporter's arms, and they talked and planned and laughed – sorted out when they each knew they loved the other. For a precious hour they were simply a man and a woman who loved each other and reveled in the fact of it.

A discreet knocking at the door pulled them back into the present. Helen said, "We'll have to tell some of the Secret Service. They'll need to plan."

"That will be an inexorable part of our lives together, won't it?"

"It's funny. I'm used to it, to them, now. Which reminds me, do you play volleyball?"

Not seeing the connection, Jack nevertheless replied, "Yes, I do."

Helen's face took on a mischievous look. "Then it is time you learn about one of the great secrets of the Conner White House."

They were at the door. "Follow Agent Smith and he will provide you with suitable clothing. I have several phone calls to make and then I will be joining you."

"Are we going to play volleyball?"

Helen just smiled as Smith led Jack away.

Smith pointed out a room. "Everything you need should be there. When you're ready, come outside."

Did Jack detect a hint of annoyance in Smith? And who was he going to play volleyball with? Were there other guests here? On the bed in the room were appropriate athletic clothes. But no shoes, just thongs. Jack changed and came outside to find Smith waiting for him outside. Beyond the main building was a well-maintained sand volleyball court. Ah, no shoes needed. Smith asked him to wait and then disappeared back into another part of the complex.

There were comfortable benches and chairs out of the way under the trees. Jack sat down and contemplated this latest twist to the Helen Conner/Jack Kelly story.

Helen was the first to join him. He'd never seen her out of the simple, elegant presidential clothes she always wore, except that time at the airport. Now she had on sweat pants and a tee shirt. Understanding his look, she twirled for him as if she were modeling a couturier collection. He said what he'd been meaning to say for a long time. "You are so beautiful."

She smiled her acknowledgement and then said, "I know you are wondering about this."

"Well, yes."

"From the first there has been an on-going volleyball tournament. The teams are made up of me, the boys sometimes, and mostly the Secret Service. We play hard, serious power volleyball. However the agents have developed an amazing technique of appearing to play normally with me, but they never spike a ball hard at me. I tell them I'm not fragile, but, well, you can see their dilemma."

"Not wanting to be the one who knocks the President senseless."

She nodded. "This is the first time I've played since..." a shadow crossed her thoughts, but she made a conscious effort to remove it "...the shooting. Don't worry. The doctors say I'm fit. It's poor Jenkins who can't play yet. But we'll take it easy today."

Men and women, some agents Jack recognized, others not, were drifting out onto the playing area. They were jostling and joking and bumping volleyballs to each other. Jack saw several furtive glances in his direction. He was the outsider here, and not a very welcome one at that.

"Let's warm-up," said Helen, inviting him over to one of the groups. They stood in a circle bumping and setting, warming up their fingers and arms and legs. Silently blessing a good coach in college and all the hours of press league play, Jack held his own. After 5 or 10 minutes, someone said, "Let's play," and everyone sorted themselves out on the court.

Helen spoke up, "Before we start, I want to introduce you to Jack Kelly. Some of you know who he is. All of you will be knowing him soon. Tomorrow, Mr. Kelly and I will be getting married. The ceremony will be held here with only the bare minimum of guests."

The news sunk in and Jack watched the expressions, some of surprise, some knowing, but pretty much all happy for the President. There were murmurs of congratulations and one said, "Should we be playing?"

"Jenkins is organizing the necessary security. Mrs. Kramer is making the other arrangements. Mind you, this is to be an absolute secret until after the fact. Now — let's play ball."

These were all skilled athletes, and the competition, although friendly, was fierce. Jack was on the same team as Helen. She was too short to be a serious spiker, but her ball handling skills were exemplary. She asked where he liked his sets and then put them there, soft and easy and just hanging in the air waiting for him smash down on the other team. And as the games progressed it was clear that during this time at least, she was very nearly just 'one of the guys'.

After an hour or so Helen said to the group, "I'd better stop now. I don't want to overdo it. I've got to be ready for the next championship round." Still in the flush of competition, the players called out various comments including well-wishes for Jack and Helen. The agents regrouped and continued playing as Jack and Helen walked away. Jack sensed that the feelings toward him were more openly accepting. Had Helen planned it that way?

"I enjoyed that. Thank you."

Understanding his thank you, she said, "I started this for purely selfish reasons. I wanted to be able to play without the world watching me. It turned out to have all kinds of other benefits." With a laugh she said, "We do softball, too. How are you at that? Equally skilled?"

"I've played the odd game here and there."

As they reached the house Helen said, "Have a shower and then we'll have lunch, outside don't you think? The boys will be here by then."

"Sounds good."

After showering and changing, Jack went back out to the patio. Helen had not returned yet, but Alex and Chris were there. They saw Jack and rose to meet him. Their faces showed that they knew about the engagement. Jack was grateful to see happiness in their eyes.

Chris spoke first, his enthusiasm spilling out, "Mom told us the good news. I think it's wonderful."

Alex smiled and said, "Me, too," as he shook Jack's hand.

As instant families go, Jack couldn't have hoped for better. "I'm honored and pleased to be part of this family."

Mrs. Kramer came up and added her congratulations, and then added, "Helen will be out in a few minutes. A small Presidential matter came up." As an afterthought she said, "That dreadful Mr. Quinlain. She's been able to put him off, but finally had to see him. Some congressman begged..."

Jack's voice was low, holding in his emotion, "Albert Quinlain? Is the President with Albert Quinlain?"

Mrs. Kramer was confused by his intensity. "Yes."

Jack looked at the boys and their stricken expressions gave him the answer even as he asked, "Haven't you told her?"

He turned back to Mrs. Kramer, "Where are they?"

"In same room where you were this morning. What...?"

"Boys, go get the agents. Mrs. Kramer, find Jenkins." Even as he ran back toward the house, Mrs. Kramer had out her phone and was paging Jenkins.

Agent Smith was lounging against the wall outside the living room door. He snapped upright, reached for a weapon, and then relaxed as he saw it was Jack running toward him. Jenkins opened a door down the hallway and came out, nearly colliding with Jack.

"What's going on?" He sounded annoyed.

Not wanting to alert Quinlain, Jack said in a low voice, "The man in with the President is very likely the one behind the assassination attempt."

Smith was sputtering a confused denial of how he had been checked through security. Jenkins looked in Jack's eyes and drew his gun as he moved to the door.

Jack held him back. "Wait. If we burst in them, he might do something rash. I have an idea. Follow my lead."

In a loud, quarrelsome voice, Jack shouted, "I will see her if I want. You can't stop me," and began rattling the knob before pushing open the door. Jenkins understood and said back, "The President is with someone now. You have no right."

Meanwhile they were both in the room moving toward the President, who stood up in amazement. Jenkins still had his gun out and was pointing it in Jack's general direction. Quinlain face darkened in rage. He didn't understand this interruption, but he had no intention of being thwarted again. Hoping to be covered by the confusion, he slipped a razor sharp ceramic knife from a sleeve sheath, and jumped toward the President. Jack's momentum propelled him between them. He grabbed the knife hand and twisted. Quinlain was strong and desperate. Jenkins couldn't take a chance firing as the two struggled. Anyway, his first job was to protect the President, so he pulled her away from her attempt to aid Jack, and literally propelled her into the arms of two agents who had just arrived. "Get her out of here now."

Jenkins turned back in time to see Jack finally breaking Quinlain's grasp on the knife. It skittered across the floor and under a chair. Jack loosened his grip long enough to pound a fist into Quinlain's belly. Jenkins was there to catch the man as he doubled over.

The room was suddenly filled with agents, guns out, eyes searching for the menace. Jenkins had his knee in Quinlain's back and his arm twisted back and up. Jack thought he actually saw a smile as Jenkins looked up at him and said, "I hope you will be able to explain this."

"Me, too," replied Jack but his thoughts were turning to Helen. Knowing he was of no immediate use here, he turned and walked out, going to find his bride.

EPILOGUE

Jack married Helen the next day. Sam and Carol came, not knowing what to expect until they arrived. Alex and Chris were the only other guests if you don't count the Secret Service. They had a private ceremony, but that was the end of any privacy they were to know for years to come. Of course, that is not entirely true. They learned how to snatch moments of quiet togetherness, behind closed doors that were guarded very well — from the outside.

Jack writes books and only occasionally misses the journalistic world. Walter accused him of being a sly dog, but never turned down invitations to dinner at the White House with the family. Jack gave Mrs. Kramer's phone number to Sam, and he used it with discretion.

Quinlain's hatred of Helen only grew, destroying his mind, as it had destroyed his life. He died in a maximum-security mental ward. It was established that the Green Eagles, while militant and occasionally vicious, had nothing to do with Quinlain's worst excesses. However, several of their less well-known members were convicted of assisting Quinlain. The people he had managed to place in sensitive positions were found and dealt with according to their crimes.

Helen served eight years as President, achieving some of her dreams, leaving others to be realized by the next generation. She remains one of the premier statesmen of the world, much sought after. Chris's software company, which specializes in computer security, makes piles of money, and he uses some of it to help finance Alex's political career. Their wives and kids bring the beach house to life.

Made in the USA
Charleston, SC
22 July 2014